AF441742

About the Author

Dr. David A. Salomon holds a PhD in English literature from the University of Connecticut and an MA from the City University of New York. A specialist in the literature, religion and culture of the Middle Ages and Renaissance England, he is the inaugural Director of Student Research and Creative Activity at Christopher Newport University. In addition to podcast and lecture appearances, he is the author of several articles and four books. He can be reached at www.davidasalomon.com.

Why Sin Still Matters

David A. Salomon

Previously published as *The Seven Deadly Sins: How Sin Influenced the West from the Middle Ages to the Modern Era* (Praeger, 2019).

Contents

Preface

Growing up Jewish in the Bronx, New York, one of my favorite films was Cecil B. DeMille's 1956 epic *The Ten Commandments*, which I dutifully watched on television every Passover/Easter season. I was so intrigued with Charlton Heston's portrayal of Moses that I even fashioned my own desert "robes," staff, and stone tablets. My father and I went to see the film when it played in a theater in the Bronx in the early 1970s, not realizing until the film began that it was being shown dubbed in Spanish. No difference—I knew the entire script by heart.

It wasn't the story of the "prince of Egypt" that fascinated me but Moses's exile, journey to Sinai, and his conversations with God. I was trying to understand the nature of faith and, with it, the nature of sin. It seemed harsh to me that at the end of the film Moses was not permitted to enter the Promised Land, all because he had destroyed the original tablets in a fit of rage. His ascent of Sinai to "see" God provided me with a mystical grounding for the relationship one might have with divinity, regardless of the spiritual tradition.

It is no surprise then that I went on to a life studying religion and religious and spiritual literature or that the lives of the passionately devout have continually fascinated me. I began this book with several misgivings, first and foremost that I am not a trained theologian. Religious studies, philosophy, and theology were originally ancillary to my education but eventually became central to my work. I also began work on this book at a significant transition point, refocusing my career as an English faculty member to an administrative position directing undergraduate research and creative activity. I moved my family from upstate New York to coastal Virginia. As I began considering this work, my mother passed away. Crises of faith, whether of the traditional religious flavor or the personal crises of my faith in myself, pervaded.

Each chapter of this book is devoted to discussion of a different "deadly sin." The order of the chapters may appear random because they appear here in the order I wrote them, not according to any of the standard classification systems. This order is therefore organic and the result of my own prioritizing of the sins. I make no argument for this order other than that it reflects my own take of the current cultural and spiritual landscape.

A keen reader will note my predilection for citing two authors in particular: the English novelist D. H. Lawrence and the French poet Paul Valéry. I first read Lawrence under the careful guidance of Dr. Duane Edwards, an English professor as passionate about Lawrence and his work as Lawrence was passionate about art and existence. Over the years, I have found Lawrence's insights, particularly during the long arc of the 20th century, to be both intellectually stimulating and spiritually uplifting. I came to Paul Valéry much later after reading his novel *Monsieur Teste* while writing my doctoral dissertation. I knew Valery's poetry, often anthologized, but not his nonfiction writing, and in his essays and other short pieces, Valéry responded to the cultural unsteadiness of his time. The two writers, then, hover in the background of this book both as thoughtful commentators on social mores and as prophets for our time and beyond.

I am thankful to have a strong support system of friends, colleagues, and family who guided me through a difficult two years to conclude the writing of this book. My thanks to several colleagues and friends at The Sage Colleges, including Christopher White, Deb Lawrence, Steven Leibo, Kate Kagan, Nancy Cumo, Nina Marinello, Gail Hughes-Morey, Sara Schuman, Tom Sweeney, Carol Pett, and Don Richards. At Christopher Newport University, I would like to thank Lynn Lambert, Quentin Kidd, Bill Kelly, Geoffrey Klein, Grace Godwin, Michaela Meyer, Mary Sellen, Rebecca Wheeler, Carolyn Davis, Gina Polychronopoulos, Jay Paul, Andrew Falk, Sean

Heuvel, and my administrative assistant Terri Johnson; the project could not have been completed but for the expert interlibrary loan work of Jesse Spencer and the wonderful circulation staff led by Bethany Young.

No one accomplishes anything in this life without good friends, and I am fortunate to have many: Amy Pass, Natalie Farina, Linda Allbee (missed every day), Tom Jolly, Fran Colombo, Christine Smith, Cindy Casper, Kathy Heenan (gone too soon), Gene Kannenberg, Corey Jamison, Richard McCambly, Joan Sohn, Joyce Gauthier, Amy Fuqua, Nicholson Baker, Elizabeth Brundage, Susan Daitch, Tama Janowitz, Kristen McCloy, Jill Eisenstadt, Tim Sandlin, James Morrow, Sara Clemens (formerly at Penguin), Linda Larrabee (formerly at W.W. Norton), Shane Brisson at W.W. Norton, Lori and Tim Maki, Kethley Parlegreco, Louie B. Free, and Susannah Chewning. Professional friends have provided advice, good counsel, and tough love when needed: Donna Heald, Nancy Hensel, Sally Lawrence, Terry Weiner, and E. Ann Matter. Former students continue to enrich my career and my life: Cara Forrest, Kyra Fitzsimmons, Katie Kiger, Este Pope, Amelia Mello, Andrea Laurencell Sheridan, Courtney DeNobile, Kayla Nelson, Robyn Finnicum, Cariann Drake, Destinee Udelhoven, Heather Hanson, Vanessa Slocum, Lisa Jenner, Sarah Turner-Pogozelski, Courtney Primmer, Jodi Hill, Heather Rozmierski, Paola Sposito, Emily Woerthman, Hannah Geyik, Claudia Gagnon, Emily Miller, Marita Breen, Karen Faiman, Ashley McHenry, Alexandria Wachunas, Lily Holley, Brooke Nixon, Rachel Little, Olivia Brubaker, and Lara Deveraux. Catherine Lafuente of ABC-CLIO has been with me on this project from the first phone call to discuss the proposal through to the final drafts; she possesses the best characteristics for an editor: understanding, patience, knowledge, a keen eye, and humor.

My professional life has largely been the result of the mentoring and inspiration of Dr. Thomas Jambeck, who not only influenced the direction of my intellectual pursuits in graduate school, but whose example of the teacher-scholar continues to provide a model for me each and every day. I miss Tom's Finnish good counsel, his Minnesota humor, and his unwavering encouragement.

Finally, and most importantly, my supportive and nurturing family: my deceased mother and father, Sheila and Robert, my brother Steven, and my sister Lynda. My own morals and spiritual life have been greatly influenced by the examples set by my father and mother.

Pema Chödrön opens *When Things Fall Apart* with "Embarking on a spiritual journey is like getting into a very small boat and setting out on the ocean to search for unknown lands." Always first, my wife Kelli and my daughter Phoebe are my refuge and safe harbor in the storm of life as I continue on the journey.

I dedicate this book to all of the great thinkers who have come before me whose ranks I continue to aspire to stand among.

Thanks to all who read pages as the work developed. Any remaining errors or omissions are my own sins to bear.

Portions of Chapter 3 are adapted from my "'A Bad Counselor': Anger in the Bible," *Understanding Angry Groups: Multidisciplinary Perspectives on Their Motivations and Effects on Society*, ed. Steven A. Leibo and Susan C. Cloninger. Santa Barbara, CA: Praeger, 2017, 111–129.

The original edition of the book was completed in 2019, just before the COVID pandemic, the murder of George Floyd and the racial unrest in the United States, and the unprecedented presidency of Donald Trump.

Introduction

*That was the birth of sin. Not doing it, but KNOWING about it. Before the apple,
[Adam and Eve] had shut their eyes and their minds had gone dark. Now, they peeped
and pried and imagined. They watched themselves.*

—D. H. Lawrence[1]

Society is a tissue of illusions and every organized society a sort of collective dream.

—Paul Valéry[2]

Coming from a good Bronx Jewish family in the early 1970s means that
between the ages of 8 and 12 I went to Hebrew school in preparation for my
Bar Mitzvah on my 13th birthday. We were not a particularly religious
family—we were more "cultural" Jews (we enjoyed a good bagel, had a Seder
every Passover, but also ate ham) than religious Jews (I had friends whose
mothers "kept kosher"; if we had pizza at their house, it had to be on paper
plates so as to not contaminate the kosher dishes). Nonetheless, my father
prayed every morning, silently and alone while he got ready for work, wearing
his *tallit* (prayer shawl) and *yarmulke* (skull cap) as he silently thanked God and
asked for another day.

The early 1970s were a period of steady decline in the Jewish community
in the Bronx; as a result, I attended Hebrew school where it was
convenient—and this so happened to be the orthodox synagogue three
blocks from our apartment on the Grand Concourse. We were not Orthodox
Jews at all; at best, we were Conservative. But going to Congregation Beth
Shraga would allow me to go to public school during the day and then easily
walk to Hebrew School every day at 4:00 P.M.

Lessons lasted for a bit more than an hour Mondays through Thursdays.
I would meet my friends outside the synagogue after school, so we could get
in some stickball in the street before being called inside to study not only how
to read Hebrew but also how to be a Jew. The small synagogue held both

charm and mystery and provided both answers and more questions.

The first year began with a healthy contingent of young boys—perhaps 12—taught by a young woman herself just out of high school. I believe she had just returned from some time in Israel living on a Kibbutz and was now in college. What a handful this group must have been! She was trying to prepare us for an ethical and spiritual life as a Jew; we were interested in having a good time after a long day in the classroom diagraming sentences and learning for the fourth year in a row how Columbus had discovered America. One of my clearest memories was when she decided we would all take a class trip to a New York Yankees day baseball game. We piled onto the subway car, traveled on the El down to the Yankee Stadium stop, one devout young woman and 12 eight-year-old boys forced to wear their yarmulkes in public (no one in my class was being raised Orthodox and, so, the wearing of yarmulkes in public was quite a foreign concept to us).

We paid $1.50 each and sat in the leftfield bleachers in the warmth of the late-April afternoon sun. This was before the Yankees had embraced the world of kosher hot dogs, and, as a result, our teacher would not let us eat the *tref* (non-kosher) hot dogs. We were being instructed to lead an ethical life by closely following rules set out in a mysterious text that, for some reason, was kept on big scrolls hidden in a closet in the synagogue's main room. Apparently, that text had pretty clear and rigid rules about eating hot dogs at a baseball game.

Over the course of my time at Beth Shraga, the size of my class shrank as Jewish families fled the dangerous streets of the Bronx for the lush suburban lawns of New Jersey. By the time of my Bar Mitzvah, at which point we too had migrated across the Hudson, I was the only one of the students left from that original class, tutored now by a combination of the synagogue's office manager, a diminutive woman who agreed to lead me toward my big day, and the rabbi himself, stereotypically bearded but kind and insightful; he had the demeanor of a good therapist.[3]

What in fact was the goal of this education? What was the goal of the Jewish life? Both questions seemed to be answered by cultural practice that turned doctrine into daily living. In the fall, when the sun would set earlier and earlier, requiring the old men to come for evening prayers by 4:30 P.M., the boys would file out of the synagogue oftentimes while the men were entering. Because of the decline in the neighborhood, what must have once been an ornate front door had now been replaced with a heavy steel slab with a foreboding contraption that made the building seem more a meat locker rather than a house of worship. Add to this a sizeable step up, and entering God's house was becoming more of a challenge for many of the older men, particularly those who walked gingerly. One man in particular has always held a special place in my memory.

This man, at the time probably almost 80, had undoubtedly served his country in World War II after emigrating from some Eastern European locale. At his advanced age, he walked with a cane, but his most significant physical marker was his profoundly hunched back. Each day, he arrived at the synagogue for evening prayers, just before sundown, usually in a black trench coat draped over him like an umbrella in his stooped posture. His question mark figure reflected my own curiosity and confusion.

It is traditional Jewish practice to hang a *mezuzah*, a small usually metal box with a scroll inside it on the doorpost at the entrance to any dwelling, the result of the Old Testament order to "write the words of God on the gates and doorposts of your house."[4] *Mezuzahs* are usually placed on the right doorframe, about two thirds from the ground. This man embraced the age-old tradition of kissing the *mezuzah* by putting his fingers to his mouth and then to the *mezuzah* and then back again, upon entering the synagogue. And this was no easy feat given his hunched posture. I recall watching him as he inched his fingers up the doorframe, slowly, until he had reached the mystical talisman in order to touch his fingers to his lips and then to the *mezuzah*. The entire procedure could take him as long as 10 minutes, as my friends darted past him on their way home after a long day first of public school and then of Hebrew School. I remember watching him on many occasions, from my perch on the burgundy carpeted steps that led up to the main tabernacle. What an oddity he was to my 10-year-old self! How devoted! How devout! But why? What was driving his devotion and his commitment? I was both baffled and jealous.

This book is an attempt to reconcile that upbringing with religious and secular notions of sin. We live in extraordinary times. In the first decades of the 21st century, humanity is undergoing an existential shift under its very feet. This is nowhere truer than in the Western world where language, concepts, theories, and even words themselves have been called into question, disputed, belittled, oversensitized or desensitized. Most alarming, what does "truth" mean in what some now call the "post-truth" era?[5] Building on ideas by a wide variety of scientists, social scientists, and humanities scholars in the second half of the 20th century, we can begin to understand the complexities that have developed in the ways we speak about the world and our very existence.

Never mind the orthographic confusion regarding technological innovations (is it "email" or "e-mail"?), even greater confusion has arisen regarding the more abstract concepts humanity has dealt with for millennia. The very meaning of certain words has been called into question, as their meanings swing wildly like the pendulum on a hormonally imbalanced clock. In particular, words and concepts of a spiritual sense have taken quite a buffeting. Perhaps no one word is more disputed than "sin." What does "sin" mean in the context of the early-21st century global, increasingly secularized world?

At the outbreak of World War II, the Swiss theologian Emil Brunner wrote of "the *humanistic idealistic understanding* of man," and noted "the truth of our life *here* is determined by a life *beyond*."[6] "Man," Brunner continued, "is the bearer of ideas, the shaper of ideas."[7] This view of humanity as innately transcendental, as concerned from birth with a life yet to come, is heir to centuries of philosophical and theological treatises. It also looks forward to a new conception of humanity, one that would eventually build upon the existentialist ideas emerging in the postwar world and increasingly distancing itself from the Catholic Church and organized religion of all kinds so that, by the 1980s, "New Age" religiosity[8] had taken root firmly in the Western world. A type of smorgasbord of spirituality and religious ritual, New Age spirituality reframed the goal of human life, moving its focus further from "a life beyond" and focusing more on behavior for behavior's sake, on living a "good" and "clean" life for its own sake and for the sake of others. Lacking a central governing body—no Vatican, no Rabbinical Board—this new type of spiritual belief depended on consensus and the cultural ethos. Under the heavy influence of Eastern philosophy and new religious movements, New Age religiosity encouraged a type of egotism in the individual, culminating in the sentiment that the individual himself is God, so much so that a 1970s underground publication argued the importance of "three simple words": "I am God" in which the subject "I" is the reader. The separation between the mystical One and the Self had collapsed. The distinction between subject and object was dissolving.

The great French poet and thinker Paul Valéry realized this disconnect as early as 1925 in his "Remarks on Intelligence":

It is to inquire in what way modern life—the inevitable machinery of modern life and the habits it inflicts on us—may modify on the one hand the physiology of our minds, our perceptions of all sorts, and above all what we do with our perceptions, or what becomes of them inside us; and, on the other hand, the place and function of the mind itself in the present condition of the human race.[9]

Valéry was a French essayist and philosopher, perhaps best known as one of the last symbolist poets. A model for what later became known as "the public intellectual," Valéry remained active in French cultural life until his death in Paris in 1945. As the 20th century came to a close, "the inevitable machinery of modern life" took its toll, physically and psychically, such that traditional ideas regarding the spiritual and the moral—and in particular its relationship to the concept of sin—had been significantly altered.

An increasing stress on personal responsibility in the late 20th century grew out of the existentialist movement, and the focus on responsibility for and ownership of one's own actions increased by the beginning of the new millennium. In the process, however, the old notion of sin became cloudy at best and muddied at worst. The modern legal system stirred up the mud by suggesting different measures for behavior according to complex constructions of intentionality. In an age when the only being one is responsible to is himself, how can the notion of sin still be viable?[10] There are many—most in the Judeo-Christian tradition—who would argue that responsibility goes hand in hand with sin, that without one we could not have the other. More recently, intellectuals such as Steven Pinker have argued for a more progressive view of the spiritual aspect of humans. Pinker notes that "one fear of determinism is a gaping existential anxiety: that deep down we are not in control of our own choices."[11] Pinker, an avowed believer in what he calls the "computational theory of mind," writes, "The experience of choosing is not a fiction, regardless of how the brain works. It is a real neural process, with the obvious function of selecting behavior according to its foreseeable consequences." It is, he concludes, "the existential fear of determinism that is the real waste of time."[12]

It would seem on the surface that much of contemporary psychology (including the growth of the so-called self-help industry) is divided between what I'll call the blame shifters and the blame takers. The former look to escape responsibility and blame their actions on some other factor—human or otherwise. The blame takers continue to believe, as did French philosopher Jean-Paul Sartre, that we are the sum of our choices and that we need to take ownership of that fact. The result is that the human situation becomes a creation of human beings themselves: "In another man I always meet myself and myself is reflected in him."[13]

For Sartre, responsibility is the direct result of freedom: "Man being condemned to be free carries the weight of the whole world on his shoulders; he is responsible for the world and for himself as a way of being."[14] Human beings are thus responsible for the world because the world is the result of the choices humans have made. If there is war, then "the war is *mine*"; "thus *I am* this war."[15] The key word for the blame takers is "am," while the blame shifters are all about "but." Contemporary forensic science has often fallen into the trap of using biology as an excuse; as Pinker says, biology becomes "the perfect get out of jail free card, the ultimate doctor's excuse note."[16] After all, it is much easier to blame my lapses on some pathology rather than on my own moral weakness. Nonetheless, as Spanish philosopher José Ortega y Gasset writes, "Life is then, in its own essence, responsibility for itself"[17]; put simply, there is no one else to blame. When former president Bill Clinton was asked in June 2018 whether he had ever apologized to Monica Lewinsky for the trials and tribulations she and her family navigated as the result of his affair with his White House intern, he blame shifted the question to focus on himself as victim, saying "nobody believes that I got out of that for free. I left the White House $16 million in debt."[18] The blame shifters often cast themselves in the role of victim in an attempt to absolve themselves of the guilt of their own behavior.

Biologists will argue that, without the presence of a soul (or other moral component), human beings are the products of their biology and their genetics. Thus, I am blameless for lashing out at my wife because a brain scan shows a hormonal imbalance that makes me prone to fits of rage. As Pinker says, "Biology may show that we are *all* blameless."[19] Evolutionary biologists, like E.O. Wilson, would argue that our actions are the result of generations of genetic mutation. If my genes made me do it, how am I responsible? This appeal to and reliance on absolution of responsibility is not only morally questionable, but it is even dangerous to the future of the species. Without personal responsibility, what prevents society from decaying and falling into moral disarray?

This conundrum of humanity's responsibility for their actions connects directly to the question of sin. If, as Romans 6:20[20] has it, humans are all "slaves to sin," then what of responsibility? "Slaves" have no rights and little control over their behavior and are thus absolved of responsibility. The very concept of responsibility is interwoven with the contract or, in theological terms, the covenant, an agreement between two parties in which both agree to some accountability and consequences for violation of that contract. Let us take as an example the original contract in the Garden of Eden.

Some will object to my overuse of religious texts for this discussion, so let me explain my rationale. These stories in the Bible, particularly the early stories in the Old Testament (Adam and Eve, Cain and Abel, Noah, etc.), whether read as history or myth, form the foundation of our Western cultural ethos. I argue that they are also at the nexus of a mythology of Western thought. Separated from theology, they are central to our history of ideas.

It is in a simple Genesis story in the Garden of Eden that we first see the shirking of responsibility for a forbidden act. Given all of the created world as theirs, Adam and Eve are granted "dominion over the fish of the sea, and over the birds of the air, and over the cattle, and over all the earth, and over every creeping thing that creeps upon the earth."[21] The so-called Edenic Covenant is an exchange of obedience for safety. As long as the pair do not eat from the Tree of Knowledge of Good and Evil, they will remain in the security of the Garden.

Once the serpent invites Eve to eat and she then shares the fruit with Adam, the two hide themselves as a first indicator of shame. The covenant has been broken, but the importance of the incident is in the ways the two react to what they have done. When asked if he had eaten of the tree, Adam's response is, "The woman whom thou gavest to be with me, she gave me fruit of the tree, and I ate."[22] Adam is the original blame shifter: "I ate, but . . ." Here we find the foundational responsibility myth of the Western world. What are we to learn from this?

Adam is explicitly told not to eat from the Tree of Knowledge of Good and Evil "for in the day that you eat of it you shall die."[23] The Genesis text has Eve eat after being offered the fruit by the serpent, an animal "more subtle than any other wild creature that the Lord God had made."[24] Eve eats and, in almost absurd concision, "she also gave some to her husband, and he ate."[25] There is no elaboration or exposition. Neither takes responsibility when they hear "the sound of the Lord God walking in the garden." They hide themselves in shame at which point Adam places the blame on Eve, and Eve places the blame on the serpent. And, indeed, it is the serpent who is punished first, followed by Eve and finally Adam, both of them told "you are dust /and to dust you shall return." The punishment for breaking the contract is severe, but is it unwarranted? Didn't Adam and Eve have as much freedom to obey as they did to disobey and break the contract? Didn't they have "free will"? Isn't the violation of the contract and their original sin their own responsibility?

Adam is stuck in the tines of what philosophers call "Hume's fork": a distinction between the relationship between ideas and matters of fact.[26] Either my behavior is predetermined, and so I am not responsible, or my behavior is the result of random events, and so I am not responsible. Either way, it is not my fault. For Adam, to be a responsible human being in Western culture had no precedent. We have seen Adam skirt the burden of his actions and imagine him thinking, "it's not my fault, they made me do it" or "it's not my fault; you made me this way." As novelist and journalist Tom Wolfe writes, "Don't blame me! I'm wired wrong!"[27]

Given the bare text of Genesis, the calculus is simple:

Man is told not to eat from a particular tree + he eats from that tree = punishment for transgressing the commandment.

Is Adam guilty? Yes. Does he accept blame? No. Does that unwillingness to accept blame incur a more severe punishment? Not exactly. Of course, the world of sin is much more complex than this, but this is after all "original sin." We are a long way here from complex philosophies of good and evil in which right and wrong are more clearly delineated, as in early Western films where it is always easy to tell the good guys from the bad guys by the color of their white and black hats.[28]

So transgression—and sin—is innately tied up in the nature of the excuse. Adam's excuse is "the woman you gavest me"; Eve's excuse is "the snake made me do it"; the snake has no excuse, is punished first, and slithers away: "Upon your belly you shall go, and dust you shall eat all the days of your life."[29] This excusatory culture has blossomed in the early 21st century with everyone from the president of the United States to the four year old invoking "it's not my fault because . . ." to the student who argues for a paper extension because her printer ran out of ink, which is not an excuse for behavior; it is a reason. Arguably, millennials, in particular, have conflated and confused the two, the excuse and the reason, seemingly believing that every reason is an excuse. Again, Hume's fork: "If behavior is not utterly random, it will have some explanation; if behavior *were* utterly random, we couldn't hold the person responsible in any case."[30] The student with the inkless printer is not absolved of responsibility—she did not plan ahead to make sure she had printer refills on hand. The printer issue is the reason her paper is not on time; it is not an excuse. She is expected to claim responsibility.

Discussions of responsibility, in philosophical, theological and—indeed—mainstream circles blossomed in the long shadows thrown by the Holocaust, and it seems no contemporary discussion of the subject can ignore the magnifying impact of that horrific event. Who was responsible for the horrific components of the Holocaust? Of course, it is easy to prosecute Nazis who were complicit in the killing, but what of the responsibility of humanity as a whole? And what of the responsibility of a divine being? I once had a Jesuit philosophy instructor who told us that after World War II American Catholics were questioning their parish priests: "How could God have let this happen?" The professor said that the Vatican convened meetings to discuss an answer. They ultimately came up with "God didn't let this happen. You let it happen. You could have stopped it and you didn't." The responsibility, the Church claimed, lay in humanity's own hands.

If we think of human existence as having a particular goal or *telos* (in Greek), what is that goal? Aristotle thought it was happiness, *eudaimonia*, although Paul Valéry later averred that happiness is "an animal notion" and that "the happy organism is oblivious of itself."[31] As science journalist Robert Wright suggests, if we are "to know how humans should behave, we must first ask toward what end evolution is heading."[32] Each discipline has its own answer to the question, "What is the goal of human existence?" For the biologist, it is procreation; for the Buddhist, it is escape from the cycle of rebirth; for some Christians, the goal is converting as many nonbelievers as possible; for some Jews, it is to live the Torah. As British philosopher Julia Annas writes, "While there is consensus that our final end is happiness (*eudaimonia*), this is trivial, for substantial disagreement remains as to what happiness consists in."[33] The role of happiness in modern morality remains unclear. More than "happiness," modern human beings strive for balance, what the Middle Ages called "the middle way."[34] In *Nicomachean Ethics*, Aristotle tells us that "moral excellence is a mean" negotiating between "excess" and "deficiency."[35] He mentions as well that it is "no easy task to find the middle." Swiss psychologist Carl Jung notes "the median degree of modesty which is essential for the maintenance of a balanced state."[36]

Human beings strive for balance regarding so many aspects of daily and long-term living. Balance in eating, sexual activity, work, play, in fact, many of the very activities that arise when we talk about sin. I suggest that one of humanity's most difficult balancing acts concerns morality and finding the sweet spot between doing right for self, others, and the world, and being focused on one's own welfare and happiness without falling into narcissistic solipsism. Regardless of the *telos* of human existence, sin acts as a disruptor, what German Catholic philosopher Josef Pieper calls "a disturbance in man's relationship to his final goal."[37]

Charles Darwin believed that humans are the only moral animal, though he argued for a natural morality that occurs as the result of the evolution of the species. Darwin wrote that what he called "higher social animals" "would inevitably acquire a moral sense or conscience."[38] How such instincts were acquired, through natural selection or "the indirect result of other instincts and faculties, such as sympathy, reason, experience, and a tendency to imitation," Darwin was unsure.[39] Then again, he wonders, morality could be "simply the result of long continued habit."

What does it mean in this context to be a moral animal? Self reflection would seem to be key to meaningful existence. That we have "self awareness, memory, foresight, and judgment"[40] is all well and good, but we must also exercise the ability to reflect on our thoughts, actions, and beliefs. "We have, at least, the technical capacity for leading a truly examined life."[41] E. O. Wilson has argued that "individual selection favors what we call sin and group selection favors virtue."[42] Human beings, Wright writes, have "a moral gyroscope, to hold fast to our values, come what may."[43] While I agree with Wright, that gyroscope, sometimes mysterious, requires constant recalibration based on experience and knowledge.

To be sure, much of this book comes down to a deceptively simple but longstanding question: what does it mean to lead a good life? This is a question that has been asked at least as long as Plato and as recently as the OpEd pages of *The New York Times*. But what is a "good" life, and how has human history coped with very real temptations, many of which philosophers and theologians have come to call "sin." Is sin real? Are these concepts even definable or recognizable? Or are they like Justice Potter Stewart's 1964 definition of obscenity: we know them when we see them.

Any investigation of sin in the West must begin in Eden, travel through the early Jewish and Christian interpretations, meander through the fire and brimstone sermons of the Middle Ages, find itself lost in the Enlightenment, only to be reintroduced to discussion with Darwin, and then have its very existence questioned in postmodern thinking. We begin in the fourth century with a Greek monk who fled Constantinople for Jerusalem in 383 before moving on to Egypt.

Evagrius Ponticus and the Codification of Sin

We have a fourth century monk to thank for any notion of a list of sins. Living first in Jerusalem and later in Egypt, Evagrius Ponticus combined classical Greek thought with Christian philosophy to create a distinct monastic theology that embraced a particularly metaphysical cosmology. The greater portion of his extant work focuses on the minutiae of monastic life, presaging the *Rule of St. Benedict* not to be written until the early sixth century. His corpus provides an early foundation for the rule of the monastic life, a kind of daily handbook for monks and nuns. One important aspect of Evagrius's mystical theology was the notion that souls were once part of a great divine unity; it is through their fall that they join to a body. Evagrius felt that through ascetic principles and deep contemplation the soul could return to union with God.[44] As one of Evagrius's modern scholars puts it, "Evagrius' justly famous 'psychology' has one aim only: to make the human being capable of loving again, and thereby capable of God. But this is not possible without overcoming the distortion of human existence and the passions that kill love."[45] Central to Evagrius's writing is the codification of sin, which he of course saw as the greatest obstacle to achieving the love of and union with the divine. Evagrius scholar Kevin Corrigan refers to Evagrius's list of sins as "eight forms of dangerous reasoning" instead of as deadly sins.[46] "What Evagrius means by these reasonings is not so much the great sins themselves, as the associated temptations toward them along the particular trajectories of the soul."[47] The "dangerous reasonings" are temptations from the ascetic practice central to Evagrius's theology.

Evagrius provides us with a list of eight sins in his *On Eight Thoughts*: gluttony, fornication, avarice, anger, sadness, acedia, vainglory, and pride. "The nature of the exposition of the eight thoughts in the treatise suggests that the work was intended as an introduction to the subject for a reader or audience still engaged in the initial stages of the struggle against the passions or the 'practical life,' as Evagrius called it."[48] It is in this way that we can easily see how Evagrius's list made the move from the monastic world to the wider religious world beyond the monastic enclosure.

His origin stories for the eight sins are familiar. He traces gluttony to the Garden of Eden: "Desire for food gave birth to disobedience and a sweet taste expelled from paradise."[49] Women are the object of the sin of fornication (apparently, only men are susceptible to sin): "The sight of a woman is a poisoned arrow." In what reminds me of Hamlet's railing against women ("God has given you one face and you make yourselves another. You jig and amble, and you lisp, you nickname God's creatures and make your wantonness your ignorance"), Evagrius writes that women "speak softly, cry emotionally, dress modestly, and moan bitterly"; "they raise their eyebrows and bat their eyelashes; they bare the neck and use the entire body in an enticing manner."[50] Avarice is, of course, "the root of all evils,"[51] so that the monk should be free of all possessions. Anger "leads to madness,"[52] and "the psalmody of an angry person is an irritating noise."[53] Sadness "is a worm in the heart, and consumes the mother who gives it birth";[54] those afflicted by sadness can gain no spiritual pleasure. Acedia (what would become sloth) "is a relaxation of soul which is not in accord with nature."[55] Vainglory "gets tangled up with any work of virtue," and "the virtue of a vainglorious person is like a flawed sacrificial victim."[56] Finally, pride "is a tumour of the soul filled with pus."[57] "The soul of a proud person mounts a great height, and casts him down from there into the abyss."[58]

Although Gregory the Great is said to have originated the concept of the seven deadly sins by reducing Evagrius Ponticus's list to seven, we already find a list of seven spirits/sinful inclinations in the Jewish Christian Greek *Testament of Reuben* probably written sometime after 250 BCE. The text provides a list of "spirits of error" that nearly correlate to our concept of the seven deadly sins: "promiscuity" (lust), "insatiability" (gluttony), "strife" (anger), "flattery and trickery" (avarice), "arrogance" (pride), "lying" (vainglory), and "injustice, with which are thefts and crooked dealings" (acedia/sloth).[59] In coordination with "the spirit of sleep," these seven spirits form "an alliance, which results in error and fantasy. And thus every young man is destroyed, darkening his mind from the truth, neither gaining understanding in the Law of God nor heeding the advice of his fathers."[60] As we see later in the writings of the Christian Middle Ages, women are the target of blame:

Do not devote your attention to a woman's looks, nor live with a woman who is already married, nor become involved in affairs with women.[61]

Evagrius's list included melancholy and apathy (*tristitia* and *acedia*). These were later conflated by Gregory the Great to the single sin of acedia or sloth. There is a significant difference in the way that Old Testament Hebrews viewed sin versus early Christians. For the Hebrews, sin was a public affair, an affront to God that would be punished in very visible ways, often resulting in punishment of the many for the sin of just one. For early Christians, sin had become a much more personal, interior matter, between the individual and God. Ancient Hebrews also believed that the punishment for sin was imminent, would be coming sooner rather than later, while Christians instead subscribed to the idea that the punishment for the sin might be delayed, as long as after death in some cases. Later, when the job of punishment shifted to the state, the nature of sin itself morphed, becoming less a question of morality and more one of legality. The moral sins were handled by religious authority, while the illegal sins were the purview of the government and the court. Thus, much of what was once considered "sinful" behavior has now become almost solely "illegal." Murder is illegal and is prosecuted by the courts and punished by the state. Pride is a sin and is prosecuted in one's heart and in dialog with either the Church or divinity itself. Illegal acts are public matters; sins remain private. Clearly, then, the codification of sin is not new to the Christian Church but had been a concern in ancient Hebrew literature as well.

Nevertheless, it is Gregory whose name is most closely associated with the phrase "seven deadly sins." One of the most important figures in the history of Christianity, Gregory was probably born into a wealthy Roman family around 540 CE and is generally credited with founding the modern papacy when he served as Pope Gregory I from 590 until his death in 604. His papal reign was witness to a unification of the East and the West, and

Gregory worked diligently to erect a bridge from the ancient Church to the medieval Church.

As a young monk with little interest in the papacy, Gregory was focused on the contemplative life of the monastery when he was called to wear the papal pallium. Liturgical reform, Gregorian chant, more structured and effective administration of the Church—all are Gregory's legacies, but it is his explication of the sins in *Morals on the Book of Job* (commonly referred to by its Latin name *Moralia on Job*) that will more than likely make him a final Jeopardy answer.

Essentially a commentary on the book of Job, *Moralia on Job* is one of the longest works in the patristic corpus, filling 35 books and some six volumes. Gregory's work is an attempt to reconcile monastic spirituality with the life of the Christian in the world, essentially extending Evagrius's intentions. "The *Moralia* is an attempt to be an encyclopedia of the Christian life."[62] Gregory is the one of the earliest popes to leave an extensive written legacy, a legacy that includes more than 800 extant letters detailing his involvement in the myriad affairs of the day. The writing of the *Moralia* bridges the time from when Gregory was a monk through his time as a papal ambassador. Gregory scholar Mark DelCogliano calls the *Moralia* "a treasury of insight about the pathways, attitudes, challenges, and conditions not only of the spiritual life of the individual Christian but also of the collective life of the Church."[63] Jean Leclerq, the French Benedictine monk whose 1957 study *The Love of Learning and the Desire for God* continues to be an influence in religious studies, writes that Gregory developed "not only a theology, but a psychology of the spiritual life."[64] Gregory's work became the standard: "Everyone in fact, had read him and lived by him."[65]

Most significantly, for our purposes, Gregory abridged Evagrius's eight sins to seven and established "the seven deadly sins" as a seminal concept in the Western world. Donald Capps, noted pastoral theologian at the Princeton

Theological Seminary, suggests that the abridgement to seven sins may have had something to do with accommodating the seven day week. In line with other infamous sevens (seven virtues, seven sorrows of Mary, seven gifts of the Holy Spirit), Capps suggests, "A list of seven sins would lend itself to daily prayer, with each day's prayer focusing on the sin assigned to it."[66] Capps then suggests that the "ranking" of the sins places them in accord with the devotions of each day of the week: Sunday is the day of pride when one stresses devotion to God and humility of self; Wednesday is the day of sloth, the low point in the week; Saturday is the day of lust when the effects of Sunday's spiritual commitment have waned, and so on. Using the seven days as a memory aid for the seven sins might be expected in a society used to such devices.

One common tool used for meditation on sin during the late Middle Ages and early Renaissance was the hand as a mnemonic device. The practice is probably an adaptation of using the hand to illustrate musical notes. Several examples are extant, including a particularly striking one from an 11th century manuscript: the Guidonian hand in which the hand is used to map different musical notes with each tip and joint of the hand designating a specific note.[67] In a 1466 German print, "The Hand as the Mirror of Salvation," the viewer is instructed to meditate on different finger segments and sections of the palm in an effort to pray and repent. Latin text above the hand says, "If you know the will of God, recognize evil, so that you may avoid it. If you have done evil, regret it. If you regret it, confess it. When you have confessed it, do penance." Both Mary Magdalene and Martha are present in the woodcut sheet to assist with the *bonum* (good) and *malum* (evil) clearly marked. Such tools for contemplation are later found in the mental imagery of the 16th century *Spiritual Exercises* of the Jesuit Ignatius Loyola and are quite commonly found in 21st century guides to meditation and mindfulness.

Although the phrase "seven deadly sins" is largely identified with

Christianity, I'd like to suggest in this book that the concept has transcended religion and has been adopted by secular society, that in fact most people could not name the seven sins, nor would they know where or when the idea originated, though they easily invoke the phrase "seven deadly sins."

Perhaps most notably in this introduction, I want to outline the distinction between secular sin and religious sin. Can we have the notion of sin without religion? In philosopher Albert Camus's 1942 essay *The Myth of Sisyphus*, we find the phrase "sin without God" in his definition of the absurd. By this, he means only that the absurd is human beings' problem to deal with just as Judeo-Christians have to deal with the notion of original sin. In his 1947 novel *The Plague*, Camus's main character famously asks, "Can one become a saint without God?" It is not my intention to suggest an answer, and I mean "sin without God" in a different sense than Camus. Camus suggests in his corpus that the existence of God could only make modern life more absurd. Is discussion of sin in a godless existence a moot point? Or is sin only possible with the presence (and threat) of divine punishment? Grace Whistler argues that Camus "wanted to demonstrate the value of morality in a godless universe" throughout his work.[68] Camus's existentialist philosophy—quite different, Whistler argues, from mainstream existentialist thought—suggests, "It is clear from very early on that the lack of a guiding power should not mean the lack of morality."[69] We can in fact be moral beings without divine oversight. In fact, if there is no morality without God, the human race is doomed.

Friedrich Nietzsche saw humankind stumbling through the 20th century on the threads of what Tom Wolfe called "the old decaying God-based moral codes."[70] Two world wars in addition to several horrific genocides prompted humanity to reflect on itself and its fundamental values. The notion of the self? The notion that humanity is somehow responsible for itself and each other? Problematic at best. Wolfe notes that evolutionary biologists, what he calls "genetic determinists," believe that "an individual's happiness is largely genetic."[71] This impacts the current discussion directly because if my happiness is based on my genetic makeup, then my behavior—good or otherwise—is also a result of genetics, and both are essentially and inherently beyond my control, regardless of one's attitudes toward responsibility and free will. Such genetic determinism is a red herring in that it merely makes possible avoidance of responsibility and leads to moral decadence.

Moral bankruptcy has proven more devastating than financial bankruptcy because the latter most often affects an individual, while the former is the plague of a society. In Ernest Hemingway's 1927 short story "Hills Like White Elephants," a man has a cryptic conversation with a woman, implying that he is encouraging her to get an abortion: "'Well,' the man said, 'if you don't want to you don't have to. I wouldn't have you do it if you didn't want to. But I know it's perfectly simple." Some read the nonchalant way the pair discuss a potential abortion as an indictment of their values. Such moral bankruptcy is not uncommon in Hemingway's work and reflects the void in the postwar moral landscape.[72] In 1958, Gasset wrote, "Intellectually we are like banks in pseudo bankruptcy. Pseudo, because each one lives with his thoughts; and if these are false and empty, he is falsifying his life and swindling himself."[73]

Moral bankruptcy in the contemporary world presents in two forms: those who take advantage of others in an immoral fashion, and those whose actions are morally questionable. When the island of Puerto Rico was ravaged by not one but two hurricanes in 2017, the devastation destroyed the island's power grid, leaving millions without electricity for months. The governor of Puerto Rico estimated that the second storm, Maria, caused at least $90 billion in damage; a month after the storm, the Trump administration requested $4.9 billion to fund a loan program for Puerto Rico to rebuild some of its basic functions and infrastructure— less than 5 percent of the stated need. A month after the storm, Donald Trump tweeted, "We cannot keep FEMA, the Military & the First Responders, who have been amazing (under the most difficult circumstances) in P.R. forever!" The mayor of San Juan, Carmen Yulin Cruz, responded, "You are incapable of empathy and frankly simply cannot get the job done." It was not until a full year had passed that the entire island had power restored. The federal government's response, particularly that of the president, to the crisis in Puerto Rico is an example of moral bankruptcy.

In an extensive 1968 article published in *Speculum,* Siegfried Wenzel, professor emeritus at the University of Pennsylvania, argued that after the 16th century, the paradigm of the seven deadly sins "no longer played an important role in analysis of human behavior or in church teaching."[74] Nonetheless, notions of sin, including their codification and classification, have remained central to Western culture. To be sure, one of modernity's greatest challenges has been the adoption of a moral structure applicable to a culture that has shaken itself of ancient notions of divine punishment. Certain actions are considered sinful by virtue of their very nature and are not dependent on a theologically sanctioned moral code. Nonetheless, "It is futile to condemn the evil one has not done. This is on a par with a blind man's talking about colors."[75] In 1973, psychiatrist Karl Menninger asked *Whatever Became of Sin?* For some two decades, no American president— Kennedy, Johnson, or Nixon—had mentioned sin. Menninger catalogs the media dearth of discussions of "sin" in the 1960s and early 1970s, particularly curious in light of the atrocities of the Vietnam War. How could, during the age of the Watergate scandal, attention to sin have been relegated to the dustbin of theology?

I am going to follow Menninger's fine and simple definition for sin: "behavior that violates the moral code or the individual conscience or both."[76] Note this is not a particularly theological or even religious definition but is instead spiritual, that is, related to the human spirit, regardless of the religious belief. Unlike the days of the early Christian Church or the ancient Israelites, moral sin and social law are no longer conflated. When David slept with Bathsheba, his sin was both moral and social. He had sinned against his God, who had commanded, "Thou shalt not commit adultery," and as well as against the society in his disruption of another's marriage (and eventual murder of Bathsheba's husband). Carl Jung wrote that "real moral problems all begin where the penal code leaves off" since they "spring from conflicts of duty. Anyone who is sufficiently humble, or easygoing, can always reach a decision with the help of some outside authority."[77] The true challenge for moral behavior—and questions of sin—lay in individual decision made without the influence or external judgment. It is also the great paradox of human being.

In this study, I embrace an essentially nonreligious based definition for sin, but one that is clearly informed by centuries of religious and philosophical teaching. That is not to say that religion has nothing to do with sin; it only means that it doesn't have to. In the process of sinning, someone is harmed, either physically, psychologically, or spiritually. Because human existence is rooted in inquiry, in curiosity, in the basic two-year-old child's question of "why," it is inevitable that humans sometimes reach beyond the limits of accepted behavior. Those limits, however, differ from society to society, from culture to culture, and even from family to family. Human beings do not live in a vacuum, nor are they hermits by nature. Therefore, societies of human beings have erected rules/laws regarding the limits of accepted behavior. Over time, such rules have morphed into social constructions of morality and ethics.

Therefore, rules and the nature of sin probably differ dramatically. I grew up in a sixth floor apartment in the Bronx. If someone was in the shower, it was considered "a sin" to flush the toilet (thus, diverting all of the cold water and possibly scalding the person in the shower). I'm not sure that would have been considered sinful behavior in Fort Lee, New Jersey, or in Boulder, Colorado. Sin, if not relative, is certainly contextual. The issue of sin has always been closely connected with self reflection.

From the Oracle at Delphi ("Know thyself") to Socrates ("the unexamined life is not worth living") to José Ortega y Gasset ("To live is to find oneself forced to interpret life"[78]), human beings have struggled with the subjective "I" and how it fits into the objective world. I see this as a struggle that has only intensified since 1900—through two world wars, the rise of technology, the explosion in affluence, the development of nuclear weapons, the mapping of the human genome, and the movement into a tech-focused 21st millennium. The balance between good and evil is inherent in so many of these changes, and with that has come a battle with sin and sinful behavior. When J. Robert Oppenheimer said, after the first test of the nuclear bomb, "I am become death," he not only echoed the Hindu Gita, but he displayed the sin of pride, as I will examine further in Chapter 1.

Gasset expressed the sentiment so well in his *Man and Crisis*: "For if anything is at this moment clear, it is that man, and the very man who is most civilized, on this continent or any other, does not know what to do."[79] A feeling of impotence has washed over humanity, even more so since Gasset wrote those words in 1958. Civilized man, who has begun to doubt his very civility, is at odds with the world he himself has constructed. The chaos of the global environmental crisis, the fluctuating economic status of much of the world's population, human rights lapses—all speak to a humanitarian crisis of the spirit in which the line between "right" and "wrong" has become so muddied that we often seem paralyzed to make a choice and too often make the incorrect one.

In discussing a similar existential crisis in the Middle Ages, Gasset writes:

This fifteenth century man then is lost in himself, torn away from one system of convictions and not yet installed in another, without a solid ground on which to stand; swinging loose on his hinges, so to speak, exactly as man is today. He still believes in the medieval world, that is to say, in the supernatural otherworld of God; but he believes it without a living faith. His faith has already become a matter of habit, and inert, though this does not mean that it is insincere.[80]

I suggest in this book that humanity is at a similar tipping point today. We live in a world where the definition of sin has morphed, has been contorted, to fit our own needs and desires. "Good" has come a long way from the rigidness of the ten commandments and is as malleable today as the plastic that seems to represent the age; we make of it what we want, and if that is not good enough, it can either be melted down and reshaped or merely discarded (like so many plastic goods), only to be replaced by this year's model.

We exist at a moment of transition between what was and what could be. We certainly live in an age of potentiality. And what becomes of that potential is entirely up to us. Writing in his final work—the nonfiction *Apocalypse*—in 1929–1930, English novelist D. H. Lawrence argued that it is we ourselves who are responsible for the evil in the world: "Society consists of a mass of weak individuals trying to protect themselves, out of fear, from every possible imaginary evil, and, of course, *by their very fear*, bringing the evil into being."[81] Lawrence laments, "Our conscious range is wide, but shallow as a sheet of paper. We have no depth to our consciousness."[82] The price, he says, is "boredom" (acedia/sloth, to be discussed in chapter seven).[83] Lawrence's concern was a spiritual wasteland not unlike T. S. Eliot's broken landscape haunted by "the rattle of the bones" and the "rock without water," a land wasted of both physical and spiritual fertility.

Although my preceding examples are taken from the early 20th century, my thesis is that we are in a similar state in the early 21st century and that our notions of sin and sinful behavior again merit a serious discussion. The problem is that I don't think it is getting the discussion it demands, mostly due to the tremendous amount of cultural "noise" coming from the Internet, 24/7 news cycles, and the ever present danger that we might miss out. The cultural malaise that seemed to plague Europe between 1900 and 1950 has now descended on America and, by extension, the world.

The media reinforces this notion. A September 2018 cover story in *New York* magazine decried "The Politics of Anger." The June 2018 cover of *Self* magazine profiled Tess Holiday, a self professed "fat positivity activist," and the editors questioned whether being overweight was something to be proud of. A recent lede article for *Healthy Living* asked, "Is It Love or Lust?" The 2012 premiere issue of *Spirit & Flesh*, a magazine covering "fashion, beauty, art, music, and culture," was a "profile" of the seven deadly sins. The Fox television series *Empire* focuses on a fictional entertainment company and the drama that ensues from its founders' family fighting to control the company and its mass fortunes. Perhaps the most significant locus of sin in the media is the news itself regardless of the delivery method: print, electronic, social media. The news almost daily points out the sins of humanity, but to what end? It certainly does not appear intended to remedy the situation but only to feed on it and encourage us to feed on it like so many hungry lions fighting for a scrap of meat.

Chapter One: Pride

All men make mistakes, but a good man yields when he knows his course is wrong, and repairs the evil. The only crime is pride.

—Sophocles, *Antigone*

"Pride goeth before a fall." "Pride feels no pain." "Proud people breed sad sorrows for themselves." We all have probably heard one or more of these quotations, sentiments that have, over time, entered the popular ethos if not globally, at least in the Western world. But pride, arguably the root—and once thought the most egregious—of the seven deadly sins, is largely misunderstood in contemporary society mostly due to the lack of clarity in the meaning of the word: the original sin committed in the Garden of Eden? or a feeling of self-satisfaction as in "have pride in yourself"? For millennials, who have been consistently coached about self-esteem, pride is a positive—one can never have too much pride. For centuries of thinkers, however, including contemporary intellectuals particularly concerned with issues of morality and ethics, pride remains an odious and reviled trait to be avoided. How did we get here, and what are the ramifications for contemporary society? In this chapter, I will explore the issue of pride, from the Garden of Eden to the modern schoolyard, in an effort to better position this as a central concern of contemporary society.

The dictionary definition for pride is little help: "A high, esp. an excessively high, opinion of one's own worth or importance which gives rise to a feeling or attitude of superiority over others; inordinate selfesteem."[1] The hyperbolic language—"excessively high," "superiority," "inordinate"— raises red flags, but to what those red flags warn is unclear. Is pride equivalent to the notion of the self? In D. H. Lawrence's 1917 short story "The Mortal Coil," a soldier asks "And isn't my pride *me*? What am I without my pride?" To which another responds, "You are *yourself*. If they take your uniform off you, and turn you naked into the street, you are still *yourself*." But the first character resists: "What does it mean, *myself*!"[2] What is the self and what is its relationship to this sin of pride?

We have to wonder if it is possible to be a "self" without pride. If pride is self-esteem, then pride is a positive aspect of the self. If it is "inordinate self-esteem," it becomes dangerous both to the self and to the world. Jung wrote, "Through pride we are ever deceiving ourselves. But deep down below the surface of the average conscience a still, small voice says to us, something is out of tune."[3] Valéry noted, "Consummate pride is based on permanent dissatisfaction with one's self, treating oneself as somebody else and others as oneself—in other words, harshly."[4] Pride is the noise that disturbs the peace of the spirit that allows the intellect its creativity. In its absence, we are literally no one; with too much, we are intolerable humans.

But pride itself is not inherently evil—it is only evil, a sin, in excess. For moderns, pride is tied to what Canadian philosopher Charles Taylor calls "the ethics of authenticity" and the question of how one can live an authentic life in which one is true to one's self. Pride can certainly interfere with authenticity when an individual wears a persona of "inordinate self-esteem" and thus oversteps the boundaries of his authentic self and lives what amounts to an ersatz life.

The early fifth century Christian theologian John Cassian calls pride "first in terms of origin and time."[5] Gregory the Great wrote that "pride is the root of all evil."[6] Augustine viewed pride as "the beginning of all sin." German Protestant theologian Julius Müller calls pride "the most naked form of selfishness."[7] The heart of the matter: Western philosophers and theologians have for centuries focused on the development and empowerment of the self and its role in the relationship with the divine. Pride, however, is the result of excessive concern with the self. As is the case with almost all sin, the action itself is not wrong; only when that action is committed to excess does it become problematic. But we have to deal with an interesting problem: the concept of the "self," since about the fourth century, has been held up as a trophy of Western philosophy and psychological development. Throughout his work, St. Augustine focuses on the role of the self in developing a complete concept of the individual and connecting that individual to the divinity. Augustine scholars have had much to say. Phillip Cary has argued that it is Augustine who is responsible for the "invention of the inner self";[8] Sarah Spence examines the role of the *corpus* as both body and text in the 12th century contribution to the self.[9] Most recently, Brian Stock has written of Augustine's use of the inner dialogue as it fosters the development of the self.[10] The ancient Greek maxim "know thyself" is the key to unlocking so much in Western knowledge, while Polonius's "to thine own self be true" seems solid advice to his son Laertes as he embarks on a journey to France. The rise of the inner dialogue—a discussion of the individual with the individual— marks the true growth of humanity and is central to Augustine's philosophy. It is not, however, until the 12th century Arthurian tales of French writer Chrétien de Troyes that characters begin to display an inner life.[11] It is in these tales that we first witness the interior dialogue of literary characters rather than stories being simply linear narratives of action. The power of intention rose in importance.

In many ways, as Stock has shown over the course of several insightful studies, Augustine is indeed responsible for giving us a concept of the self, facilitated mostly through the reflective acts of meditation and reading. Most recently, Stock writes of what he calls "the integrated self": a melding of the physical and spiritual selves, mediated by insightful reading, intellectual development, and spiritual dialogue.[12] This integrated self fosters self awareness, self knowledge, and thus encourages the growth of a whole individual, one that includes a consciously and intentionally formed self.

It is notable that in his monumental study *Sources of the Self*, Charles Taylor notes Plato's sentiment that the good person "is collected" and "enjoys a kind of self possession, of centring in himself."[13] I'm particularly taken with Taylor's choice of "in himself" rather than "on himself," and I think that is the difference between pride and narcissism. Colloquially, we say one has pride "in himself," but in narcissism, as in Jung's Shadow, "one meets with projections, one does not make them."[14] The narcissist is consumed with the projections of his or her own self. Pride indicates a connection with the external world, but a connection in which the individual sees himself or herself as superior to all others encountered. The narcissist barely acknowledges the existence of others and might instead be living in an entirely self-constructed interior world—a fantasy, a simulation of reality.

The human ability to move from external to internal is a true marker in the development of the self. Taylor argues that it was Augustine who "introduced the inwardness of radical reflexivity" to the West, a singular moment in which the division between objectivity and subjectivity becomes the driving force in the individual's relationship with self.[15] This is perhaps represented later in the Middle Ages in the mystical turn toward God (found in, among others, English mystic Richard Rolle— about whom more later in this chapter).

Augustine characterizes pride simply as "love of self." What is termed the "inward turn" can only be viewed as positive in Augustine. As Taylor puts it, "Augustine is always calling us within."[16] Augustine suggests reflection and contemplation, not submersion in the self. That submersion into the self is what Freud indicates as narcissism. Perhaps Augustine's "inward turn" is more akin to what Jung terms "introversion," while Freud reads narcissism as primarily, if not exclusively, related to sexual impulse. I prefer to read narcissism in a contemporary context as overinvolvement with the self, combined with an almost paralyzing inability to operate with any kind of objectivity.

One who is "guilty" of the sin of pride is one who has made the inward turn but then is unable to turn back. He or she is caught in the snare of subjectivity, unable once he or she has examined the self, to return to the world of objects and objectivity. "In other words, the dark side of individualism is a centring on the self, which both flattens and narrows our lives, makes them poorer in meaning, and less concerned with others or society."[17] Alexis de Tocqueville saw this almost two centuries ago when he wrote in *Democracy in America*, "Each person therefore retreats within the limits of the self and from that vantage ventures to judge the world."[18] When Taylor writes in *The Ethics of Authenticity* of a "flattened world," I think he indicates a world that lacks moral dimensionality, a world where the ethics of existence have collapsed. Taylor credits Augustine with introducing "radical reflexivity."[19] A kind of exaggerated inwardness, radical reflexivity leads us to think on a higher plane, perhaps either the plane of Plato's forms or the world to which many hopeful intellectuals had aspired.

It is somewhat ironic that as the individual has grown, people have lost the broader vision," which has led to "a centring on the self," what Taylor calls "the dark side of individualism."[20] This is the result of "the massive subjective turn of modern culture, a new form of inwardness, in which we come to think of ourselves as beings with inner depths."[21] This brings us into the complex and contentious area of identity theory[22] and the ways in which moral ambiguity has risen steadily concurrent with the rise of the individual. Taylor states again: "Individualism as a moral principle or ideal must offer some view on how the individual *should* live with others."[23] Taylor argues that individualism has a responsibility to provide a moral system; without that moral system, the individual risks falling into a completely subjective existence, an existence driven and supported by pride.

In his seminal study of the seven deadly sins, medievalist Morton Bloomfield notes pride as "the sin of exaggerated individualism."[24]

Particularly in the Middle Ages, "exaggerated individualism, rebellion against the will of God, was considered particularly heinous."[25] Bloomfield goes on to argue that since the Renaissance, "with its emphasis on individualism," the culture has looked at pride as a relatively slight sin that does not require serious punishment. Pride, to the medieval mind, meant rebellion against the will of God. As the centuries passed, and with the rise of the individual, pride came to mean "dangerous independent thinking, setting up one's own interest as supreme."[26] In this way, pride, like all sin, is a threat to order and discipline.

It is when focus on the self becomes exaggerated that one risks crossing from awareness to pride. Being "self aware," in the parlance of contemporary pop psychology, is a positive; being "self obsessed" is a step toward what D. H. Lawrence refers to as egoism, a kind of radical, overreaching individualism: "We become trashy, conceited little modern egoists."[27] Once we view existence through a purely subjective lens, it becomes increasingly difficult to appreciate a world in which we are anything but its center as well as the best—this is the sin of pride. Jung notes that "inflation of the ego" can result in "puffedupness."[28] Twentieth century philosophy had long concerned itself with the problem of subjectivity; French phenomenologist Maurice Merleau-Ponty linked it to the phenomenology of perception, that is, how it is that we view the world and distinguish subject from object.[29] But this in turn relates to early conceptions of the self. It is this topic I would like to tease with for a bit.

Questions of the self and identity dominate philosophical writing. From Plato to Daniel Dennett, the topic sits at the center of most philosophical systems. In the *First Alcibiades*, Plato notes, "At times, I fancy that anybody can know himself; at other times, the task of self knowledge appears to be very difficult."[30] Having control over one's self, what Taylor calls "self mastery," is gained by having "the higher part of the soul rule over the lower, which means reason over the desires."[31] "To be rational is truly to be master of oneself."[32] The concept of a self developed from myriad discussions of soul and mind and evolves from a combination of both. Without a concept of self, the sin of pride has no meaning. If I have no sense of self, then I have no particular identity and would be unable to have an inflated sense of that identity—pride. For Jung, however, "the more consciousness insists on its own luminous nature and lays claim to moral authority, the more the self will appear as something dark and menacing."[33]

"In the beginning was the self." Well, not exactly. The Genesis text explains that Adam was created in the image of God. By extension, then, the greater aspect of Adam's existence is tied into his existence as an image of the divine. Part of Adam's self is God's self (but does God have a "self"?). In *Secrets of Heaven*, Swedish philosopher and mystic Emanuel Swedenborg writes, "Human selfhood, viewed from heaven, looks completely bony, lifeless, and hideous—inherently dead. But once the Lord gives it life, it appears to have flesh. Human selfhood is in fact nothing more than a dead trifle, even though it seems to its owner to be significant and indeed allimportant."[34] It is not my intention to get into an anthropology of the divine but instead to look at how the Genesis myth suggests the notion of a self in light of humanity's creation in God's image.[35]

Albert W. Fields articulates the gist of the matter in discussing John Milton's epic poem *Paradise Lost*:

> Milton's view of man distinguished between his rational part, or self-like God, and his passional nature, the latter being that aspect of self most easily subverted by Satan. By means of self knowledge, a person might maintain a harmony between the two aspects of self.[36]

The dual nature of the self is one explanation for the creation of gender in the original human. In many ancient cultures, the male became associated with reason and the female with passion; in others, the male represented humanity's divine nature, while the female represented carnal nature. A fairly strong Genesis tradition has it that the original human being lacked sexual distinction and that the division of male from female was a divine afterthought. None of these schema preclude the existence of a self.[37] The Genesis commentary tradition presents humanity as divided in a different way, having two aspects: the spiritual and the physical. The spiritual is the connection to the image of God, while the physical is the dust he is made from. It is with the "breath of life" that the Genesis text says humans became "a living being." As a result, humanity's sense of self is often at odds as in Socrates's explanation in *Phaedrus* where the self is likened to two horses driven by a charioteer; one horse represents restraint, reason, and morality, while the other is driven by appetite and passion. The two are perpetually at odds and result in a bifurcated and conflicted self.[38]

With the progression of the Middle Ages—and widespread education and private reading that developed after the printing press—the notion that the self could be holistic and whole became a guiding principle in religious writers from the 14th century English mystic Richard Rolle to the founder of the Jesuits, Ignatius Loyola. In point of fact, by the time Ignatius Loyola put together his *Spiritual Exercises* in the mid-16th-century, the idea that any individual (not just royalty or clergy) could have a developed sense of self had become ingrained in the culture. The age of the individual had truly begun.

In his autobiographical mystical work *The Fire of Love*, probably written in the 1340s, Richard Rolle tells us that "the conceited and touched consider themselves so magnificent as to be beyond any possibility of suffering. They cannot be persuaded by reason or authority because they are not going to be seen to be beaten or ridiculous." He pleads, "Give up this mad pride, and proud madness!"[39] In one of the most evocative passages in the book, Rolle, a reclusive monk, tells of three lustful experiences he had with women: one whose clothing he "inspected too closely"; one whose "great bosom" he

37

admired; and a third he attempted to touch. He was reprimanded by the third woman who "deservedly made me feel uncomfortable." Rolle notes his realization: "When I came to myself."[40] The original Latin here is "*Nam rediens ad meipsum*," but when we parse the Latin *meipsum*, it is actually two words: *me* and *ipsum* as in "my self." I have always read this passage as telling in Rolle's development, but more importantly, I think it says a great deal about the epiphanies a human being experiences, particularly those that bring us to a greater understanding of "self." It is perhaps ironic that, with all the time spent focused on the self in today's culture, many have little sense of their true self; it is through epiphany that many receive that flash of understanding.

The epiphany, a sudden realization, is well illustrated in James Joyce's 1914 short story "Araby," where the first person narrator, a young teenage boy, has a crush on a neighbor girl and foolishly promises to bring her a trinket from the local bazaar "Araby." After paying to get in, and with barely any money left, he stands before a stall studying wares, knowing his "stay was useless." As the bazaar closes for the night, he comes to a stunning self realization: "Gazing up into the darkness I saw myself as a creature driven and derided by vanity; and my eyes burned with anguish and anger." The young man has come to "his self" in a telling reflection (the story is told by the adult speaker reminiscing) and has realized his behavior was driven by vanity, a realization that is both extraordinarily painful and insightful.

Indeed, it is in the darker side of the self, Plato's horse that pulls to the left, that we find the nascent seeds of the sin of pride. It is here that commentators lay the blame; if humanity could remain entirely and wholly spiritual, sin would cease to be a concern all together. This is the very goal of the journey of the mystic in the mystical tradition, to achieve union with the divine, to experience ecstasy (literally the Greek *ex stasis*, out of body), and to exist, if but for a moment, at the level of pure spiritual being. By the English Renaissance, knowledge of one's self had become "the absorbing problem."[41]

In fact, the balance between the inner human and the outer human, the private and the public, has become a driving concern till this day. One only has to look at contemporary American politics where a candidate's morality and personal life are balanced against his or her professional accomplishments and abilities in a bizarre kind of crucible. We continue to struggle with human beings' dual nature— whether that duality is physical and spiritual, rational and emotional, or public and private.

At the start of the 20th century, Oscar Wilde noted the shift from the ancient ethos of "know thyself" to the modern one of "be thyself."[42] Indeed, this would seem to be a move from the intellectual to the emotional, and the 20th and 21st centuries have increasingly focused on the subjective self, as Kurt Andersen argues in his recent *Fantasyland: How America Went Haywire: A 500 Year History*. Andersen's "fantasyland" is increasingly a self-constructed existence, one in which organized religion has actually served to distort values and morph society into an increasingly self-centered, and thus, more pride-centric, culture. When I lived in western South Dakota in the early 2000s, it seemed to me that the local shopping mall's tag line—"It's All About You"—encouraged narcissism and contributed to Andersen's "fantasyland."

In her recent study of pride, psychologist Jessica Tracy calls pride a "two-sided emotion"—it is both sin and badge of honor—but she argues that it has "shaped our nature. We humans are by far the most cultural species in existence, we are better than any other animal at learning from those around us and making what we learn our own. We would not have gotten here without pride."[43] Indeed, the history of modern humanity is rife with examples of pride-motivated achievements—from Edison's lightbulb to flight to radio.

Initial conceptions of pride in the West directly linked the sin to Adam's transgression in Eden beginning with the earliest interpretations of the Genesis story. For the early Church—and through the Middle Ages and

Renaissance—the math was easy. Adam and Eve eat the fruit of the Tree of Knowledge of Good and Evil after being told not to. Tempted by a serpent that the fruit would make them "like God," they aspire to a position beyond their appointed station. As a punishment, God expels them from Eden, condemns them to death, and causes their progeny to inherit the punishment (and guilt) for the sin without having actually taken part in the act. This initial fall from grace was an act of pride that became the main root of the tree of vices for humanity: a simple story that not only generated much of the Augustinian *raison d'etre*, but one that compelled philosophers (like Aquinas and Hegel), theologians (like Emanuel Swedenborg and Karl Barth), and poets (like Dante and John Milton) to pick up the biblical gauntlet in an attempt to further explain why eating a single piece of fruit should cause so much chaos.

Although we now live in what Charles Taylor calls "a secular age," the specter of Adam and Eve and that piece of fruit continues to loom large in the collective unconscious. The "Adam's Apple"—the one that stuck in Adam's throat because he knew he wasn't supposed to eat it—is biologically prominent in males. The continued theme of temptation of men by women (which isn't even biblically accurate—there is no actual "temptation" in Genesis) became a driving force in Western misogynism.[44] This also implies that pride is an innately human characteristic, highlighted in the culture's origin story.

Early rabbinical interpretations of what Christians would come to call the "fall" focus less on pride but instead are taken up with the nature of the dynamic between Adam and Eve as it set the standard for the marriage relationship between man and wife. Philo of Alexandria, the influential Greek Jewish contemporary of both Jesus and Paul, provides the litmus test here. In his *Allegorical Interpretation of Genesis II*, Philo reads the text as an allegory of reason versus pleasure (Adam and Eve respectively). Pride only comes into

Philo's discussion when he discusses the nature of shame. Essentially, he argues that Adam and Eve could not have experienced shame because they had "not yet attained to the apprehension of good and evil."[45] In *The Decalogue,* Philo calls pride "that most insidious of foes" and "the creator of many other evils."[46] But, without knowledge of right and wrong, intentional sin is not possible.

Much of the extracanonical material on Genesis reads the fall story through the lens of Christianity or, at least, is messianic in its anticipation of salvation. Thus, 2 Baruch: "For, although Adam sinned first and has brought death upon all who were not in his own time. For truly, the one who believes will receive reward."[47] Pride's grip reaches far into the future; although much later, the 12th century Spanish philosopher Moses Maimonides would refer to the fall story as "absurd in its literal sense."[48]

If there is no pride without a self, as I suggested earlier, then what of Adam's self? Adam's identity in the Genesis text is indeed spare—it is only when we appeal to apocryphal and literary texts that we see his "character" fully fleshed out. So how can a one-dimensional figure, one only just created, who knows only one other human, and who has lived his entire life in a protected bubble, know the self and, thus, experience (and even be guilty of) pride? The short answer: it's a myth. But that does not make the story or its impact any less real. As Joseph Campbell said, "Myths are closest to the spiritual potentialities of human life."[49] Myths provide us with the color of our existence, allowing us insight into some of life's greatest mysteries in ways that don't always make rational, objective sense. Although we might currently live at a time when myth is frowned upon, we cannot dismiss the importance of these foundational stories and the power they continue to have over us.

Several fine recent studies have examined the development of Adam and Eve as myth and legend in the West. These include Stephen Greenblatt who in his recent book, *The Rise and Fall of Adam and Eve,* goes so far as to argue that when the story of original sin was deemed not powerful enough to change people's behavior, the story itself was changed.[50] Greenblatt suggests that the "master text" required elaboration and enhancement to carry the gravitas needed. Theresa Sanders reads the Adam and Eve story through current popular culture in texts as disparate as the Harry Potter series and *The Cosby Show*.[51] All this tells us that the impact of a story of a fall from grace via the transgression of pride has in no way faded.

In a culture still centered on the myth of the fall, the role of pride as sin versus the role of pride as self esteem has become clouded. How much pride is too much pride? If I tell my daughter to "be proud of yourself," am I encouraging her to sin? Perhaps this was the sinkhole a generation fell into with awarding so-called participation trophies to children just for taking part in an activity or sport. This was intended to boost their confidence; instead, it seems to have backfired and created an entire generation of entitled adults who cannot but imagine that they are all "number one." And it has contributed to the affluencing of a generation. Many college campuses no longer house institutions of higher learning—they increasingly resemble resort spas with lush dining halls, on-campus entertainment, well-appointed dorm rooms, and even housekeeping at some schools.

As I often tend to do when encountering a conundrum that has me stuck in a dark room, I go back to the beginning, back to the ancients. The oracle at Delphi counselled: "know thyself." This powerful dictate not only motivated Augustine to engage in inner dialogue but has also compelled educators to instruct students to pursue education as personal development—the stereotypical college student who is looking to find himself. In fact, the relationship between knowledge and pride again brings us back to Eden, where, as the biblical writer has it, it is the unreasonable desire for knowledge that catalyzes the downfall of the original pair. This is perhaps nowhere as evident as in Milton's *Paradise Lost*, where the couple's sin is pride, in this context their desire to "know too much."

First published in 1674, when Milton had already gone completely blind, *Paradise Lost* is an epic poem intended to "justify the ways of God to men" through a retelling of the fall story and man's redemption by a benevolent God. Ironically, Milton has little to say in the poem directly on the sin of pride other than to note it as Satan's downfall. Instead, Milton frames Adam and Eve's pride in the context of the desire for knowledge. As Satan wonders upon hearing them for the first time, "Can it be sin to know"?[52] In many ways, the real sin here is the desire to be God, seen first in the fall from Heaven of Satan who thought he was as supreme a being as God and should be running the show. Upon hearing of the creation of the Son, Satan "through pride" cannot bear the idea and begins his revolt. It is Satan's desire to be God that compels him to revolt. The sin here is the desire to know as God knows—upsetting the ordered chain of being and attempting to rise on that chain from humanity's appointed position.[53] Once again, sin is about disrupting order.

In fact, it is not pride that motivates Adam to eat the fruit in Milton's poem but love. Adam cannot imagine life without Eve and so consents to partake in the fruit with her, fully aware of the consequences. When later questioned by God preceding his punishment, Adam is asked, "Was shee thy God."[54] During the sin itself, Adam wonders:

How can I live without thee, how forgoe

They sweet Converse and Love so dearly joyn'd,

To live again in these wilde Woods forlorn.[55]

Driven by his love of Eve—"Flesh of Flesh/Bone of my Bone"[56]—Adam sees no other solution but to eat. Milton is clear; Adam knows what he is about to do is wrong: "he scrupl'd not to eat / Against his better knowledge, not deceav'd, / But fondly overcome with Femal charm."[57]

Adam commits the sin of his own free will, paradoxically an indication of his human nature. Milton here endorses the Augustinian connection between pride and free will: "By their free will, and only thus, can humans prove the greatness of creativity and creation that Augustine identifies with God."[58] Free will allows humans the ability to make choice, but it is complicated when the distinction between the choices is not black and white. As a species, we live in the gray zone.

Humanity Becomes God:

Twentieth century humanity, armed with science and technology, seemed almost obsessed with turning itself into God. Indeed, the modern world's inclination for humanity to make itself God, the impulse toward self-deification, is some of the early occurrences of "pride." Certainly, as the 20th century progressed, the technological evolution and revolutions affected everyday life and increasingly turned humanity into all-powerful beings, setting up a standoff between humanity and divinity. The American theologian Reinhold Neibhur notes, "Religion is not simply . . . an inherently virtuous human quest for God. It is merely a final battleground between God and man's self-esteem."[59] Religion—and spirituality as a subset—is not only about getting closer to God, but it is about becoming one with God, the original mystical impulse of union from the ancient Greeks. Once humanity achieves union with the divinity, the only further step in this evolutionary journey is for humans to become the divinity. Humans can control their environment, their physical being, their emotional and psychological being, and, ultimately, they can control others. This impulse to control, to wield power and authority, has led us to the dangerous situation in which we currently live, a time when each political leader believes his or her country is superior and, indeed, should be supreme, dominating the others who would then only exist to serve. Be a "proud American"? Indeed. The America First Committee founded in 1940 opposed U.S. involvement in World War II. Let us never forget that "America First" has occasionally been a motto of the Ku Klux Klan. There is a fine line between pride and arrogance. It is a razor's edge.

If we consider the scientific innovations of the last hundred years, it is easy to understand how some intellectuals argue that humanity's ultimate goal has been to turn itself into a god, one that controls, has the ability to alter, and can even create an alternate reality. Neibhur succinctly summarizes the problem regarding modern humanity:

> He [i.e., humanity] assumes that he can gradually transcend finite limitations until his mind becomes identical with universal mind. All of his intellectual and cultural pursuits, therefore, become infected with the sin of pride. Man's pride and will-to-power disturb the harmony of creation. The Bible defines sin in both religious and moral terms. The religious dimension of sin is man's rebellion against God, his effort to usurp the place of God.[60]

It is in humanity's attempt to mold its world that it goes too far. Paul Valéry brilliantly outlines all of human history in three short pages of text including a stage in which "all living creatures adapt themselves. But Man does more; he adapts things to himself and bends them to his will, using their own laws against them."[61] After Trinity, the first successful test of the atomic bomb in 1945,[62] Robert Oppenheimer, one of the bomb's chief architects, famously remarked, "Now I am become Death, the destroyer of worlds." This line, actually a misquote from Chapter 11 of the Hindu spiritual text Bhagavad Gita, suggests that the impulse to control life and death—in this case in the form of apocalyptic annihilation—reflects a classic flavor of pride, that is, that desire to move higher on the chain of being and control creation. Once such complete control over life and death has been gained, humanity is left to finally and completely control its own destiny. While James Hijiya has made the case for Oppenheimer's devotion to the Gita and his study of Hinduism, I find it more telling that Oppenheimer's choice reflects both humanity's disgust and pride with itself at finally rising to control life and death in the sense of creation and destruction.[63] Oppenheimer elsewhere noted "the prevalence of newness" that hovers over the culture.[64] The speed with which that newness dominates is also noted: "What is new is that in one generation our knowledge of the natural world engulfs, upsets, and complements all knowledge of the natural world before."[65] Valéry completes, in his words, his "history in a nutshell" with the following:

> Next to come on the scene will be a Bellerophon who will reduce Death to its primitive role simply by reducing the value of the individual. For the children of the year 10,000 of our era will be moved to laughter by our notion of the "I"; Death and the Ego will be on a par with the setpiece *Monster versus Hero* of all conceivable mythologies. And once this is done, Homo will feel happy and cease being *sapiens*.[66]

Our very desire for knowledge—like Adam's in Milton's poem—has the potential to catapult our pride to destructive levels.

If physical comfort is a singular barometer for happiness, then it is no surprise that attempts to manipulate the world have blossomed. From the seemingly mundane faux nature of the shopping mall, which attempts to simulate an old neighborhood feel (complete with fake trees, plastic benches, and kiosks selling wares) for teeming shoppers, to the more recent work to alter the world at the level of the microscopic in the field of nanotechnology, several paradigm shifts have heralded new ways of thinking about humanity's relationship to the world around it. And each of those paradigm shifts has been subsequently derided by intellectuals with accusations of pride and concerns with what it would mean to our very humanity. Technological advancement masked as economic growth (as well as economic growth masked as technological advancement) has indeed affected the human nature of the species. An overly facile example: the disconnect caused by introducing artificial intelligence to company's telephone trees whereby it is no longer necessary (or, in most cases, even possible) to engage with a live human being. Instead the computer listens for your responses which it then processes. We are reduced to talking to (and fighting with) machines. We are dangerously close to becoming robots ourselves.

Indeed, such "innovations" have slowly chipped away at what makes human beings human and humane. A cavalcade of popular articles, books, and scholarly studies has looked at the technological revolution begun with the introduction of the personal computer, Tim Berners-Lee's invention of the World Wide Web,[67] and, more recently, the conspicuous presence of the smartphone and wearable technology. The majority of these studies, while lauding the "progress" we have made, have also acknowledged that we have become "dumber" and more vacuous as a species.[68] The damage done to humans' capacity to remember and be thought-full may be irreparable.

It is almost cliché to look at historical figures such as Napoleon, Hitler, and more recent political phenomena like Donald Trump. And while I see the value in looking at pride in such figures, it is perhaps more important to examine pride in the ordinary individual because it is there that we find the true endemic damage done to humanity. Contrary to what Ani DiFranco sings, everyone is not a Napoleon.[69]

Technology Becomes God:

As the 20th century closed and the 21st century dawned, humanity seems to have turned over much of the responsibility for the mundane tasks of existence to technology. Ceding the control over life and death that they earlier longed for to technology, humans have in many cases turned the reins over to artificial intelligence—self driving cars, automatic vacuum cleaners, "smart" thermostats. No longer satisfied with a doctor's deductive diagnosis, procedures such as CAT scans and MRIs have become the norm or are indeed required for insurance reimbursement. It is no longer enough for one human to question another human about his or her pain level; we now require disinterested, seemingly objective proof in the form of technological assessment. The reasons for this are not a mystery—money, the driving force behind much of human behavior. However, there is a positive case to be made as well. Technology has arguably made us a healthier and more enduring species.

In 1945, while working as the director of the government Office of Scientific Research and Development, Vannevar Bush wrote the brilliant essay, "As We May Think," first published in *Atlantic Monthly* that July, the same month as the Trinity atomic bomb test. Bush proposed a fictitious machine he calls the "memex": "a device in which an individual stores all his books, records, and communications, and which is mechanized so that it may be consulted with exceeding speed and flexibility. It is an enlarged intimate supplement to his memory." What a glorious idea: a "supplement" to the memory of an individual. Bush's vision was that such a machine could free up human beings' minds from the mundane minutiae of everyday life so that they might move their brains to more higher level thinking.

Flash forward some 70 years and most are walking around with Bush's "memex" in their pockets—the smartphone and the tablet computer have revolutionized not just the way that human beings retrieve memory but also how they store memory. This "enlarged intimate supplement" could be a fantastic growth opportunity for humanity. But what has humanity made of it thus far? In what significant ways have human beings taken advantage of this fantastic tool? Have they taken the opportunity to engage in higher level thinking? Not exactly.

Instead, smartphones (the very fact that the phones are called "smart" and not the users is telling) have encouraged a kind of narcissistic existence into which people continue to fall as Alice did into the rabbit hole. This narcissism, what the social critic Christopher Lasch predicted in 1979 would become a "culture of narcissism," has contributed to a culture of pride in which humanity consistently believes it to be and know better than anyone else, including proven scientific facts like climate change or vaccinations for children. "The egomaniacal, experience devouring imperial self regresses into a grandiose, narcissistic, infantile, empty self."[70] For Lasch, this was a condition of cultural malaise; I'm not sure he had any idea how deeply the culture would fall into this malaise in the following decades and into the next century (Lasch died in 1994). Not only has the self regressed into an empty shell, the ability to distinguish fact from fiction, truth from lie, and real from virtual has so deteriorated that polls continually show the individual's lack of ability to discern truth. In the age of fake news and election meddling through social media, the monster is once again out to kill its creator.

What Daniel Sarewitz, codirector of the Consortium for Science, Policy & Outcomes, and Professor of Science and Society in the School for the Future of Innovation in Society at Arizona State University, calls "the pride of modernity," science is, as he writes, "in deep trouble."[71] Sarewitz encourages scientists to emerge from the artificial environment of grant funded laboratories and classrooms to deal with real world issues and confront future crises. Citing another important piece by Vannevar Bush, Sarewitz notes science as "the free play of free intellects," something integral to the future of humanity as it confronts a possible "sixth extinction." In fact, Sarewitz's ideas follow from a genre of writing by scientists like E. O. Wilson, who declare it necessary that science work in tandem with the humanities in order to counterbalance increasingly prideful behavior on behalf of public policy shapers. A move to a problem-based intellectual model, not unlike the atmosphere embraced in the 19th century French salon culture, will be integral to solving humanity's most threatening ills, whether that be access to clean water or finding the cure for cancer.

So what does that all have to do with the pride of human beings? In order to shift to such a problem-based model, the species will have to move past its pride, past thinking that, just because one has a smartphone, he or she "knows everything." In actuality, the smartphone does not reflect knowledge at all, only access to information. It is for human beings to synthesize information and make it into knowledge. Knowledge is "made"—it is a creative act, and it is one of the characteristics that distinguish *Homo sapiens* from nonhuman animals.

Sarewitz provides examples of the ways in which the American scientific community collaborated in the past with the U.S. government and military complex to produce new technologies, but he leaves out an important component—the role of the humanities in the process. Steve Jobs, founder of Apple, once said, "It's in Apple's DNA that technology alone is not enough—that it's technology married with liberal arts, married with the humanities, that yields us the result that makes our hearts sing."[72]

Unfortunately, it would seem that the only way to draw humanity away from the mirror is through threats to its very existence—nuclear holocaust, pandemic disease, climate change. And perhaps the only way to do that in the United States is through collaboration with the military industrial complex. Thus, in the war to combat cancer, the National Breast Cancer Coalition president realized that the best avenue to encourage more research and win the war is to join up with the U.S. military.[73]

Sarewitz poses a probing question for a culture seemingly obsessed with assessment: "But if there is nothing by which to measure scientific progress outside of science itself, how can we know when our knowledge is advancing, standing still, or moving backwards?" His response: "It turns out that we cannot." Is that indeed true? I don't think so. We are currently a culture focused on quantitative data. It is human pride that stands in the way of accurate reflection and assessment, for as long as advances are rewarded only with monetary or frontpage accolade, it will remain difficult to make genuine and meaningful human advancements. Consider the most basic advancements in humanity's history: the wheel, fire, cooking—we know little of the process and even less about the players in such monumental moves forward. No one individual invented fire. These inventions were cultural and were part of a tradition of craft studied by archaeologist and historian Alexander Langlands. In his recent *Craeft: An Inquiry into the Origins and True Meaning of Traditional Crafts*, Langlands writes that "craeft is a form of intelligence, an ingenuity that can shift in accordance with a changing world."[74]

Susan Fitzpatrick, president of the James S. McDonnell Foundation, says we have "the sense that we're gaining knowledge when we're not gaining knowledge."[75] Again, this is the result of too much time spent in front of the mirror. When one is driven by economic benefit and thrives on self congratulation and external validation, it is difficult to engage in an accurate assessment of just what we have in fact gained by having, say, self driving cars. The disconnect from *techne*, the Greek word for "craftsmanship" or "art," has only widened. As philosopher Martin Heidegger wrote, technology is a "revealing" that "never comes to an end."[76] We cannot, however, forget that technology can effectively impact "our relationship to its essence" and that the danger is that man "exalts himself to the posture of lord of the earth."[77] Thus, Heidegger concludes, "questioning is the piety of thought."[78] If we blindly accept every technological "innovation," we run the risk of becoming slaves to the machine. Instead, we cannot relinquish our role as questioners; in this way, the danger of pride can be tamed through doubt.

One model to avoid pride and invite progress is the philanthropic Artemis Project, a research initiative launched by the National Breast Cancer Coalition to find a cancer vaccine by 2020. "The Artemis Project is different from science as usual in many ways. It is small, collaborative, and focused not on producing good science for its own sake, nor on making a profit, but on solving a problem."[79] That "solving a problem" approach to existence, particularrly in the world of scientific inquiry, is what prevents human beings from falling into the abyss of pride, narcissism, and solipsistic thinking. The Artemis Project is a "grassroots   action and advocacy" campaign working through a variety of modes including the "collaborative efforts of various stakeholders."[80] The all-too familiar complaint—that researchers and scholars live in ivory towers, once removed from the reality of everyday life— is, I hope, receding into history as we realize that the solutions to our problems can really only be discovered through physical, intellectual, and even spiritual collaboration.

I do believe that the key to avoiding damaging pride is collaboration, collegiality, and commitment to the truth. That may sound pie-in-the-sky in the age of post-truth, ritual obfuscation, and outright lies, but I agree with Chaucer who wrote, "Truth is the highest thing that man may keep."[81] With our eyes on truth, we can easily avoid the dangers of pride and the kind of cultural narcissism Christopher Lasch presaged. Mired in the technology of the future, a future we seem to encounter anew every day, it is more important than ever to be wary of those who try to sell us the truth like "Dr. Seth Arnold's Cough Killer," a late-1800s remedy claimed to cure coughs that contained morphine and "works like magic." Truth with a capital "T" seems to be, if not dying, at least under attack. Without access to the truth, it is easy for us to be led down "the primrose path of dalliance"[82] to a narcissistic existence in which pride is the first and only motivation for behavior.

Chapter Two: Lust

I sometimes think of what future historians will say of us. A single sentence will suffice for modern man: he fornicated and read the papers.

—Albert Camus[1]

The great third-century scholar Origen of Alexandria developed one of the earliest hermeneutics of biblical scholarship, a multimodal theory of reading that influenced thinkers into the Middle Ages and beyond. Origen's many achievements include the *Hexapla*, the first critical edition of the Hebrew Bible; *On the First Principles*, one of the earliest systematic theologies in the Church; and a lifelong attempt to blend pagan, Jewish, and Christian thought into a coherent whole. One of the most prolific thinkers the Christian Church ever produced, in addition to his biographical labels of theologian and scholar, Origen is a historical precedent for the Christian ascetic—one who engages in the oftentimes extreme punishment of the physical body in an effort to edify the soul. It is in this context that this keen reader of the Bible, reports the ancient historian Eusebius, a contemporary of Origen, appears to have read in "an absurdly literal sense" the verse in Matthew 19:12: "For there are eunuchs who have been so from birth, and there are eunuchs who have been made eunuchs by men, and there are eunuchs who have made themselves eunuchs for the sake of the kingdom of heaven. He who is able to receive this, let him receive it." According to Eusebius, upon reading these words, Origen committed a "headstrong act," that is, he had himself castrated.[2] All to curb his feelings of lust.

Although there is disagreement over the veracity of the story—some modern scholars believe it to be apocryphal[3]—this story persisted for thousands of years as an exemplar for the extreme lengths a good Christian might go to quell the evil physical yearnings of lust. To be certain, the ancient world clearly felt as if the soul and the body were at odds, that the soul needed to "exercise gentle violence on the body" to balance spiritual virtue with physical cravings.[4] Ascetic practices were not new to the Christian Church; pagan and Jewish communities had a long history of engaging in such practices.[5] In his work on Moses, Philo of Alexandria, the Hellenistic Jewish philosopher contemporaneous to Jesus, explains that the priest has to be "clean, as in soul so also in body, to have no dealings with any passion, purifying himself from all the calls of mortal nature, food and drink and intercourse with women."[6] Indeed, early Christian attitudes toward the body grew from the ancient Greek virtues of restraint and renunciation. The Greek word *ἀκράτεια* often translates as "self control," but in the present context, a better translation is "continence," specifically self control over the body. In the second century, Clement of Alexandria wrote that Christians went even further than Greek continence: "Our ideal is not to experience desire at all."[7] Nonetheless, it is ironic that Origen, expounder of an allegorical method for reading the Bible, would so grossly misread a passage as he did. Peter Brown, brilliant scholar of early Christian theology, notes "transformation" as a dominant characteristic in Origen's ethos, and it is clear that Origen saw that transformation in sexual renunciation and the squandering of carnal desire.[8] Eusebius reports Origen's ascetic practices that include "patiently enduring cold and nakedness," walking around without shoes, and abstaining "from wine and all else beyond the minimum of food."[9] One has to wonder, however, how feared might physical desire be, how horrific the notion of lust, to drive one to perform self castration in the name of the Divine.

In this chapter, I will discuss the sin of lust, relying on the issue of sexual renunciation, both historically and in the contemporary world, as well as on the sexual dynamics of the contemporary world.

The English word "lust" is derived from the Latin *luxuria*, a cognate for the English "luxury." The Latin *luxus* had connotations of luxury and excess, even debauchery. An interesting secondary meaning is "disjointed" as in misaligned. An 1828 etymological dictionary connects the Latin word to *luo, luxum* and relates "From its dissolving and loosening the powers of the body and mind."[10] *Luxuria*, then, implies unbridled and potentially dangerous freedom. Where there is freedom, there is sure to arise restraint and, ultimately, repression and, in this case, renunciation.

To be sure, the medieval Church regarded *luxuria* as luxury, not merely related to sexual activity but related to all types of excessive licentious behavior. As Church doctrine entered the mainstream consciousness by the 18th century, it became clear that *luxuria* almost exclusively referred to a sin of excessive physical desire—lust. The topic of sexual renunciation has fascinated theologians and scholars for millennia. One of the most notorious examples is the Essenes, that infamous group responsible for the Dead Sea Scrolls, who had apparently taken devotion to sexual renunciation and chastity as one of their communal rules—with the result the group disappearing by the end of the second century CE.[11]

The very word "lust" has come to carry both positive and negative connotations. A "lust for life" is desirable, while Jimmy Carter's "lust in my heart" for women other than his wife was deemed scandalous. The Catholic Church was left to deal with Paul's many dictates in his epistles. Pauline scholar Fernand Pratt includes a veritable laundry list of Paul's "lists of vices and sinners" in which "fornication" makes several appearances.[12] Pratt includes it in "works of the flesh," "vices unworthy of Christians," "sinners to be avoided" and several others including "sinners excluded from heaven." Most famously, perhaps, Paul writes in 1 Corinthians 6, "Flee from sexual immorality. Every other sin a person commits is outside the body, but the sexually immoral person sins against his own body. Or do you not know that your body is a temple of the Holy Spirit within you, whom you have from God? You are not your own, for you were bought with a price. So glorify

God in your body."[13] What does it mean then when the temple that is the body is defiled or defaced by lust?

Matthew 5:28 explains that anyone who even "looks at a woman with lustful intent has committed adultery in his heart." The world in which we currently live is woven throughout with sexual and sensual temptation. Madison Avenue advertising, particularly in the "Mad Men" era of the 1960s, has long professed that "sex sells," a fact that is evident in campaigns of myriad clothing companies such as Calvin Klein, whose provocative advertisements for its jeans in the 1990s were decried,[14] and Carl's Junior, which employs reality star Paris Hilton washing cars in a bikini in order to sell hamburgers.[15] Documentaries such as Jean Kilbourne's series *Killing Us Softly* continue to expose the ways in which women are sexually objectified in advertising.[16] Print magazines have long used images of women and men in sexually provocative poses to rouse lustful curiosity in order to sell magazines. The culture preys on the titillation factor with the knowledge that the lust button is not only easily accessed but hypersensitive to activation.

Thus, the dynamic between men and women suffers under the burden of lust. Harry, Billy Crystal's character in 1989's *When Harry Met Sally*, argues with Sally over the question of whether men and women can "be friends":

Harry: Because *no* man can be friends with a woman that he finds attractive. He always wants to have sex with her.

Sally: So you're saying that a man can be friends with a woman he finds unattractive?

Harry: No, you pretty much want to nail 'em too.

Harry and Sally struggle to be "just friends" throughout the film, only to end up together, romantically, at the film's conclusion. On television, late-1990s dramedy *Ally McBeal* toyed with the lust-ridden shenanigans among lawyers in an urban office; in the series, "The most frequent special effects signifier of lust is a giant tongue extending from characters' mouths. Special effects stretch the tongue's utility from its relatively private uses to a 'public' display of unmentionable desire, shown for the audience's benefit alone."[17] The series had us believe that such behavior was a daily common occurrence in the modern workplace.

Contemporary society is so inundated with temptations, encouragements, and taboos that it is often difficult to parse the current cultural ethos and attitude. This has most recently been more complicated by the sexual harassment scandals and the #MeToo movement in Hollywood and Washington, D.C., not to mention the corner office. A complete survey of that issue is beyond the scope of this study, and since it is a moving target that is currently in chaotic flux, it is probably too early to comment on it in the context of the current study. So, let's begin at the beginning.

Sexual Renunciation in the Ancient and Biblical Worlds:

The ancient world is rife with proscriptions regarding lustful behavior. The hero-athlete in the pagan world renounced sexual activity in the name of spiritual and physical strength.[18] As Michel Foucault writes, "This abstention was linked directly to a form of wisdom that brought them into direct contact with some superior element in human nature and gave them access to the very essence of truth."[19] We have to look no further than the voluminous words in the Pauline epistles to find the source for the Church's often repressive and oppressive attitudes toward sexuality. Much of the Pauline debate centers on distinctions between "body" and "flesh" in which "body" is identified as the person, while "flesh" usually refers to a human's pride. But in Paul's work, "The body and flesh are not synonyms. The body is the organized matter, living or dead, of men and animals. The flesh is the body minus the idea of organism, with, in addition, the ideal of life."[20] To be sure, Paul viewed the body as innately weak, what Brown describes as "a photograph taken against the sun: it is a jet-black shape whose edges are suffused with light."[21] That Pauline dualism of body and soul does not seem to have arisen from Hebrew thought but instead grew from Plato. The ancient Hebrews viewed man as the single product of an outer (body) and an inner (soul) being.[22] In fact, ancient Hebrew theology posited an evil impulse and a good impulse, the former living in the body and the latter in the soul. In Pauline theology, this translated as the good impulse dwelling in the inner man (the *nous*) and the evil impulse controlling the physical body. It is Plato where we first find a clear line between body and soul, evil and good, respectively, in relation to spiritual concerns. For Plato, if we are able to conquer lust, "life will be bliss."[23]

Paul provides lists of sins in two different places: 1 Corinthians 6, 9–10, and 1 Timothy 1, 9–10. Lust is included in Paul's "sins against the human body." These sinners would appear to be the immoral, idolaters, adulterers, and "sexual perverts."[24] Jerome's word for "sexual perverts" in the Vulgate translation is *molles,* Latin for "softness" or "passiveness." The verse has often been interpreted, after Michel Foucault, as implying prohibition against homosexuality. Philip Ariès suggests, "The Roman citizen . . . must never play a passive role in love, whether homosexual or heterosexual."[25] Although passivity is not necessarily the sin of lust, it is an ancillary "sin of the flesh" and was often considered sinful behavior in the context of homosexuality.[26]

Passivity appears as a negative trait throughout ancient Greek and Roman literature where the concept of male power was linked to male virility. Slaves and children were passive; passivity implied weakness. Men were active, strong, and assertive.[27] It is curious that Paul mentions only male homosexuality. Next on his list in 1 Corinthians are *masculorum concubitores—*that is, men who have sexual relations with one another. Women are nowhere mentioned here, curious given Paul's infamous misogyny, starting with his explicit laying of blame for the fall directly on the head of Eve. Paul writes that the woman was created "for the man" and that wives should submit themselves to their husbands.[28] This focus eventually developed into repulsion for the body, particularly the female body, in a duality in which the body is evil (and to be punished—thus ascetic practices) and the spirit is good. This set in motion a tradition in which the body in pain, to use Elaine Scarry's phrase,[29] indicated religious devotion.

The body in pain persists in the modern world where self-imposed mutilation, including diseases such as -, binge-eating, and extreme fasting have become commonplace. This is reinforced by millennia of attitudes that the flesh is weak, inferior, transitive, and even the earthly embodiment of evil in the dualistic theology of various Gnostic sects, including the Manichees.[30] The idea that flesh is evil and to be punished persists in many contemporary cultures, either explicitly (as in some fringe Hindu sects in India[31]) or liminally (as in "body haters" in the West).

How did we arrive at this spot? What traces can we find in the ancient world that connect to the modern attitudes toward the body and, more specifically, to lust? Let us look at one of the seminal stories in the Western world related to lust: the Old Testament tale of David and Bathsheba. Recounted in 2 Samuel, the story of the already-married king of Israel and his unbridled lust for a woman he first sees bathing transmuted from the story of a creepy stalker to one of passionate love. "David" in fact means "beloved" in Hebrew, a word itself whose root means "to boil," reflecting the fiery nature of David's passion. David first sees Bathsheba after he himself has arisen from an afternoon nap. "From the roof," he sees the woman bathing, "and the woman was very beautiful."[32] David's lust is immediate. After sending a messenger to Bathsheba, he "took her; and she came to him, and he lay with her."[33] Famously, in order to be with Bathsheba, David sends her husband, Uriah, "in the forefront of the hardest fighting" so that "he may be struck down, and die."[34] Bathsheba, who conceived after that first bedroom encounter with David, laments her husband's death, but is then brought to David's house where "she became his wife, and bore him a son."[35] This all sounds delightfully salacious, but we are then told, "But the thing that David had done displeased the Lord."[36]

What is "the thing that David had done"? Does the writer refer to David's lust, his covetousness of Uriah's wife, his adultery with Bathsheba, his ordering of Uriah's death? Perhaps all of the above. Explicit judgment is never given. In the next chapter, the prophet Nathan asks David, "Why have you despised the word of the Lord, to do what is evil in his sight? You have smitten Uriah the Hittite with the sword, and have taken his wife to be your wife."[37] David is chastised for being ungrateful, but he is nowhere reprimanded for his sin of lust, which actually set the story in motion. David J. Zucker and Moshe Reiss characterize the episode as "among the most morally problematic events in David's life."[38]

The lust for power and physical lust are almost conflated in the story. David failed in being able to control his physical lust, noting only, "I have sinned against the Lord."[39] According to the law of exact retaliation (*lex talonis*) outlined in Exodus and Leviticus, David should have been killed for his order resulting in the death of Uriah. Instead he is told, "The Lord also has put away your sin; you shall not die." Curiously, love is never mentioned in the story—it is instead a story about the ramifications of power-driven lust.

My point in recounting this tale is to wonder whether this is then the exemplar for lustful behavior in ancient Hebrew culture. This is tricky to answer. "Because they deal with specific situations, the biblical laws give us only a partial picture of the norms and values of ancient Israelite society."[40] It is worth noting that the Talmud regards lust—what the Talmudic author calls "evil inclination"—as one of the four things God is said to have regretted creating.[41]

There is another, lesser-known, tale in the Old Testament of lust in the Genesis story of Reuben sleeping with his father Jacob's wife. Genesis 35:22

is fairly succinct on the whole matter: "When Israel [Jacob] dwelt in that land, Reuben [his son] went and lay with Bilhah, his father's concubine; and Israel heard of it." The story ends abruptly, is not elaborated, nor is the punishment clearly stated. "One would expect some mention of *what happened* as a result of this sin—all the more so because similar, indeed lesser, offenses recounted in Genesis are sometimes accompanied by vivid accounts of the consequences suffered by the offenders."[42] Early scriptural scholars note that Reuben was the firstborn and would have received a special inheritance— twice the normal share of his father's possessions. Ultimately, Rueben does not receive a double portion; instead, it is Joseph who receives the firstborn's share. Talmudic commentary on the story chides the reader for misreading the passage: "Apparently, Reuben did not sin."[43] Instead, the writer claims, "Reuben rearranged his father's bed in protest of Jacob's placement of his bed in the tent of Bilhah and not in the tent of his mother Leah after the death of Rachel." Still, the focus of those early writers is rarely the sin itself, which seems to linger in the periphery, and blame shifting runs rampant in the commentary.

The story of David and Bathsheba is treated differently. One modern scholar remarks, "To infer that David succumbed to lust is challenged, paradoxically, by the biblical text itself," in that the text says very little about David's reaction—lustful or otherwise—to Bathsheba.[44] Cohen, shifting blame himself, recasts David as a tragic figure in the story: "David was the tragic hero who vainly grasped at sex as a means to preserve his ebbing self-esteem."[45] David was experiencing a midlife crisis, and thus, his behavior is explained and excused. Cohen continues, "Though we may call him a sinner and thereby dissociate ourselves from him, we nevertheless must sympathize with him in his desperate effort to forestall the destiny to which we are all heir." To his credit, Cohen never blames "the victim" (Bathsheba), but neither does he ever implicate David's behavior as anything other than masculine. Alexander Izuchukwu Abasili questions whether David's action would be considered rape.[46] Other scholars, like G. G. Nicol, shift the blame to Bathsheba, arguing that Bathsheba "was deliberatively provocative" in bathing so closely to the royal palace.[47] Many others consider David's act as rape and the result of an abuse of power and a misuse of authority.[48] A sculpture depicting the pair appears on the 13th-century Cathedral of Auxerre, about which art historian Wayne Craven concludes, "In the eyes of the people of the Middle Ages, these . . . scenes did not, therefore, represent a story of lust and sin."[49] Instead David was read in the story by the medieval Christian as a *figura* for Christ: "David, in his lust, had sinned; but his desire is rather to be seen as a prefiguration of Christ's desire for his peoples instead of David's lust for Bathsheba."[50]

What morals were to be learnt from this story? The Hebrew word for lust is תְּשׁוּקָה, but the word lacks positive or negative connotation and is used in both contexts of loving desire and carnal hunger. In Exodus 15:9, for example, the word translates as "desire," a need to be satisfied. Proverbs 6:25 uses the same word to refer to the lust of a young man. The word is *yeçer hara*, meaning evil inclination. The inclination does not, however, have to be evil: "Man is, however, not only responsible for making the *yeçer* more evil by submission to its power; he is also capable of putting it to good uses."[51] One debate in the rabbinical literature concerns whether the body or the soul (assigned as matter and spirit) is responsible for sin.

But are the prescriptions of the ancient world also ancient fact, that is, did these people practice what they preached? Was lust really as central to the cultural consciousness as it seems to be today? Peter Brown notes that, in the early Christian centuries, most were more concerned with death than sexual proclivity. Nonetheless, in pre-Christian societies, there was a clear attitude that chastity, indeed virginity, was valued by the state. The Vestal Virgins of Rome are just one example of dedication of a select few to renounce sexuality in the name of civic duty. Such practices "filled the minds of educated Christians when they, in their turn, came to write on marriage and on sexual desire."[52] Thus, doctrinal ideas and practical manners on lust were integrated into the new Christian religion from the various ancient sources.

Lust has almost always been viewed as the enemy of serious thought. As Simon Blackburn puts it, "Sexual climax drives out thought. It even drives out prayer, which is part of the church's complaint about it."[53] Lustful thoughts and motivations cloud rational intentions and derail clear decision making. Plato was clear that humans are "impelled by needs or desires, of three kinds": for food and drink and "lust of procreation with its blaze of wanton appetite."[54] We check each of these desires by "three supreme sanctions—fear, law, true discourse" and "make the procreation of children follow on our regulations of marriages, and on their procreation, their nurture, and education." Plato's entire take on lust is fairly regimented—he goes on to discuss the goal of the bride and bridegroom: "to present the city with the best and finest progeny they may." In the Platonic world, lust is to be put into the service of the state.

Once we move to the early Christian era, we find an increase in a celibate life as it relates to devotion. The Essenes appear to have required a portion of their male members to remain celibate for the spiritual benefit of the community. This is not actually that different from Plato in that certain members of the community are chosen to represent that entire community. Such citizens "considered themselves to be warriors of Israel, subject to the vows of abstinence."[55] "The celibate state of these few stood for the embattled character of the Community as a whole."[56] This concept, essentially the scapegoat, dates to the earliest days of Hebrew thought and the story in Leviticus 16:8, in which a goat was chosen to carry the burden of the entire community and cast into the desert. This tradition of sexual renunciation in the name of the larger group would carry through the Middle Ages into the monastic community where it was often felt that monks and nuns had taken vows of celibacy in order to live more spiritual lives for the betterment of society. Brown suggests that the various restrictions on sexual behavior in early Christian groups "heightened the sense of the separation of Israel from the pagan world"[57]—thus reinforcing the special quality, first of Israel and, later, of the early Christian community.

Sexual Renunciation in The Modern and Contemporary Worlds:

In *The Art of Love*, Ovid writes that a woman's lust is "more fierce than ours [i.e., man's], and more frenzied."[58] In the influential *Art of Courtly Love*, Andreas Capellanus's 12th century treatise that updated Ovid for the Christian Middle Ages, the lust experienced by Solomon, whose lust drove him to marriages to multiple foreign women, in the Old Testament is especially dangerous not in and of itself but because it leads to the violation of the first commandment: "Idolatry, too, very clearly comes from love, as is shown by the case of Solomon, the wisest of men, who from love of women did not fear to go after strange gods and like a beast make sacrifice to dumb idols."[59] Lust is the motivating factor in the   12th century tragic love story of Abelard and Heloise. Serving as Heloise's tutor, Abelard coerces (some modern scholars feel "raped") Heloise. For his lustful intentions and actions, Abelard was castrated by Heloise's uncle, and the two were separated—Abelard went on to become one of the great philosophic minds of his time, while Heloise seemed to languish in a convent. Heloise's letters express her frustration with Abelard.[60] "You are the sole cause of my sorrow," she writes. "You alone have the power to make me sad, to bring me happiness or comfort."[61] In the same letter, she recalls her feelings of lust: "Every wife, every young girl desired you in absence and was on fire in your presence; queens and great ladies envied me my joys in my bed."[62] Even after Abelard's castration and Heloise's exile to a nunnery, she maintains her lustful feelings: "How can it be called repentance for sins, however great the mortification of the flesh, if the mind still retains the will to sin and is on fire with its old desires?"[63] She realizes that the intention to lust is as sinful as the action: "Men call me chaste; they do not know the hypocrite I am. They consider purity of the flesh a virtue, though virtue belongs not to the body but to the soul."[64] In what is probably the most comprehensive Catholic theology ever written, virtually contemporary to Abelard and Heloise, Thomas Aquinas quite clearly argues that sin can be the result of intention as well as action.[65]

Lustful intention is put into action in the story of Arthur, Guinevere, and Lancelot, with Lancelot betraying his king by lusting after and having an affair with the queen Guinevere, Arthur's wife, and subsequently bringing an end to the idealized kingdom of Camelot. In fact, the Arthurian legend is riddled with lust from Uther Pendragon's desire for (and rape of) Ygraine to Sir Gawain's failures with the Green Knight. Many Arthurian tales focus on the confusion of love with lust in Arthur's supposedly ideal knights.[66]

Aquinas is quite clear regarding the evils of lust-motivated fornication: "Since the intercourse of fornication destroys the due relations of the parent with the offspring that is nature's aim in sexual intercourse, there can be no doubt that simple fornication by its very nature is a mortal sin even though there were no written law."[67] Lust is "among the works of the flesh" and is considered a "capital vice" by Gregory the Great.[68] For Gregory, "The inward swelling of pride descends to the genitals as lust, its outward analogue."[69] Lust can have a physical effect on the body.

The English Renaissance encountered lust in heaving bosoms and with bated breath. There is certainly no shortage of lust in Shakespeare, from the fickle desires of Romeo (who pines for Juliet after supposedly being consumed by Rosaline) to Hamlet's complaint that his mother yearns for Claudius: "She would hang on him/As if increase of appetite had grown/ By what it fed on."[70] In Shakespeare's Sonnet 129, the speaker laments "lust in action," noting that it is "past reason" and is almost a mirage, a dream, that drives the lustful "to this hell." In Helen Vendler's assessment of the sonnet, "Socially, lust is of course savage in its pursuit of its object, perjuring itself, untrustworthy, and so on; religiously, it may be an expense of spirit on base matter; psychologically, it may be the occasion of shame and madness."[71]

It seems that, for most of history, lust has been particularly grievous for two reasons: (1) it distracts one from the rational focus of being; and (2) it is an affront to the nature of human beings. In his survey of 44 theologians writing between 1152 and 1327, John Dedek finds that most writing about fornication find it to be a mortal sin, the most serious of sins, one that is not committed accidentally and is punishable eternally. The distraction from rationality—the characteristic that distinguishes the human animal from the nonhuman animal—also appears in Milton's *Paradise Lost* where Adam and Eve experience an internal wrestling match between reason and passion before both eat the forbidden fruit.

Lust in the Heart:

When Jimmy Carter announced in a 1976 interview with *Playboy* magazine that he had lusted in his heart,[72] he raised an age-old question: Is lust purely a physical expression, or can it be psychological as well? Is it possible to have feelings of lust that are not acted upon, and if so, would "just thinking" be as egregious as putting thought into action? It is in Paul that we find the accusation that the pagans were slaves to "the lusts of their hearts."[73] Matthew 5:28 provides: "But I say to you that whoever looks at a woman to lust for her has already committed adultery with her in his heart." The idea that one could lust emotionally and not physically, of course, developed from modern notions of psychology and the conceptualization that humans can have an inner life—a private self—that is quite different from their outer life—their public self. These "two selves" are discussed in depth in Charles Taylor's *Sources of the Self,* where the philosopher argues that the modern notion of the self is characterized by inwardness.

Moderns are often denounced for living "only in their head"; academics particularly are often accused of living in a world divorced or disconnected from reality. Thus, the danger of the construction of an inner self with little or no relationship to the exterior life. The development of ego and superego allows humans to cultivate an inner self that can often become quite disconnected from external reality. Modern life would seem to be a tenuous balance between that inner self and external reality. Even with his focus on individuation and the discovery of the true self, Jung did feel that excessive withdrawal into the inner self was dangerous and could result in "psychic catastrophe."[74]

So we have a conflict. We have two millennia of philosophical and religious thinkers encouraging the development of an inner self as a means to union with the Divine. And then we have contemporary concerns with the dangers of introversion and alienation from society. Perhaps we should turn to Taylor's "secularism" for a solution. In his mammoth treatise, *The Secular Age* published in 2007, Taylor argues that secularism as a religio-philosophy does not necessarily negate the existence of God. Instead it places God at odds with the scientific sensibilities of the modern world. Thus, it sees God as inadequate to understanding and predicting modern morality. Because so much moral guidance is finessed by belief in the Judeo-Christian God and his laws, the secular age in which scientific fact has come to replace theological faith has pushed God to the margins of contemporary life.

Does contemporary society approve of those who feel lust in their hearts but who do not take action? Is it only the action we punish or is it the intention? Augustine and Paul would have us punish those who even think lustful thoughts. But can this be realistic in our modern, secularized and pluralistic world, a world rife with sexual innuendo and gender politics? Perhaps Hamlet says it best for the modern: "There is nothing either good or bad / but thinking makes it so."[75] If reality is a subjective individuality, thoughts are as serious as actions. Again, when Hamlet plans to visit his mother, he says that he will "speak daggers to her, but use none" but notes that his "tongue and soul in this be hypocrites." Hamlet's suggestion, that I can have intentions I never put into action, is a precursor to the kind of virtual, simulated world in which we currently live. And as is evident from the countless news stories, the line between subjective and objective is increasingly blurred so that some are unable to make the distinction. I am thinking here of instances of violence which if in a video game would be harmless but in reality are deadly. We are far past the days of the anvil falling on Wile E. Coyote in the "Looney Tunes" cartoons, though it is worth noting that when CBS showed the cartoons in the early 1980s, executives ordered violent scenes edited from the cartoons, arguing that children could not dissociate the fiction of the cartoon from their own reality.

Lust in Popular Culture:

The pre-Judeo-Christian world viewed sexual activity in much the same way that early Judeo-Christian culture did—it was a draining of energy from the male and was therefore to be avoided unless in the name of propagation. This was then perverted by the early Christian Church to be sinful behavior that reflected incontinence in both body and soul. "Marriage was treated as a concession to those who could not contain themselves, a permit to indulge in lust for those who found lust indispensable."[76] Early Christian writers are quick to distinguish love from lust—lust is immoderate and carnal, while love is controlled and spiritual. In fact, the Church writers took great pains to separate love from sex. Love is spiritual, while sex is carnal and has a single purpose: procreation.

Has such an attitude persisted in the modern world? I would argue that the late 20th century, particularly the sexual revolution of the 1960s and women's advances in the 1970s, significantly altered modern attitudes toward love and lust.[77] In order to answer this question, I look at newspaper and magazine coverage, television, and the zeitgeist of our "secular age."

The Hays Code, adopted by Hollywood in 1934 and not suspended until 1968, clearly spelled out what was acceptable regarding sex and violence on the cinema screen. Any "suggestive nudity," for example, was strictly forbidden. Television went even further. Early television shows like *I Love Lucy* and *The Dick Van Dyke Show* required their stars sleep in separate beds onscreen though married and eventually with children. The late 1950s and 1960s saw the growth of the daytime soap opera. Essentially an ongoing morality play, these sponsored serial dramas most often centered on a hospital and the randy behavior of its doctors and nurses. By the 1980s, this had developed into lust in the afternoon for millions of viewers on daily shows such as *The Young and the Restless* and *General Hospital.* Such behavior was fairly unregulated on daytime television, but observers were more concerned with the evening, when children were home. The development in 1975 by the Federal Communications Commission of the "family viewing hour" was an attempt by conservatives to curtail depictions of sex and violence on television between 8 and 9 P.M. each night.[78] Although the definition of "indecent" content was never settled upon, one goal was "to reduce the level of gratuitous TV violence and sex."[79]

By 1993, it seems the "family viewing hour" had dissolved not only in concept but in practice. Steven Bochco's police drama *NYPD Blue* included nudity and erotic material from its pilot episode, but in 2003, an episode included Detective Connie McDowell (played by Charlotte Ross) standing nude for seven seconds. The FCC proposed an indecency fine against ABC, the network airing the show, of $27,000 for each of its 52 affiliates with a total fine of $1.4 million. The offending material in the show, the FCC wrote, was intended to be "titillating and shocking." The case was ultimately dismissed in 2011 by the U.S. Court of Appeals, but that did not stop other groups such as the Parents Television Council from working to make sure that children were not exposed to what they felt was objectionable material on television, most often characterized by sexual content and even glimpses of nudity. Then, in 2004, we all saw Janet Jackson's exposed nipple during her Super Bowl halftime show, and the world stood still.

Referred to as a "wardrobe malfunction," "Nipplegate," and "the boob seen around the world," the incident was broadcast to an audience of some 143 million viewers. At the end of her performance, Janet Jackson's breast, adorned with a nipple shield, was exposed by Justin Timberlake for about half a second. The outrage in the media and from politicians was almost deafening with many suggesting the incident reflected declining morality in the country. The fetishizing of the female breast in America contributed to the furor—unlike most countries, in the United States the female breast equals sex, something quite evident in the current debates over public breastfeeding. Arguments range from "it's an intimate act that should be performed in public" to "women who breastfeed in public are inviting harassment" to "it's a completely natural act." The Janet Jackson incident and the more contemporary discussions of public breastfeeding reflect an American public uptight with its own sexuality and convinced that any suggestion of nudity, particularly female, evokes lust.

In 2013, Paris-based fashion company Vicomte A., an online retailer of women's clothing, wanted to reach a wider audience through social media. Fred & Farid Shanghai, the company's advertising agency, intended to get men to share the company's collections by promising them a model would remove a piece of clothing if they clicked on it. Within 48 hours, 150,000 pieces of clothing were shared on Facebook and 300,000 people tweeted about the campaignn.[80] Although the company primarily sells women's clothing, the advertisers were appealing to the male viewer's lustful curiosity, and it clearly worked. Traffic on the company's website increased by five times during the campaign. Lust makes money.

It is interesting that over time the use of the word "lust" in the mainstream media has experienced a considerable shift. Since 1980, it is rare to find the word used in *The New York Times* in the sense of a sin. Instead, "lust" is used in the more generic sense of a desire for anything, not necessarily sexual. In fact, during the last 30 years or so, in a quick survey of *The New York Times* online archive, "lust" is most often used in discussion of business and business dealings, an example of how the corporate world has coopted religious language. Even the myriad recent scandals of the political and entertainment world have rarely invoked the word but instead regard these actions as legal violations, not necessarily moral ones.

In the opening pages of his history of sexuality, Michel Foucault argues that sexual freedom is antithetical to what he calls an "intensive work imperative,"[81] a clear response to the "Protestant work ethic." Thus, a hardworking person has the ability to repress or control sexual desire. In Foucault's mind, of course, there is a direct link between repression of sexuality and power. The management of lust is integral to the power dynamic. Nevertheless, writing in *The Guardian*, art critic Jonathan Jones says, "We live in a world that fears erotically charged images."

The cornerstone of modern attitudes toward lust remains the image of woman as temptress, the descendant of Eve and the embodiment of lust itself, so much so that lust has been personified as female in myriad spiritual and artistic traditions. The Hindu goddess Rati, a wife of Kama, is the goddess of passion and lust. The Aztec goddess Tlazōlteōtl represents lust, carnality, and sexual misdeed. In Jacques Callot's 1635 *The Temptation of Saint Anthony*, the sin of lust is personified as two nude females amidst a whirlwind of alluring activity.[82] In a separate etching and engraving of "Lust," Callot presents the figure as a partially disrobed female with a goat (a classic symbol of virility and fertility) to one side, a bird in hand,[83] and a demon arranging her hair; the Latin word *Luxuria* appears prominently at her feet. In a series of wood sculptures made in the early 16th century, Pieter Bruegel the Elder carved a series of wood sculptures of the seven deadly sins; "lust" is a bawdy dancing peasant girl lifting her dress.

In his work on sin and fear, Jean Delumeau surveys the late Middle Ages and early Renaissance where he notes that lust was at one time thought to be a sin worse than murder or theft.[84] One thing becomes clear: lust has been on "the list" since Evagrius Ponticus, often ranking as high as fourth in severity. Sin itself has hung over humanity like a dark cloud, at times intensifying into a storm.[85] Not surprisingly attitudes toward lust are almost relationally concurrent with societal attitudes about the body. In times of overt sexual repression, such as Victorian England, lust is vilified.[86] In times of "free love," such as the 1960s, lust is viewed as trifling.

Of course in the 21st century, particularly with the rise in fourth wave feminism[87] and movements regarding bullying and sexual harassment, it has become much clearer that lust transcends gender, that it reaches beyond pure sexuality and has innate relationships to power and authority. Foucault was correct. In fact, in a current adult online video game called "Lust and Power," the avatar is a young man who has inherited a mansion and proceeds on exploits involving both sexual and economic conquests, often difficult to differentiate.

A 2016 piece directed by Nick Knight celebrates *British Vogue* editor Edward Enninful in a 14-minute video titled "The Seven Deadly Sins of Edward Enninful" in which seven famous female models depict the sins "through the lens of Internet culture."[88] Model Kate Moss poses provocatively as Lust in red, while a voiceover reads, "Lust is an intense and uncontrollable desire for sex." Images of cellphones, sex toys, the "Parental Advisory" and other warnings blend with Moss's body as she eventually undresses and writhes on screen. Knight noted, "Kate wanted to be lust; I mean she IS lust."

Augustine writes that "there are lusts for many things" but that physical lust "is the lust that excites the indecent parts of the body. This lust assumes power not only over the whole body, and not only from the outside, but also internally."[89] This is a lust that "disturbs the whole man." Augustine derides lust because it indicates "an almost total extinction of mental alertness; the intellectual sentries, as it were, are overwhelmed," leaving the individual susceptible to other temptations and transgressions because reason has been "overwhelmed." This would seem to be excellent support for those claiming Internet sex addiction.[90]

Does lust not have a positive place in the contemporary world? This is a question I kept coming back to as I read more and more through the rules, punishments, and chastising of Christian and other theologies. Surely, according to the laws of evolution, human beings would not have retained this characteristic if it had no benefit to the species at all. Religion has taught for millennia that love is the epitome of righteous existence. What then about its squatter-neighbor lust? While love is proclaiming itself through the neighborhood, lust aims to remain behind closed doors, tightlipped, and, often, ashamed.

Perhaps the most characteristic reason lust is seen as bad is its ability to shift thinking and control away from topics more rational and spiritual. In the medieval Church, this was an easy calculation—lust drove out prayer. Today's take is that it is distracting. In a world filled with distractions, many of them technological, we should not be surprised that lust, then, is not at the top of the list of modern-day distractions—it is one of many. It is in fact difficult if not impossible to think rationally and/or spiritually when engaged in a state of lust. Biologists will cite the rush of blood from the brain to the sexual organs. Psychologists will note an imbalance in brain chemistry when one is engaged in lustful behavior or even thoughts. Here is one of the most significant reasons lust is at odds with a spiritual life, such as the ones led by early monks for whom St. Benedict wrote, "Do not carry out the urgings of the flesh"[91] and "Love chastity."[92] In fact, Benedict condemns carnal desire several times in his *Rule*. If the aim of the monastic life is devotion to God, any distraction from that devotion is to be avoided. I recall my graduate school advisor's story of his uncle, a Benedictine monk in Minnesota. When his class of Catholic teenaged boys visited the monastery, the monk lectured the boys on the evils of lust and lustful thoughts. Nudity, in particular, was singled out as especially heinous. "Don't you see yourself naked when you bathe," the boys asked the monk. "No," he responded, "I don't look down there." Ignorance is bliss.

Lust, indeed all forms of sin, is a distraction. In an age of myriad distractions, perhaps this is why lust is no longer viewed by contemporary society as the scandalous misdeed it once was. At any given moment, a member of today's society has a phone vibrating, a computer in front of him with a consistent influx of data and demands, the murmuring and buzz of both the electric and the human activity around him. An accidental erection or even intentional sexual thought is probably least of his or her worries.

As did the Greeks, the medieval mind seemed to regard lust as acceptable if regulated. The problem was the "excess" aspect of lust because it implied a lack of human control or agency. Human society implies a framework of self-control within which certain behaviors are taboo, if not expressly forbidden—legally or morally (or both). The degree to which lustful behavior has been accepted or vilified has certainly changed with the times and adjusting social mores. What I'll call "self-regulated lust" seems specious, even in today's world of constant sexual distraction.

As already noted, one of the most effective uses of lust in the modern world is in the world of advertising. Jean Kilbourne's series of documentaries, *Killing Us Softly*, have highlighted the exploitation of women in advertising since 1979. She has written, "It is almost impossible to imagine what our popular culture would look like if women's bodies weren't objectified and dismembered."[93] In her study, *Breasts: A Natural and Unnatural History*, Florence Williams suggests that the female human breast evolved as it did as a sexual attractor. Others argue that the development of the female breast was a matter of survival. The explosive effect of the Internet has propelled pornography from the seedy magazine hidden under the mattress to a multi-billion dollar, and largely accepted, business.[94] "The porn industry makes more money than Major League Baseball, The NFL and The NBA combined."[95] One might argue that the increasing presence of evocative sexual imagery has only served to equally increase lustful feelings in the general spirit of the culture.

Although it is a violent crime, not a sexual one, reported rapes in the United States have actually declined from more than 97,000 in 1995 to fewer than 85,000 in 2014.[96] In fact, I do not believe that lustful inclinations have risen but that in our fast-paced, connected world, it is easier to tap into those feelings on a daily, on an hourly basis. And those feelings, largely chastised when Jimmy Carter mentioned them in 1975, now result in a seat in the Oval Office.

Donald Trump has a long and well-documented history of impropriety with women, from his three marriages to "grabbing women by the pussy" to the countless accusations of physical and verbal abuse made by dozens of women. This is a man who has built his career on lust, from the glistening gaudy, self-important logos of his properties to the unrestrained ways he brags about his own successes. Trump seems to believe, as he said in the notorious *Access Hollywood* interview, that "when you're a star, they let you do it. You can do anything." With such a man in the most powerful seat in the free world, traditionally a locus for model behavior, standards of decency have sunk. Interviewed by Howard Stern in 2004, Trump called his daughter Ivanka "a piece of ass" and said he'd date her if she weren't his daughter.

Writing in *The New Republic*, Ted Gup notes the difference between Trump's and Carter's admissions: Carter's feelings were intentions "in his heart," while Trump admits to having acted on his feelings.[97] Here is a clear distinction between Aquinas's concerns regarding intention and action. It is, I think, without doubt that in current society, the action is held to more scrutiny than the intention alone.

It is not my intention here to rebuke Donald Trump. Instead, I'm using the example to indict the people who supported and elected Donald Trump. After Carter's comments in 1975, he claims his poll numbers dropped 15 points. One month after the Trump *Access Hollywood* tape surfaced, he was elected 45th president of the United States. This says more about public attitudes toward lust than it does about Donald Trump— attitudes that have been in continual flux since the 1970s.

The appearance of cable television and the VCR in the American home in the late 1970s brought nudity and sexuality to the living room as never before. The 1960s brought a change in sexual mores to the American public. These phenomena are all well documented. It should come as no surprise that the public's attitudes toward lust have shifted with those significant changes. As Paul Bloom put it in *The New York Times*, "The real worry that people have with pornography—and with lust more generally—is that the targets of the arousal are seen as losing certain uniquely human traits."[98] That is my concern here. As the result of these increased lustful behaviors (and, to some degree, thoughts), we are becoming less human.

In fact, if we recall my introduction, that is what sin does in general terms: it makes one less human. Lustful intentions and lustful actions can both result in shame and disgust. Pornography does objectify women, and lustful behavior is often demeaning, but perhaps of even more significance is the lasting effects on the individual's sense of self. Lustful intentions are inwardly detrimental, while lustful actions are detrimental to all. Thus, lust leads us down that "primrose path" to many other social troubles, psychological problems, and even physical injuries.

Chapter Three: Anger

Anger is one letter short of danger.

—Eleanor Roosevelt

"We are aware that a civilization has the same fragility as a life."[1] When Paul Valéry wrote those words in 1919, he had no idea how prescient his words were. Within just three short decades, civilizations would rise and some would fall; cultures would struggle to remain alive and relevant, while others would attempt to blot them from existence. Those decades, between 1910 and 1950, were indeed angry times.

In fact, much of Western history has been predicated on feelings of anger—if not envy, but more on that in Chapter 6. The 20th century was rife with repressed anger, explicit displeasure, and uncontrolled rage, and the 21st isn't looking much better. Part of my argument rests on a creaky hinge: I suggest that the modern person's dissatisfaction with themselves and the world—evidenced in the modern obsession to make life faster, more efficient, and ironically less active for human beings— has resulted in feelings of anger. We always seem to be looking for the next technological solution to our existence, whether that be self-driving cars, automated vacuum cleaners, or so-called smart homes. We are so dissatisfied with the slow pace of life that we have invented ways to accelerate the drudgery of daily existence. Microwave ovens cannot cook the food fast enough (do you have your hand poised on the release button, waiting for the first beep?). Traffic lights don't change quickly enough. Email has increased the speed of commerce and communication to an almost lightspeed rate (have you followed up an email with another email asking if the person received your first email, which had only been sent minutes before?). This pace has exacerbated and magnified angry sentiments in the general population.

This is hardly new, nor is it only reflective of the age of computers and global communication. The earliest days of factory automation in the 19th century were another indication of human beings' dissatisfaction with the speed with which goods were produced. The Luddite movement, formed in the early years of the 19th century, was a reaction by a group of textile weavers who destroyed weaving machinery in protest of automation they believed would threaten their jobs and their livelihood. In modern parlance, the label "Luddite" denotes those who are essentially antitechnology and resist the integration of computer technology into daily life. Some denigrate today's Neo-Luddites as "backward," "behind the times," and "ignorant," while others increasingly appreciate the philosophical backbone of the movement as cautionary.[2]

The entertainment world has provided us consistent commentary on the role of technological "advances," from the slapstick comedies of the 1920s (which often lampooned the latest craze, from automobiles to assembly lines) to the *Jurassic Park* movie franchise (and its cautionary tales of genetic engineering). Perhaps no one portrays cynical anger as clearly as Charlie Chaplin in 1936's *Modern Times* in which the Tramp works in a factory and is put on an assembly line only to himself get caught up in the gears of the massive machine. As he attempts to turn bolts on the assembly line, he ends up tweaking the buttons on his coworker's coveralls in a fit of repetitious mimicry—he himself becomes like a machine. The film opens with images of workers scurrying to work who then morph into images of sheep. In another iconic scene, the factory boss brings in a salesman to demonstrate the "Billows Feeding Machine," a machine that will allow employees to continue their monotonous work while being fed their lunch through automation. The machine, of course, goes haywire, shoving food into the Tramp's mouth before buffeting him with the device meant to clean his mouth. After a four-minute demonstration that leaves the Tramp covered in food, panicked, and on the floor, the boss says, "It's no good—it isn't practical." Chaplin said the film "started from an abstract idea, an impulse to say something about the way life is being standardized and channelized, men turned into machines—and the way I felt about it."[3] In this case, the subdued anger at an increasingly mechanized world is presented in almost satiric form. Earlier films such as Fritz Lang's *Metropolis* (1926) were less restrained in their hostility.

Lang's film opens with the workers marching, like prisoners, to elevators that transport them below ground where they labor to operate the machinery that runs the city. So dehumanized that they walk with heads slumped and eyes facing the ground, their hands clenched into fists, the workers are quickly contrasted with the wealthy powerful and elite who work in high rise buildings that tower over the city. Writing about the film in 1985, critic Roger Ebert said, "*Metropolis* is one of the great achievements of the silent era, a work so audacious in its vision and so angry in its message that it is, if anything, more powerful today than when it was made."[4] The film also contains scenes of rioting and angry mobs attempt to destroy the machines.

In the newborn age of television, in the 1950s, Lucille Ball paid homage to Chaplin in a memorable *I Love Lucy* episode in which Lucy and Ethel get jobs working on a candy wrapping assembly line. The candies speed by at increasingly rapid speeds. When the conveyor belt speeds up, Lucy has no choice but to stuff her mouth and blouse with unwrapped candies. The forewoman then comes in and bellows "speed it up." In all of these cases—from Lang to Chaplin to Ball—technology serves to dehumanize the workers, either transforming them into machines or making them dispensable in lieu of machines. Paul Valéry predicted our dissatisfaction with what he termed "a terrible future" in which "the machine, with its demands will subject even the most lighthearted, most elusive to its disciplines. It records and foresees; it regulates and hardens."[5] The result is an increasingly angry populace.

The hostility that has grown from our frustration with the pace of life is,

I think, palpable. As Ferris Bueller notes, "life moves pretty fast," and with that speed comes increased anxiety and increased anger. It is in this sense that anger has transformed from historical sin to modern addiction. Many become addicted to anger, unable to transcend the sharp spear of the emotion. Eastern philosophy's antidote to anger is patience, practiced through meditation, yoga, a holistic perspective on existence, and a current cultural focus on mindfulness for everyone from kindergartners to senior citizens, from phone apps to costly retreats. Patience not only allays anger but leads to tolerance. The American Psychological Association publishes a webpage titled "Controlling Anger—Before It Controls You" that includes "strategies to keep anger at bay": relaxation, cognitive restructuring, problem solving, better communication, using humor, and changing your environment.[6]

We in the West are taught to capitalize on anger from an early age. Elementary school recess games like dodge ball reward anger as do increasingly competitive activities (sport and otherwise) right through high school—being "chosen last" is not only a badge of shame but a motivation for anger and revenge; in *Rhetoric*, Aristotle makes the explicit link between anger and revenge: "Anger, according to Aristotle, is a man's longing for revenge when someone appears to slight him or one of his relatives or friends and when the slight appears undeserved."[7] Nonetheless, one popular argument is that, on the whole, the West is angrier than the East, Eastern cultures are more accepting and are more likely to let the flowing river go its own way, while the West tries desperately to control that flow. A travel site called "Global from Asia" counsels: "People in the West are more open to express their feelings. If they are angry, they may express. But, people in the east may cover it for tact and good manners."[8]

Robert Thurman has shown, however, that almost every ancient Eastern text focuses on battle of some kind.[9] Cultures that went on to develop what

Thurman calls "Inner Science" aimed to understand the relationship between poisonous emotion and biology—a kind of depth psychology (i.e., a study of the unconscious mental process and its motivations) familiar in Jungian thought.[10] Such thinking was rooted in a fairly dualistic approach to existence in which the physical is in constant struggle with the spiritual.

Of course the Judeo-Christian Bible significantly shifts its focus on anger, from the Old Testament where anger is a precursor to sin to the New Testament where anger itself is a sin. One of the initial questions we must broach is, "From where does the modern West get its notion of 'anger'?" There are myriad possible sources: Western philosophy, the Bible, genetics and human biology, external influence, and modeling, just to name a few I would like to consider here.

Anger in Western Philosophy:

Many of our most respected and oft-cited philosophers address the question of anger in their work. Plato felt that anger is at war with our other emotions; Aristotle looked at anger as an entrée to revenge. But perhaps no other ancient writer took on the subject with more thought and more depth than Seneca. In his work on anger, written in the middle of the first century CE, the Stoic philosopher toes the party line in arguing that any passion needs to be eradicated and that the passions themselves are innately evil.

Anger, Seneca opens his book, "consists entirely in aroused assault."[11] It is, he goes on, "a brief madness." And we are only four sentences into the work. A few paragraphs later, he compares anger to a pestilence. Curiously, although anger is uniquely human (animals, Seneca, argues, "lack human passions"), anger "is not natural."[12] Anger indicates a weak mind,[13] one that should instead make an appeal to reason, which is "well-balanced."[14] Anger "betrays human nature," "urges us toward hate and bids us to do harm," and detracts from the "lofty mind" that is "ever peaceful."[15]

Seneca spends large portions of his work engaged in a kind of how-to approach, advocating for an early Roman behavioral therapy to help those overcome with anger. "People inclined to anger should give up unusually demanding fields of study . . . or at least shouldn't pursue them to the point of exhaustion."[16] The fine arts (in Seneca's words, "the pleasant arts") can be used therapeutically: "Let them be soothed by reading poetry and beguiled by legends from history."[17] He would seem to presage our modern age of information overload: "It's not a good idea to hear and see everything that goes on."[18] Instead, "don't be inquisitive." "Most things should be turned into a joke"—Lenny Bruce would smile.

A group of "angry comics," including Lewis Black, Russell Brand, Richard Pryor, and even George Carlin, have made careers out of turning anger into humor. In the 2003 dark comedy *Anger Management*, Jack Nicholson's psychologist character tells Adam Sandler, his patient, "Let me explain something to you, Dave. There are two kinds of angry people in this world: explosive and implosive. Explosive is the kind of individual you see screaming at the cashier for not taking their coupons. Implosive is the cashier who remains quiet day after day and finally shoots everyone in the store." But the relationship between humor and anger has been culturally masculine. In her critically acclaimed 2018 HBO show *Nannette*, Australian comic Hannah Gadsby notes, "People feel safer when men do the angry comedy." In a 2013 interview with television personality Sonny Fox, George Carlin explained that he isn't "personally angry" but instead that his anger is a "reflection of disappointment" in humanity.[19]

One of the greatest vehicles for anger in the contemporary world, especially political anger, is the comic stage. From the vitriolic put downs of Don Rickles to the political sarcasm of Samantha Bee, anger can be funny, and comedy can be angry. Why are the two such good bedfellows? This is actually nothing new—the link between satire and anger is woven throughout the writing of Horace and Juvenal, the originators of the genre. By the English Renaissance, satire could take on a very angry tenor, such as in some scenes in Shakespeare's *Taming of the Shrew*.

In the past 30 years, comics Andrew Dice Clay and Sam Kinison both presented anger in a comedic context, but they were essentially playing characters. Today, Louis C. K. and Lewis Black weave comic tapestries with angry fiber. I remember the first time I saw Lewis Black; I was genuinely concerned for the man's health and checked on line to see if it was merely an act or he was actually that angry (and funny), only to discover that his stage presence is a persona. Notably, Black was the voice of "Anger" in the 2015 hit *Inside Out*, an animated film that delves into the mind of a young girl and reveals her five personified emotions. Watching and listening to such anger can be cathartic for the audience, especially when the material is political or social in nature. After the February 2018 school shooting in Orlando, FL, comedian Samantha Bee asked her audience "Is it okay if, instead of making jokes, I just scream for seven minutes until we cut to commercial?"

If we consider the results of anger on a global scale, we understand Seneca: "Many have been slaughtered . . . when the anguish shared by a whole people drove them to unify their anger."[20] In asking for time, Seneca backs off Aristotle's assumption that anger leads to revenge: "How much better it is to heal an injury than to avenge it!"[21] But he does ask that we consider "the basic terms of our human condition" in that "the person who reproaches individuals for a vice we all share is unjust."[22] Anger, he says plainly, "is also a form of insanity."[23] Seneca's solution is "self examination" and daily scrutiny,[24] a process later developed in the 16th century by Ignatius Loyola in *Spiritual Exercises*, which is largely a meditation on sin.

Some four centuries before Seneca, Aristotle had framed anger by classifying the individual as either "hot tempered," "choleric," "sulky," or "bad tempered."[25] It is with the "bad tempered" that Aristotle finds most fault for they "are worse to live with." As in many things, Aristotle recommends "the middle state" in which "we are angry with the right people, at the right things, in the right way, and so on." As is the case with all sin, Aristotle argues "excesses and defects are blameworthy"; thus "we must cling to the middle state." Elsewhere in the same work, Aristotle argues that anger is voluntary because "the actions which proceed from anger or appetite are the man's actions."[26] Here are the seeds of our modern discussions of responsibility for action in both personal and public life.[27]

This has of course become central to modern jurisprudence, particularly in prosecution of so-called crimes of passion, crimes supposedly committed in the throes of passion and thus somewhat absolving the criminal of his behavior. Is it possible for anger to build to a breaking point where it becomes largely involuntary, and the individual can no longer control his or her impulses? Western legal systems seem to think so. However, in *The Blank Slate* and elsewhere, cognitive psychologist Steven Pinker has argued that violence "has nothing to do with human nature but is a pathology inflicted by malign elements outside us." Violence, he says, "is a behavior taught by a culture."[28] This leads us down a rabbit hole regarding the roles of anger and violence in human evolution. One side argues anger and violence are evolutionary and have developed into necessary and useful aspects of humanity to ensure survival.[29] The other side, for which Pinker is a spokesperson, feels violence is a learned behavior which, since it is taught, can be controlled by humanity or, at least, a culture or society. "Violence is a social and political problem, not just a biological and psychological one."[30] Pinker has actually gone on to argue that violence in human culture has declined substantively, though the claim is not without its detractors.

Of course, I don't mean to argue here that the only cause of violence is anger, nor that anger must result in violence. History is littered with examples of both, but neither is the norm. Perhaps if we look to the East, we can find resolution. Eastern religion—particularly Buddhism—has long been noted for its peaceful practice. One of the Four Noble Truths states implicitly that anger can be one cause of suffering: "No evil is there similar to anger/No austerity to be compared with patience."[31] A central tenet in most Eastern thought is that anger causes harm—to both others and the self. So, anger is a "sin" regardless of where we are on the globe.

Anger in the Bible:

In *The City of God* Augustine writes, "The poets give such a distorted picture of the gods that such deities cannot stand comparison with good humans."[32] Nowhere is that comparison more evident than in discussions of the anger or wrath of God in the Judeo-Christian Bible. Augustine here highlights the problem of anger for religious writers: anger is sinful, and the anger of God seems inconsistent with his beneficence. Elsewhere, Augustine writes, "We do not worship a God who is repentant, jealous, needy or cruel."[33] Nonetheless, God's "anger" or "wrath" is mentioned repeatedly throughout the canonical books of the Old and New Testament. "The radical dissociation of divine wrath and human anger, for instance, represents a strong refusal to allow Scripture to legitimate destructive, hateful human behavior, while admitting the possibility of acting on divinely inspired anger."[34] The Old Testament text is no different: "A fool gives full vent to his anger."[35] And the New Testament echoes: "In your anger do not sin."[36] The Old Testament, however, presents anger in quite a different light; while God's anger in the New Testament seems aimed at the sin, the Old Testament God's anger focuses on the sinner.[37]

Nonetheless, other than the occasional news story reporting a copy of the Bible protecting a victim from a shooter's bullet, or in the pages of theological linguists studying Hebrew, Latin, and Greek etymological roots in biblical texts, anger and the Bible are not conventionally discussed together. In fact, in many pastoral situations, priests and ministers are encouraged to downplay the anger of God in their interpretations and sermons. Certainly the relationship of the Judeo-Christian Bible with radical fundamentalism (in any religious tradition or sect) raises ire and has often inspired anger and violence.

Anger plays a central role in several central narratives in the Judeo-Christian Bible, particularly in the Hebrew Bible or Old Testament. Perhaps that is because anger has traditionally been so closely connected with discipline and judgment, with which much of the Old Testament is concerned. By contrast, the New Testament, with Jesus as the physical representation of redemption and forgiveness, hardly relates characters or tales of anger at all but instead includes sermonizing, mostly in the epistolary writing of Paul, on the dangers of anger. From the anger of Yahweh to the anger of Moses, the Old Testament is rife with stories of dissatisfaction, dismay, and downright rage. In the figure of Jesus, on the other hand, the exemplar for human behavior as Aquinas would later write, anger itself might be considered a sin and thus contrary to the nature of the sin-free Jesus of Nazareth, particularly as a model for ideal human behavior. It is not until the Book of Revelation, the final book of the New Testament, that the wrath of God returns as a key player.

Although Jesus teaches in the New Testament that the meek will inherit the earth, it is also clear that it is the aggressive Old Testament figure, an often angry figure like Samson (whose achievements include slaying an army with the jawbone of an ass and destroying a pagan temple with his bare hands), who achieves advances for the people in God's name. In fact, an early judgment must be made on the value of anger, positive or negative; it is clearly not an absolute in that the very ethos embedded in many biblical texts encourages the *via media* or middle way between absolute anger and absolute passivity. A qualified anger therefore plays an important role in the history of

Western thought.

The Old Testament presents three types of anger: anger toward individuals (e.g., Cain and Abel); anger of an individual toward God (e.g., Job); and the anger of God at his people (e.g., the Flood). The New Testament, on the other hand, rarely indicates the anger of Jesus; instead, when anger is mentioned, it is more likely in the context of a lesson or teaching, and not as an exemplar. Anger most frequently appears in the New Testament in narratives related to God's wrath at the apocalypse in Revelation. Human anger is clearly a sin and is almost always portrayed as such, particularly in the Pauline epistles. Divine anger is often interpreted as "wrath."[38]

Anger was not understood as explicitly psychological by the ancients but was viewed as a physical ailment. Most often, as in the work of Galen and others, anger is categorized as one of several "passions of the soul": "anger, wrath, fear, grief, envy and violent lust."[39] Such passions, he writes, "arise by an irrational impulse."[40] In *Rhetoric* Aristotle defines anger as "an impulse, accompanied by pain, to a conspicuous revenge for a conspicuous slight directed without justification towards what concerns oneself or towards what concerns one's friends."[41] It seems, however, that these readings of anger apply only to human beings. It was left to the early rabbinic and patristic writers to explicate the anger of God in the biblical texts. In the second century CE, Tertullian would argue that human and divine emotions are radically different; thus, "God's wrath must be distinct from what we generally understand as anger."[42]

Studies of anger in the Bible have conventionally focused on one character or book, and such studies have rarely examined the New Testament. Is there something about anger that is particularly Hebrew or Jewish? The 12th-century Jewish philosopher and Torah scholar Maimonides noted that "our sages refer to anger as idolatry." And, of course, Sigmund Freud categorized anger as a form of displacement. The "angry Jew" is almost a stereotype in theater, film, and television.

Rather than merely catalog instances of anger in the Judeo-Christian Bible (a feat that can be easily accomplished with online concordances and wonderful biblical scholarship aids such as the *BibleWorks* software package), I attempt here to first give a broad overview of the types of anger in the Bible and then focus on the anger of God. The theological debate, played out on the pages of the Church Fathers and the Talmudic scholars, often questions the appropriateness of anger in the holy text. Although interesting as philosophical and linguistic discussions, these writers often get caught up in abstraction, sometimes ignoring what is clearly evident in the text: both humans and God, regardless the possible anthropomorphic heresy, experience anger. All anger has ramifications and consequences, some good, many not. Behind the stained glass windows of modern churches and synagogues, there has developed an awkwardness, an embarrassment, particularly regarding the anger or wrath of God in the Bible. Many apologists attempt to compensate for this liturgically through a kind of avoidance, often by omitting "offending" passages from readings and sermons.

The wrath of Yahweh in the Old Testament and the anger of Jesus in the New Testament are not as easily contrasted as assumed in the work of late-19th century biblical scholars. The traditional assumption of Old Testament wrath versus New Testament mercy is actually flawed. This assumption, which dates to the heresies of Marcion in the second century CE, claims two divinities: "An inferior Hebrew God, who created the world but behaves in a reprehensible manner, and a supremely good God, whom Jesus came to reveal."[43] In other words, the love and mercy of the New Testament (the Beatitudes, for example) correct the stern, authoritative voice of the Law handed down at Mt. Sinai in Exodus. As a result of this, Marcion dropped the Old Testament entirely from his Bible, choosing instead to focus exclusively on the "supremely good God" of the New Testament.[44] Origen of Alexandria, quite concerned with linking the New Testament to the Old, would eventually posit a way of reading the Bible "spiritually" in order to justify, some would say "correct," interpretation inconsistent with the apparent beneficence of the divinity. Marcion himself was later corrected by Tertullian in the third century in his argument that God's justice requires God's anger. We might suggest the equation "anger balanced by justice tempered by mercy."

To be sure, it is easier to find Old Testament examples of God's anger with humanity's sin since the Old Testament is an account of thousands of years of living while the New Testament recounts a much briefer history.[45] The anger of God in the Old Testament is immediately felt, while it is most often delayed in the New Testament. Thus, we are able to see God's wrath more clearly in the Old Testament in a cause-and-effect relationship, while the New Testament wrath of God appears later, generally delayed until Revelation. A mere catalogue of Bible verses on anger is not needed here as such an enterprise is now easily accomplished with databases. Suffice it to say that the word "anger" appears in some form in the New Revised Standard Version no fewer than 450 times. In the first part of a three-part essay on anger, David Powlison writes, "The Bible is about anger. Who is the angriest person in the Bible? *God.*"[46]

There are ten Hebrew terms used 714 times in the Old Testament to describe anger.[47] Of these, the majority—that is, 518—refer to divine wrath, with the remaining 196 describing human anger. Divine anger differs greatly from human anger in the Old Testament, with the latter innately being of a more visceral nature—individuals "burn" with anger, or anger is reflected in blushing or flushing of the skin; the Greek Septuagint uses *orgē* for anger, a word related to the Greek *ragō*, denoting a swelling, reinforcing the etymological connotation of anger as a physical manifestation. Thus, the word's derivation implies that anger may result in a physical change to the individual as in Moses's "hot anger" at Pharaoh in Exodus 11:8.

Although, by a ratio of more than two to one, the word is used to describe the anger of God, the first explicit appearance of anger in the Old Testament is the story of the murder of Abel by his brother Cain in Genesis. While God appears displeased with Adam and Eve after their transgression in Genesis 3, his punishments of the pair (and the snake) are expressed calmly, some might say without affect, and the writer indicates nothing of the divine wrath we find later in the book.

The outward manifestation of anger is often displayed violently and swiftly as in Cain's anger with his brother. And that physical manifestation is often reflected in a physical change in the angry individual. Anger's effect on the physical body of human beings is illuminated in the work of early writers on physiology such as Galen, who warned that anger in infants was a precursor to severe disease and disfigurement. In the biblical account of the first murder, Cain's offering to God is rejected, and the writer claims, "Cain was very angry, and his countenance fell";[48] the text, however, provides no elaboration on what "angry" means here. The Hebrew word used is חָרָה a word that can also mean to burn or be kindled with fire.[49] Bible scholar Matthew Schlimm notes this as the "most common verb" for anger in Genesis, appearing 93 times.[50] Suffice it to say that Cain's anger has a visceral quality to it, and God uses the same word in the next verse in an attempt to calm Cain where he questions Cain's anger and advises him, "If you do well, will you not be accepted? And if you do not do well, sin is couching at the door; its desire is for you, but you must master it."[51] Cain's fallen countenance implies his behavior or demeanor has shifted as a result of his emotional distress. The image of sin "couching at the door" is a startling one that evokes either a Freudian sense of repressed anger and memories or Jung's Shadow self, ready to reveal themselves and pounce at any moment. Cain's identification as the first murderer and the first person physically affected by anger is elaborated in Regina M. Schwartz's insightful study, *The Curse of Cain*, where she argues that "the origins of violence" can be found in "identity formation."[52] Anger clearly forms an integral aspect of that identity formation in the Old Testament.

Jungian psychologist Stephen A. Martin expresses well the Jungian dichotomy of the archetypal complex of anger particularly as it relates to the physical manifestations:

> One aspect of this dichotomy is characterized by a seething, red-hot emotionality that pumps blood into our faces and hands and pushes us ever closer toward impulsive and regrettable acting out. Its complement is a quite different hardness of heart, a disturbing stillness of icy emotional withdrawal that shuts us down and in.[53]

The latter is reflected in God's response to "the wickedness of man" in Genesis 6: "And the Lord was sorry that he had made man on the earth, and it grieved him to his heart. I will blot out man . . . for I am sorry that I have made them."[54] After explaining to Noah that he will "destroy all flesh in which is the breath of life from under heaven," God tempers his anger with an offer to "establish my covenant with you."[55]

An interesting contrast to God's calming covenant with Noah is his punishment of Cain, who is to be "a fugitive and a wanderer on the earth."[56] God's anger with the collective group is expressed in more reflective sorrow in the Noah story—"I am sorry that I have made them"[57]— whereas his anger with Cain's murder of his brother is marked by focused and external anger resulting in exile. The two stories, which follow each other in Genesis, seem to note a shift in the anger of God from impulsivity to reflexivity and thoughtfulness. In fact, the writer does not indicate God's protection of Noah, but only that, once the waters begin to recede, "God remembered Noah," "remembering" often a euphemism through the Old Testament to indicate God's care for and protection of his creation.[58] That remembrance and Noah's successful sacrifice[59] cause God to promise never again to destroy the creatures of the world "as I have done."[60] Nevertheless, the anger and resulting punishment are immediate: a flood kills instantly.

The recurring pattern in the Old Testament of sin, repentance, and deliverance seems to come to an explicit head in God's commandment in Exodus prohibiting idol worship: "For the Lord your God am a jealous God";[61] the second account, in Exodus 34, even notes that God's "name is Jealous" and that he "is a jealous God."[62] In fact, the noteworthy relationship of jealousy to anger in the Old Testament God is clear from early in the Old Testament where the Hebrew Yahweh is one of many available deities and that Yahweh is indeed jealous, a jealousy that leads to anger and seems to evoke fear in his creations.

God's anger is not always released externally. As the Old Testament progresses, God's anger becomes more repressed, reflective, thoughtful—less impulsive and instantly putative. Curiously, the golden calf episode, occurring late in Exodus 32:14, evokes not palpable anger but instead contemplative anger: "And the Lord repented of the evil which he thought to do to his people." This echoes God's reaction to man's corruption (leading to the Flood) in Genesis 6:6: "And the Lord was sorry that he had made man on the earth, and it grieved him to his heart." Gary Heiron among others refers to "the overall anthropopathic character of Hebrew descriptions of Yahweh," that is, God's actions are described through human emotion, something early Christian writers such as Marcion found heretical.[63]

The Exodus passage on the golden calf is followed by Moses's anger, which "burned hot" and compelled him to throw "the tablets out of his hands."[64] It almost seems here that Moses's anger has become the physical manifestation of the anger of God, who has by Exodus removed himself from much direct interaction with his creation. The entire episode evokes the language of the Flood. Here God said to Moses, "Whoever has sinned against me, him will I blot out of my book,"[65] resulting in "a plague upon the people, because they made the calf."[66] Moses's punishment for destroying the tablets is indeed harsh: God will no longer speak with Moses "face to face, as a man speaks to his friend,"[67] a punishment patristic and Talmudic writers also noted in Adam and Eve's expulsion from the Garden of Eden. Again, God's anger is immediate and tangible.

God's anger in the Pentateuch is vindictive and vengeful, and although there is anger between human beings, examples pale in comparison to God's anger and punishment, which is not only paternalistic but fatalistic. One finds a disappointment in God's anger, often including mention of the broken covenant, followed by judgment and punishment or penalty. That disappointment evokes the psychological guilt of a child toward a parent. Divine anger, "the wrath of God," is almost always a response to the breaking of the covenant and is clearly less immediate than earlier cause-and-effect anger (as in the story of Cain and Abel) but is more overwhelming and overarching. Biblical scholar Dennis McCarthy notes one of the few examples where divine wrath results in "reaffirmation of covenant":[68] 1 Samuel 12:8–12, where the transgressions of the Israelites are recalled. Samuel recalls his people's history since Moses and notes, "If you will not hearken to the voice of the Lord, but rebel against the hand of the Lord, then the hand of the Lord will be against you and your king."[69] Samuel then instructs, "Only fear the Lord, and serve him faithfully with all your heart. But if you still do wickedly, you shall be swept away."[70] The wrath of God is directly related to the people's actions, implying a clear cause-and-effect relationship between human sin and divine anger.

This causal relationship is nowhere more evident than in the book of Leviticus, a compilation of rules and regulations regarding ritual and law. Leviticus 26 outlines the punishments beginning with an "if" statement in verse 3 and changing tone to a sequence of "but if" statements in verse 14 and after: "But if you will not hearken to me, and will not do all these commandments I will appoint over you sudden terror." The breaking of the covenant in verse 15 will cause the estrangement of God from his people: "I will set my face against you."[71] Once again, God's anger is manifested in a literal turning away from his creation.

This ramification of God's anger is also clear in the earliest biblical story of sin. After Adam and Eve have eaten of the Tree of Knowledge of Good and Evil, they are expelled from the Garden of Eden, prompting many patristic writers to read the estrangement from God as representing God's anger. God will no longer walk with Adam as he did earlier in the Garden. In the early books of the Old Testament, especially, God's anger is depicted as disappointment, regret on God's part for having created sinful beings, but also disappointment on the part of humans. Interestingly, in Genesis 3, once Adam and Eve admit their sin, implicating the serpent who "beguiled" Eve, the rest of the chapter is given to God to lay out punishment. God "drove" Adam and Eve out of Eden.[72] The separation, noted later in Exodus 33 ("Thus the Lord used to speak to Moses face to face, as a man speaks to his friend"), is the direct consequence of human transgression and God's anger as previously seen in Genesis.

It is important to note that God's anger in the Old Testament is always tempered with justice, recalling the ethos behind Dante's *Inferno*: God created Hell for justice. This tempering is indicated by contrition and confession even in Leviticus 26: "But if they confess their iniquity. . . . then I will remember my covenant."[73] It is also interesting to note that God never becomes angry in the opening chapters of Genesis; through the Fall of Adam and Eve, the sin of Cain, the travesty of Sodom and Gomorrah, God's "anger" is never explicitly mentioned. Not to belabor a metaphor, but if we look at the earliest characters in the Old Testament as humanity in its infant and toddler stage, then God fulfills the parental role. As anyone who has raised children can testify, those early years are not only filled with education but with frustration. Like the parent guiding the crawling child away from the stairs, God in these early tales attempts to adjust the course of humanity without directly interfering in its growth and curiosity. By the time we reach the story of the Flood, it seems that humans have entered adolescence and must endure punishment for their transgressions—humanity is sent into a "timeout." The parent whose child runs out into traffic will react with anger, although it is an anger tempered by love and justice.

At the same time, we must recall early Rabbinic and Patristic discussions of the linguistic and theological inaccuracy of attributing human traits (i.e., anger) to the divinity. This anthropathosing (i.e., using the concept of human emotion/pathos to describe a nonhuman being) of God is viewed as dangerous by many and as openly heretical by others. Perhaps one of the most important voices here is Lactantius, the fourth-century CE North African theologian whose "Treatise on the Anger of God" warns about the arrogance of boasting that human beings can ever know the same emotional sensations as the divinity, particularly anger.

Lactantius also posits that if we decline to attribute anger to God, we can neither attribute kindness: "both alike must be taken from Him."[74] But he also suggests that as humans cease sinning, God's wrath declines.[75] Lactantius actually suggests that "the loving of the good arises from the hatred of the wicked."[76] One of his more startling conclusions reiterates Proverbs 9.10: "There can be no religion where there is no fear." Lactantius clearly links fear to divine wrath.[77]

Anger is a human emotion. Thus, the chief problem with discussing God's anger is the question of anthropomorphosis. Can we attribute a human emotion to a divine being? Or is it, as Augustine would argue, that God's anger is of a different character and definition. Augustine also suggests that we look at concepts such as God's anger as metaphors, reading such passages in Origen's *sensus spirtualis.*[78] Essentially, Augustine argues that the language of the Bible is necessary so that human beings might understand it: "If scripture did not employ such words, it would not strike home so closely, as it were, to all humanity."[79]

When considering the role of anger in the Bible, we might be prone to default to the story of Job and his anger at a God who seems to be using him as a pawn in a game. For Jung, this was the prototypical discussion of anger in the Western world. But we can see anger in the Hebrew Bible as early as Adam and Eve when, in Genesis 3, God doles out his punishments for Adam, Eve, and the serpent. However, the first mention of anger occurs in the Cain and Abel story when we are told that "Cain was very angry"[80] when God "had no regard" for Cain or his offering. God asks Cain, explicitly, "Why are you angry"[81] and warns him that "sin is couching at the door."[82] Thus, at its first mention, anger is comingled with sin. To be angry is, if not a sin, then certainly not a positive attribute.

As Regina Schwartz, American scholar of religion and literature, mentions, the sacrifices of Cain and his brother "suggest propitiation, that is, an offering to ward off divine wrath."[83] But, we might ask, at this point in the Hebrew Bible, is there an underlying assumption of divine anger that must be placated, as Schwartz continues, "to invoke his blessings of prosperity"? Schwartz echoes our frustration when she asks, "What kind of God is this who chooses one sacrifice over the other?"[84] This can all be contrasted with the thought of the ancient Greek Jew Philo of Alexandria, following Plato, who wrote that because God is without passion or emotion, he cannot be angry.[85]

The result is an atmosphere of fear in which the Israelites constantly anticipate the wrath of the father. Nonetheless, as exhibited in the stories in Judges, they continually displease God, endure his wrath, suffer through punishment, experience redemption, and begin the cycle anew. As just one example, in Judges 2 the angel of God tells the Israelites, "I brought you up from Egypt and brought you into the land which I swore to give to your fathers. I said, 'I will never break my covenant with you, and you shall make no covenant with the inhabitants of this land; you shall break down their altars.' But you have not obeyed my command. What is this you have done? So now I say, I will not drive them out before you; but they shall become adversaries to you, and their gods shall be a snare to you."[86] In response, the people "lifted up their voices and wept."[87]

There seems to be no summative effect of this transgressing, as God's anger, exhibited in his consistent plaint that the Israelites have "transgressed my covenant," seems quelled with each new generation. Even the worshipping of other gods, in the form of the Ba'als, which would seem a gross transgression and violation of the first of the commandments, results perhaps in severe immediate punishment, but no enduring punishment.

Ultimately, God's anger in the Old Testament is not entirely literal, but instead implies what German theologian Rudolf Otto termed something more "numinous," *mysterium tremendum et fascinans*, a fearful and tremendous mystery.[88] Otto is keen to relate the *tremor* root of *tremendum* to shutter or fear, noting that the ineffable divine evokes fear in human beings, partially due to its ineffability; we fear what we do not or cannot know. Otto addresses "the wrath of God": "'Wrath' here is the 'ideogram' of a unique emotional moment in religious experience," a moment Otto imagines must be "gravely disturbing" to those who "recognize nothing in the divine nature but goodness, gentleness, [and] love."[89]

The anger or wrath of the Old Testament God has had particular impact on the philosophies and theologies related to the Holocaust. In a 1999 speech in Washington, D.C., Holocaust survivor and Nobel Prize winner Elie Wiesel noted the sentiment of many survivors: "Rooted in our tradition, some of us felt that to be abandoned by humanity then was not the ultimate. We felt that to be abandoned by God was worse than to be punished by Him. Better an unjust God than an indifferent one. For us to be ignored by God was a harsher punishment than to be a victim of His anger. Man can live far from God—not outside God." So, given the choice of God's wrath or God's indifference, Wiesel chooses anger. We need also remember that Wiesel is the author of *The Trial of God*, a drama in which prisoners (not unlike concentration camp prisoners) put God on trial.[90]

Perhaps one of the most confusing instances of God's anger in the Old Testament occurs in the story of Uzzah and the Ark of the Covenant in 2 Samuel 6 where "The anger of the Lord was kindled against Uzzah" after he "put out his hand to the ark of God and took hold of it."[91] The Ark, according to Numbers 4:15, was untouchable by humans. The punishment of death seems extreme in the case of Uzzah, who reached out to steady the ark because "the oxen stumbled." Early rabbinical interpretations of the passage merely attribute the incident to the anger of the deity, claiming that Uzzah should have been aware that the Ark of the Covenant could easily have borne its own weight and did not require the assistance of human hands. The Uzzah incident in 2 Samuel is especially problematic when read in the light of the mercy of God. How could Yahweh be so vindictive as to react angrily to what is clearly a misstep on the part of a minor character moving to prevent the Ark from crashing to the ground? How indeed. The message would appear to be more closely aligned with the dictates of established rules and the consequences of violating those rules. The writer first claims it is "the anger of the Lord" that was "kindled against Uzzah."[92] Then, in a clear one-to-one relationship, "God smote him there because he put forth his hand to the ark."[93] Uzzah's fault is that he has treated the Ark as if it were any ordinary box and not the base of God's throne.

Oftentimes, it is difficult for modern people to fully appreciate what Rudolf Otto called "the idea of the holy" in the ancient world, particularly when it comes to the holiness of objects and their connection to the divinity. The Israelites understood that wherever the Ark of the Covenant was, Yahweh was present. The Old Testament prohibition from seeing God certainly extends to physical contact as well. Thus, Uzzah violates several edicts in his efforts to prevent the Ark from crashing to the ground. God's anger at this—the death of Uzzah—is then followed by the anger of David, who refuses to continue the trip to Jerusalem with the Ark, fearing the power of its very presence.

To be sure, in early books of the Old Testament, divine wrath is roused by the willful disobedience of God's creation[94] and by worship of other gods.[95] Later, outside the text of the Pentateuch, God's anger is especially provoked by the sin of the people.[96]

The effects of divine wrath in the Old Testament clearly illuminate the poor choices and actions of the Israelites. In what sounds like a Zen Koan, Jung cites the Midrash on Genesis 18:23: "If thou desirest the world to endure, there can be no absolute justice, while if thou desirest absolute justice, the world cannot endure. Yet thou wouldst hold the cord by both ends, desiring both the world and justice."[97] This paradox is at the heart of the "problem" of a divine wrath often expressed in parental terms and many times implying shame and disappointment. We need only to compare the anger expressed by Cain in murdering his brother Abel with Yahweh's reaction to Moses's destruction of the stone tablets to see both the differences. It would seem that humanity was created in Genesis without the ability to express anger. Biblical exegesis, both Jewish and Christian, indicates that the Fall introduced an unnatural conflict between body and soul and, with that conflict, anger.

Perhaps, ultimately, the paradox of anger in the Old Testament is part of the *mysterium tremendeum* in that it is consistently inconsistent with the loving nature of the being who gave life to Adam and Eve. And perhaps it is a paradox akin to theodicy, the phenomenology of perception, and the inability of the Chicago Cubs to win a World Series (until 2016). God's loving anger in the Old Testament is one of his defining traits; without it, Yahweh would transform into the Christ of the New Testament. Just as John Hick, the English philosopher and theologian who wrote so eloquently on "the problem of evil," recalls that the human attempt to understand theodicy is "a foolish pretension . . . under the illusion that [humans] can judge God's acts by human standards," so too is comprehending God's anger at his creations.[98] Anthony Hanson suggests that in the Old Testament, "where the divine wrath is met with, it is thought of as not necessarily accountable or rational, or morally motivated."[99]

Anger presents quite differently in the New Testament where Jesus is only explicitly angry in one verse: after critics accuse him of healing on the Sabbath, he "looked round about on them with anger."[100] Perhaps this scene is most succinctly explicated as follows: "Compassion fueled it. He was both angry at the Jewish leaders' hypocrisy and grieved at their hardness of heart."[101] In fact, the Greek word **ὀργή** used here suggests more frustration or exasperation than true anger. In fact, "the reason for anger in this situation fits the pattern for God's anger."[102] Jesus's anger here is "to set things right, it had a constructive purpose."[103]

Otherwise, discussions of divine anger or wrath are confined to the Pauline Epistles and the Book of Revelation, a fact that should not come as a surprise given the merciful stories recounted in the Gospels compared with the many horrific events experienced by the Israelites throughout the books of the Old Testament. Even when, in Matthew, John the Baptist urges the crowd to "flee from the wrath that is coming,"[104] it is to the eschatological Day of Judgment that he refers and not to an immediate manifestation of that wrath. Again, as C. H. Dodd reminds us, Rudolf Otto's *tremendum mysterium* is relevant here: "When religion reaches the point of personifying the objects of numinous feeling, such phenomena [i.e., natural phenomena such as earthquakes] are explained on the analogy of the irrational passion of an angry man: they are the anger of the gods."[105] Thus, the "wrath of God" is the thunder and the pestilence of the Old Testament, and it is, as in Romans 1:18, "God's anger . . . revealed from heaven against all the impiety and wickedness of those who hinder the Truth by their wickedness."

What of Jesus's displays of anger? The most notable instance of Jesus's anger appears when he overturns the tables of the moneychangers in Mark 11:15; however, the gospel writer [106] does not make Jesus's anger explicitly clear.[107] "In point of fact, however, none of the Synoptic accounts attributes any emotion whatsoever to Jesus in connection with this incident."[108] In John's account,[109] Jesus's anger is interpreted as "zeal." "Zeal is more than anger. It is the ardor of red hot passion."[110] The Synoptics describe "an incident of well managed outrage," not anger in the traditional sense.[111]

"It is with Paul that the conception of the 'wrath' of God becomes prominent."[112] Jesus's anger is, as noted, rarely alluded to. Instead, it is Paul who, looking back to the God of the Old Testament, evokes God's wrath anew in the Christian world. This suggests, from the New Testament perspective, that God uses his anger as a threat, punishment in the future for current transgressions, whereas in the Old Testament, the anger of God is felt almost immediately: for example, Adam and Eve are expelled from Eden, Moses is forbidden to enter the Promised Land. MacGregor argues for "wrath" as an "attribute of God, but, if we may so put it, an attribute held in reserve."[113] Although God's wrath is certainly effectuated by human sin, it is a wrath immediately present in the Old Testament, whereas it is delayed, perhaps until Judgment, in the New Testament.

John suggests in 3:26 that those who do not "obey the Son shall not see life, but the wrath of God rests upon him." Divine retribution in the New Testament is long term, whereas the Old Testament God might immediately lament his creation fresh on the heels of his transgression. The Old Testament sinner has violated an explicit law and is so punished in a cause-and-effect relationship. "We shall remind ourselves that, according to the New Testament, God vindicates his own justice and righteousness . . ., not through his 'wrath,' but through his forgiving love."[114] So then, the relationship between anger and justice, a pairing so often evident in the Old Testament, shifts in the New Testament to connect justice with love. After all, it is the New Testament God who grants humanity redemption (out of love) for its sin, instead of dooming humanity to an eternity of pain and punishment. And so John 3:16, "For God so loved the world that he gave his only Son" in order to, as the poet John Milton writes, "end the strife/Of Mercy and Justice."[115]

The Pauline Epistles have much to offer on the question of anger. In Ephesians 4:26–27 Paul counsels to "be angry but do not sin"; however, that anger is not to percolate beyond the end of the day: "Do not let the sun go down on your anger."[116] In Galatians 5:19–23, Paul lists anger as one of the "works of the flesh," a list that includes "fornication, impurity . . . drunkenness, carousing." Paul warns "those who do such things will not inherit the kingdom of heaven." As Scottish theologian James Denney put it, "In the NT itself there are far more warnings against anger than indications of its true place and function."[117]

The connection of divine anger to the Day of Judgment harkens to the Old Testament Prophets who suggested that God will "sit to judge all the nations round about"[118] at which "the terror of the Lord"[119] will be present. Certainly it is in the book of Revelation, a text Swiss psychiatrist Carl Jung called "a veritable orgy of hatred, wrath, vindictiveness, and blind destructive fury," that the divine wrath is clearly felt, although it does differ in nature and tenor from the Old Testament divine wrath in one significant way: the wrath of God in the Old Testament (outside the books of the prophets) is recounted historically, while the divine wrath in Revelation is a fiction, something yet to come. This and this alone may account for the more elaborate and involved descriptions of the anger of the deity in Revelation, particularly considering its author, John, was in prison on the island of Patmos at the time of writing. His own bitterness and anger are palpable from the opening verses. However, the wrath in Revelation is not purely eschatological: "It is a process, stretching from the Cross to the Parousia."[120] Hanson goes on to argue that in the New Testament wrath is never disciplinary: "The wrath is not an attitude of God, but a condition of men."[121] In fact, biblical scholars have consistently drawn parallels between the divine wrath in Revelation and the representation of divine wrath in the Old Testament, almost as if the writer of Revelation is looking to the Old Testament and not the Gospels for inspiration and influence.

Greater insight to and understanding of anger in the Bible can certainly help us to better grasp the nature of anger in the Judeo-Christian traditions, but also speaks to a larger context: the role of anger in Western religion in general, including Islam where the hadith sacred text counsels, "Do not be angry. He is not strong and powerful who throws people down but he is strong who withholds himself from anger." For mainstream Christianity, anger is one of the seven deadly sins. In Rabbinical Judaism, the Babylonian Talmud identifies anger as one the characteristic traits of an individual: "Rabbi Ila'I said: A person is known by three things: his cup (by how he holds his wine), his pocket (by his generosity) and his anger."[122]

For several centuries, human beings have often credited natural evils to the anger of God, most notably after the 1755 earthquake in Lisbon.[123] God's wrath, derived from the myriad stories in the Old Testament in particular, is, they claim, evident as punishment of human beings for perceived transgressions. However, as we have seen, the Old Testament stories of divine wrath lack moralizing and often seem the impetuous reaction of an impatient character.

As result of the varied representations of anger in the Bible, it is difficult indeed to emerge from study of this issue with a broad or general conclusion. The Old Testament God is wrathful and impetuous; the New Testament God is more understanding and delays his wrath until the end times. That assessment is too black and white and does not account for the many shades of gray in the text. We might look instead at a progression of divine behavior, implying growth of the divinity from the punishment in Eden—part of an historical narrative of the Israelites birth and growth—to the apocalyptic end in Revelation—a fictional progression of an event yet to come.

What does all of this mean for contemporary conceptions of anger as they relate particularly to concepts of sin in the West? I might suggest that the especially Jewish approach to the anger of God is an immediate reaction, within one's very lifetime. Perhaps the Christian perspective is more a delayed response, in either the next life or at Judgment. This could explain the very different approaches to action in Jewish and Christian societies and governments, the Jewish approach being more immediate and the Christian more nuanced.

Much of the hermeneutic complexity comes not in the canonical Bible but in the multitude of peripheral interpretive texts produced in more than 2,000 years. If indeed, the Bible text is meant to serve as an exemplar for human behavior, it is confusing and spurious on the issue of anger. Perhaps that is why the topic has been central to patristic and rabbinical writing for some two centuries. The same text- based religious tradition that purports to exemplify love, forgiveness, and mercy has to wrestle with apparent inconsistencies.

The ancients as well as modern psychologists concede that anger operates as a necessary, if unpleasant, aspect of human being. Seneca notes that some examples are to be avoided, while others are to be imitated;[124] one wonders whether some instances of anger in the Bible are intended as examples to avoid. As Seneca notes, "many men have been incapacitated by their anger, many disabled, even when their victims have yielded to such treatment."[125]

In his study of the decline of violence, Pinker notes that the Old Testament is rife with violence and anger, almost from the opening pages.[126] Perhaps this can be explained by the multiplicity of gods the ancient Israelites were dealing with. In order to express the dominance of Yahweh as *the* only God, the writers of Old Testament tales are pressed to display that dominance through a metaphorical battle with the other gods (not unlike similar conflicts amongst the Greek and Roman gods). As the text of the Old Testament progresses, and the New Testament arises, the need to exert power through anger and violence is reduced. Countries battle for primacy only when they are threatened by each other; in times of peace both the rhetoric and the actual events are smoothed over or made calmer.

Genetics/Human Biology:

If anger is an innate aspect of human being, coded into the DNA of *Homo sapiens* like brown eyes or baldness, then we do grave injustice by chastising and punishing those who display their anger. On the basis of this argument, then, it would be as unfair to tell a person to make their hair less brown as it is to tell someone to be less angry. If I am unable to control my ability to curl my tongue, why should I be expected to control my anger?

To be sure, we live in an angry world today. Terrorism. Random shootings. Twitter wars. Road rage. Bullying. Many believe that anger is something to be managed—"anger management" courses abound. Others think it needs to be somehow cured. But how can our angry society become less angry? Two factors would need to be involved. One is more global and social; the other is more personal and internal. First, a change in the way people interact. Second, a change in the way people reflect.

The daily life of humans in the 21st century is filled with anxiety, stress, and constant demands. From driving through rush hour traffic to choosing which cell phone carrier to go with to the ever-present bombardment of news and information, human existence today is rife with stressors that trigger anger. Again, we come back to the rate of speed of contemporary living. We seem to have two gears: fast and faster. And, I argue, that speed can only serve to ramp up anger innate in human beings. Just think: if you are working hard, and your boss stops in the office and says she now needs the report that was due at 3 P.M. at noon, it triggers a response—adrenaline rushes, the brain shifts gears, and you become more sensitive to annoyances that would have otherwise been slight. The computer program will not perform the function needed—the response is frustration and then, if unresolved, anger.

On February 24, 1924, an article in *The New York Times* reported that flirting with the female students at Barnard College "makes them angry." Gates, the article reporter, looked at 145 "anger experiences" in 51 girls. "She found that 115 of these experiences were caused by persons rather than things, and that the anger caused by persons was more violent than that caused by things." Gates also reports more anger on holidays rather than school days. In a letter to the editor published days later, M. Hirschthal writes, "These Barnard girls are on their good behavior as regards one another for the five days of the week . . . but when they arrive home constraint is thrown off and the spleen and anger stored up for five days give rise to the series of expulsions directed at their relatives." The writer notes Gates's "anger tests" should more accurately be called "irritability tests."

Regardless of the clearly sexist and misogynist attitude of this study—and the reporting of it in *The New York Times*—observations regarding anger and the attempts to assess its causes are as old as Aristotle who writes in *Rhetoric*, "Anger may be defined as a desire accompanied by pain, for a conspicuous revenge for a conspicuous slight at the hands of men who have no call to slight oneself or one's friends."[127] There is in Aristotle's mind no "anger for anger's sake"; instead, anger "must always be felt towards a particular individual."[128]

What, then, of the so-called angry young man who according to musician Billy Joel "struggles and bleeds as he hangs on the cross."[129] The martyr who will never surrender to his doom, the angry young man says he will neither bend nor crawl. Although the song asserts that the angry young man has a place in the world, he does not learn from his mistakes and is extremely boring. And it is true—the perpetually angry are indeed "boring as hell" in that they seem unable to allow any pleasure into their lives and are always (in Aristotle's thought) feeling as if they are being slighted by the world. Not to mention that modern medicine believes such individuals to be putting their health in danger with heightened risk of heart attack and high blood pressure.

This angry young man is Jim Stark as played by James Dean in 1955's *Rebel Without a Cause*. Or Marlon Brando's Johnny Strabler who is asked in 1953's *The Wild One*, "what are you rebelling against" and answers with "Whadda you got?" Is there an angry young woman? According to the Barnard study in the 1920s, the angry young woman is frowned upon if not taboo. Is that still the case in the 21st century, in the midst of the fourth wave of the feminist movement? When one million women marched on Washington, D.C., only days after Donald Trump's inauguration, a persistently sexist and denigrating complaint regarded the women as "angry." Indeed, writing in *The Daily Californian*, Grace Vogel noted that she marched in the initial march (an ancillary event in San Francisco) to "channel my anger positively."[130] *Vox.com* even went so far as to label 2017 "the year of women's anger."[131] *The Philadelphia Inquirer* called the follow-up march in 2018 "an oxymoron of anger and joy."[132] Given recent events, including the #MeToo movement and the myriad charges of sexual misconduct against celebrities and high profile politicians, the angry woman—what Donald Trump termed "a nasty woman" during the 2016 presidential debates with Hillary Clinton—is no longer   a rarity.

The issue here is how to channel anger into productive and beneficial action. The entire discipline of conflict resolution studies has been built on this principle. As one noted conflict resolution scholar puts it, "Anger can prompt nonviolent conflict resolution by stimulating people to be aware of others' feelings and beliefs about injustice, by motivating them to make amends, and by restoring feelings of self-efficacy."[133] Anger can be channeled into positive change as in Martin Luther King Jr. and the civil rights movement, Nelson Mandela's fight against apartheid, and Mahatma Gandhi's movement for an independent India.

In the postwar year of 1959, writing on the expansion of human knowledge and wisdom, the great 20th century thinker Bertrand Russell called humanity "a ferocious animal."[134] Humankind has been saved for millennia only "by virtue of ignorance and inefficiency."[135] With Russell's "expanding mental universe" and later the explosion in technological prowess, "these limitations are fading away." Just as humanity is becoming the lord of creation, it too could become a lord of destruction if its anger were to overpower its will. Russell goes on to warn that "the indulgence of hatred can lead only to disaster."[136] This would be anger uncontrolled exemplified. We are dangerously close to it in a culture that is lacking in empathy and increasingly hostile and unfeeling. Pinker has recently argued for "the better angels of our nature," saying that empathy is only one piece of the puzzle: empathy, he writes, is becoming "a sentimental idea" that is "overrated as a reducer of violence."[137] Nonetheless, I agree with Dutch biologist Frans de Waal, who in a 2009 book titled *The Age of Empathy* argued that our interdependence on one another is a fact of the species and that such interdependencies have evolved into the human ability to feel what others are feeling—both pain and joy.[138] De Waal recalls the stories of the ancient Chinese sage Mencius whose writing asks us to reflect on the origins of empathy. Mencius points to four sentiments at the root of human morality: empathy, shame, modesty, and a sense of right and wrong. Writing in the fourth century BCE, Mencius said, "The feeling of commiseration is the beginning of humanity."[139]

So, in a world in which anger is displayed in innumerable ways, what would a world without anger look like? Admittedly, it would be fairly boring. Anger is a prime motivation in most competitive sports. Perhaps it is ironic that fields such as applied sports psychology now counsel participants on controlling anger. Competitive sports live in that awkward no man's land between control and chaos. Controlled anger wins Super Bowls; chaotic anger results in expulsion and suspension from the sport. This controlled anger in sports, however, is not a novelty in contemporary contact sports but dates to the origins of competitive sports themselves.[140] Ancient cultures embraced physical and sometimes brutal contact sports for its military when there were no conflicts in progress. So-called wars without weapons gave rise to the Olympics in which countries compete to see who is best, presumably without resorting to bloody injury and heinous death. This is the epitome of controlled or focused anger.

Let us shift gears and look at anger in something much more pedestrian than war or even professional sports. Who can forget the feeling of satisfaction that came from slamming down the telephone receiver in anger? Phones, first made of Bakelite and then of heavy plastic, could certainly take a beating. An irate phone conversation would easily end when one of the parties slammed the phone down into its cradle; pay phones seem to have been made from even stronger material. Hanging up on someone with a cell phone does not yield even the closest visceral satisfaction.

Anger conveyed in electronic communication is even more problematic.

The use of emojis to indicate any emotion in emails or texts never seems sufficient and is often misinterpreted. Anger, particularly, is difficult to convey through the use of an electronic visual representation. The anger emoji, really just a variation on the smiley face, hardly relates the level of feeling and would seem to represent everything from casual annoyance to outright rage. This reminds me of when my daughter was young—perhaps 2 or 3—and she would get frustrated; "use your words," we would tell her. But somehow we are regressing to the days of pictographs of cave walls, and this regression is increasingly problematic for the expression (and possible positive channeling) of anger.

In the past decade, anger has entered the political arena where it has made a mockery of civil discourse. From the vitriol spewed from Donald Trump's Twitter account to the "debate" by the water cooler, the basic tenets of civility seem to have gone down for the count. From the white supremacists marching in Charlottesville to the *de rigueur* practice of taking a selfie in front of Trump Tower while proudly displaying one's middle finger, what it means to have control over one's angry impulses has certainly shifted. As children, we are first taught to control angry impulses and instead seek out compromise and engage in fair play. If my teammate in the schoolyard basketball game is hogging the ball, we are taught not to get angry with him but instead to calmly discuss it and develop a strategy. Such negotiation has all but vanished, particularly given the lack of reflection before action.

In a 2016 analysis of Donald Trump's personality, psychology professor Dan P. McAdams noted, "Combined with a considerable gift for humor (which may also be aggressive), anger lies at the heart of Trump's charisma. And anger permeates his political rhetoric."[141] Michael Kimmel's 2015 book *Angry White Men* wondered why this demographic was so angry, from old white supremacists to young college students. "The American Dream of endless upward mobility," he writes, "was always shadowed by the American nightmare—just as you could rise as far as your aspirations and talents could take you, you could also fall off the cliff."[142] So fear of failure escalated to anger. In his majestic *People's History of the United States*, historian Howard Zinn looks at how class anger "that came from the realities of ordinary life" in the 19th century reemerged in the 20th century.[143] Works such as Upton Sinclair's 1906 exposé novel of the meatpacking plants of Chicago, *The Jungle*, encouraged awareness of and anger toward the upper class especially by immigrants.

This class anger has reared its ugly head once again at the open of the 21st century with the ever-widening gap between "the haves" and "the have nots." The "one percenter" movement, myriad Occupy demonstrations, and Donald Trump's punitive policies on immigrants, and indeed anyone who is not white Anglo-Saxon Protestant, have only functioned to raise the barometer of divisiveness and discord. This is not to say that there is no place for anger in political discourse.[144]

Whereas anger has been an assertion of masculinity, the #MeToo movement has brought women's anger to the front page. The movement has not only magnified women's anger at men but also women's anger at the establishments and institutions that have given rise to and fostered men's harassing and discriminatory behavior for decades. In some sense, #MeToo has made everyone angrier, regardless the side of the debate they are on. Many men say they now operate in an atmosphere of confusion which can lead to fear which often leads to anger. Women, on the other hand, have worked to put their anger into action. As Senator Elizabeth Warren has said, "It's hard to be in the fight, but for me it's even harder to stand on the sidelines and watch the fight go by."[145] The #MeToo movement has come to be the signature action of a generation looking to take palpable anger and effect tangible change.

There is no explicit role for anger in the U.S. Constitution, but many interpret the Second Amendment right to bear arms as evidence that the founders endorsed the resolution of some disagreements with anger and violence. However, the text explicitly endorses gun ownership for the fostering of a "well-regulated Militia." Recent studies have linked anger and gun violence, noting that at least 8 percent per 100,000 gun owners also have what researchers term "impulsive angry behavior," a population also "more likely to be male, younger, married, and to live in outlying areas around metropolitan centers rather in central cities."[146] Putting anger into action is probably the most beneficial thing that can come out of the current situation, for women and for men. Allowing that anger to escalate to violence would seem to reinforce Martin Luther King Jr.'s statement that "'an eye for an eye' leaves everybody blind. The time is always right do the right thing."

The current political climate has promoted the angry white male, stereotypically uneducated, blue collar, and carrying a rifle. Such a figure is often connected to other angry groups in America like The Tea Party, Patriot groups, anti-immigrant protesters, and even the Ku Klux Klan. Angry white men dominate the airwaves, from Rush Limbaugh to Sean Hannity to Alex Jones, a phenomenon that seems confined to those on the right side of the political spectrum.

Terrorist attacks are the epitome of contemporary anger, provoking questions such as "why do they hate us?" Uncontrolled yet focused anger results in the inciting of fear and terror in unknown victims. School shootings evoke the same, though in some cases the victims are not previously unknown to the assailant. Anger accelerated becomes hate. ISIS. The Taliban. The Ku Klux Clan. White supremacists. All began as angry groups and morphed into peddlers of hate.[147] To be sure, anger sits on a continuum that, if left untended or stoked, will result in hate and ends with killing. The white supremacist movement in the United States has a long and ugly history. Although already present in some 17th century ideologies, it was not until that late-19th century that scientists such as H. H. Goddard, Lewis M. Terman, and R. M. Yerkes argued for the intellectual inferiority of nonwhites based on erroneous measurements of skull capacity, advancing beliefs in eugenics.[148] By the 1930s, the Nazis had coopted pseudoscience and built a racist political party. The effects have been long reaching, from the 1995 bombing of the federal building in Oklahoma City by white power advocate Timothy McVeigh to the summer 2017 marches in Charlottesville, Virginia, to the subtle anger and hatred couched in the rhetoric of Donald Trump, who once said he'd never allow his daughter to marry a Jew (although his daughter Ivanka, ironically converted to Orthodox Judaism to marry Jared Kushner and have what Donald Trump described as a "beautiful Jewish baby").

Paul Valéry wrote, "Being angry, doesn't that mean being *someone else?* Anger is another, a total stranger."[149] Seemingly arguing against Hamlet— who views the objects of his anger (his mother, Claudius, Ophelia) as loci of that emotion—Valéry distances "what takes place in the visible body with what is taking place in the conscious mind."[150]

In her recent study of anger and forgiveness, Martha Nussbaum compels us to resist anger in order to make a better world, to not fall into the trap of saying "it's too hard" to overcome angry feelings. She notes three reasons for that resignation: the tendency to believe that anger is hardwired in human nature; a "cultural reluctance to pursue non anger" because we believe "it entails an inhuman, extreme, and unloving type of detachment"; and finally, the sense that many have that anger is "good, powerful, and manly."[151] It is when we take the easy way out that we often fail in moral turpitude, relinquishing the strength of character innate in every human being.

Chapter Four: Gluttony

When eating do not gobble noisily,

Nor stuff and cram your gaping mouth.

. . . .

Express yourself with modesty—

For acting otherwise is impolite excess

—Shantideva[1]

"I just don't like anything added to my eggs." Those words from a fellow diner at breakfast this morning. I'm at an academic conference and have opted for the $16 buffet breakfast at the hotel. It's the full buffet—hot and cold, oatmeal, fruit, yogurt, plenty of bagels and bread, a selection of pastries: "All you can eat."[2] In the middle of my daily trek through *The New York Times* crossword along with my yogurt, fruit, and bagel, another conference attendee arrives. He is about 6 feet tall but weighs well over 400 pounds. He too opts for the breakfast buffet and returns from the line with two overfilled plates, at which point he informs the server of his avoidance of the buffet eggs, which have some vegetables and cheese mixed in. She offers instead to get him some made-to-order eggs. He orders six.

Is this gluttony? Is gluttony a moral issue, a biological issue, a psychological issue, or is it not an issue at all? He happens to be sitting across from and near to me, so it is impossible not to notice him in my line of vision as he pulls out a tissue into which are wrapped a handful of pills— Vitamins? Prescriptions drugs? For what? Diabetes? High blood pressure?

I'm eating lunch in the campus dining hall, which I am committed to doing about once a month. An open buffet with a panoply of choices (when did college dining halls become like resorts?), the piped in rap music is deafening, and I do not understand how students are able to simultaneously eat, study, chat with friends, and hear any of the "music." I spot one of my students, a very thin 19-year-old who has perhaps the bubbliest personality of any human being I have ever met. I have watched her in class over the past few months as she seemed to grow thinner and thinner, so I am naturally curious what her dining choice will be in this smorgasbord of fried chicken fingers, pizza, tacos, and the obligatory dining hall salad bar.

As she passes my table, I receive her standard glowing smile and "hello" and notice what is on her large white dinner plate: three slices of cucumber, four carrot sticks, and one black olive. She later confides in me that she struggles with an eating disorder. What is the relationship to gluttony? The medieval mind regarded gluttony as making the belly one's God, and such devotion to the belly can result in either eating too much or eating too little as both make the gut the focus of devotion.

■■■

The weight of the general population has historically fluctuated wildly, dependent on several factors: time, location, economics, religion, and ethical belief. It is rare, for example, to find an overweight Christian monk in a medieval illumination. At the same time, rarely does one see the figure of the Buddha who is not portly, if not downright obese—a chubby person signified wealth and success in the East; for example, Hotei, the so-called laughing Buddha, is based on an eccentric monk who lived in the time of the Liang Dynasty (10th century CE) who iconographically is always depicted as rotund. Throughout history, the full-bodied individual was usually a sign of prosperity—from Henry VIII to the buxom women painted by Peter Paul Rubens. Thomas Jefferson would reportedly eat no fewer than eight courses in a meal and is said to have spent more than $300,000[3] on wine during his two terms in the White House. In *The Art of Procuring Pleasant Dreams* (1786), Benjamin Franklin notes, "In general, mankind, since the improvement of cookery, eat about twice as much as nature requires." In an 1881 pamphlet,

The Gluttony Plague: Or, How Persons Kill Themselves by Eating, James Caleb Jackson, the inventor in 1863 of the first dry, wholegrain cereal he called "granula" and a nutritionist who endorsed what is now called a "paleo" diet, writes of Americans' excesses to "work too hard, sleep insufficiently, dress unphysiologically" and know little about taking time off. Gluttony, he writes, is "eating food which is unhealthy in itself" and is also "eating at improper times."

The modern American experience with obesity has had an interesting arc since the end of World War II. The era of prosperity after World War II has affected the baby boom generation right in the waistline. When soldiers returned from the war, they found a booming economy and increased means of mass producing and storing food through the use of preservatives, decreasing the use of fresh food in the American diet. That history might begin in 1922 with Clarence Birdseye, the Brooklyn-born biologist for the U.S. government, who patented the "quick freezing" process. An avowed "foodie" as well as a naturalist, Birdseye became frustrated with the quality of canned food. An agriculturist, while on a field assignment in Labrador in Newfoundland, Canada, he learned from the Inuits that trout fished from holes in the ice would freeze instantly in the frigid below zero air. When it was cooked later, it tasted just like fresh trout. He also noted the Inuits' practice of storing meat and hunted game in hardpacked snow, keeping it edible for months. This coincided with extensive research, in both America and Russia, on the freezing of fish.[4] After selling his interest to General Foods in 1929, 26 items appeared in the initial product line. Birdseye would end up with at least a dozen patents between 1924 and 1935, all related to food preservation.

By the 1950s, the era of frozen food had taken firm grasp of the American palate and in the American kitchen. Early on, frozen food was much more expensive than fresh food. By the 1950s, Americans with more money in their wallets were willing to pay the surcharge for the convenience of a frozen "TV dinner"[5] or of always having a steak on hand. Domestic refrigerators began appearing in the American kitchen in the early 1910s. A fairly primitive unit mounted on top of a literal ice box (big blocks of ice were delivered by the "ice man"), the early refrigerator gave way to models with separate freezer compartments to store frozen food in the early 1940s. By the time soldiers returned from World War II, most houses had some kind of refrigerator with a separate freezer compartment. With the burgeoning economy and increasing amounts of disposable income came the production and purchase of increasing amounts of prepared food. As Jonathan Rees puts it in his history of refrigeration in America, "The advent of the global cold chain coincided with post-World War II prosperity in the United States."[6] The increased use (and size) of refrigerators "served as a sign of [America's] extraordinary wealth."[7] It is worth noting that American refrigerators continue to be the largest in the world's households. Refrigerators in Europe still tend to be small units, as Europeans still tend to shop daily, spurning frozen and preserved foods, opting instead for small quantities of fresh food.

Making food at home from scratch—bread, soup, even macaroni and cheese—was viewed by baby boomers as a primitive, premodern, practice engaged by their parents and grandparents who in the 1920s and 1930s struggled through the Great Depression. The alternative to bread baked at home and made with freshly milled flour was store-bought white bread like Wonder Bread. First launched in 1921 by the Taggart Baking Company, Wonder Bread packaging did not evoke images of home or of grandma at the hearth, wooden paddle in hand. Instead, Wonder Bread came in a stark white package with colorful balloons, implying a kind of virginal cleanness and joy.[8] The bread itself matched the package: bleached white and perpetually squishy, thanks to a combination of bleached flour and preservatives. It was indeed a "wonder" to folks used to fresh bread made with ground flour and needing to be eaten quickly lest it mold. The shelf life of a loaf of Wonder Bread was 5–7 days (three months if frozen) compared with 2–3 days for a freshly baked loaf.

By the 1940s, Wonder Bread began "enriching" its product in order to restore some of the nutrients lost in using white flour; "enriching" replaces the nutrients lost during milling white flour so that it more clearly resembles whole wheat bread. But the loaf of Wonder Bread on the counter was a symbol of affluence. Americans no longer had to spend hours kneading dough and slaving over the oven like their grandmothers. The ability to purchase prepackaged, processed food was an indication of economic success. A full refrigerator also reflected wealth and prosperity, if not the equally increasing size of the humans in the house.

Nutritionists now acknowledge the drawbacks, indeed the dangers, of consuming vast amounts of white flour and processed foods, though the issue is not without controversy. Nutrition experts Amy Bentley and Hi'ilei Hobart refer to the "interest" and "anxiety" about food and attribute it, partially, to "the sheer amount of food that is available, at least in the global North, with all its ramifications, positive and negative."[9] The plethora of choice in the modern supermarket is almost stupefying. Americans can choose between hundreds of cold cereals and dozens of ketchups. Sometimes too much choice has a negative effect. "When there's no end to choices, each choice feels disappointing."[10] The stereotypical American grocery shopper enters to purchase one thing and leaves with a basket full of other things.

The correlation between the increased consumption of processed foods and American eating habits is startling, but not surprising. Since the early 1900s, the size of the American dinner plate has grown by 25 percent or more. In the early 1960s, plates were roughly 9 inches in diameter, while now they are usually 12 inches, with some even at 15 inches. In addition, between 1930 and 1950, the size of the average American refrigerator doubled in volume.[11] It is almost as if obesity was phased in by corporate America in an effort to create a society of unknowing gluttons. As we have already seen, committing a sin without intention remains a sin. The weight of the average American male in 1960 was 168 pounds. By 2000, it had risen to almost 190 pounds.

The fully stocked kitchen continues to reflect affluence, success, and supposed health. As Rees points out, "When filled with food, [the refrigerator] symbolized abundance. The size of the typical American refrigerator also indicated the extraordinary prosperity of the postwar period."[12] The argument is analogous to the break from breastfeeding in the early 1960s when baby formula became a status symbol, used by mothers who could afford to purchase it and not have to resort to the "primitive" practices of their ancestors. Never mind the fact that breastfeeding is now universally agreed to be a better source of nutrition for the newborn and have health benefits for both baby and mother. Perception of privilege trumped scientific evidence.

In today's popular culture in America, gluttony is most associated with overeating and obesity. No longer a sin, being fat in America is a sign of weakness and is now the target of comedians and ridiculers. From Fat Albert to Jabba the Hutt, from Dom Deluise's 1980 biting comedy *Fatso* to the 2001 "romantic comedy" *Shallow Hal*, those who overindulge are viewed as weak willed, sloppy in appearance, and lethargic in temperament. From the early days of W. C. Fields and Roscoe "Fatty" Arbuckle to Jackie Gleason's bus driver, Ralph Kramden, weight has often been the target of jokes and demeaning looks and sneers. We have come to euphemize gluttony in an attempt to deemphasize, to lighten, its impact—it is now "overeating" or, more commonly, "food addiction." A search for books on "food addiction" on Amazon.com yields hundreds of results dealing mostly with binge-eating, suggesting the lack of control associated with gluttony. The culture has embraced shunning the responsibility for its own poor eating habits.

Until the Renaissance, the word "gluttony" denoted overindulgence in *both* food and wine. As such, gluttony could, the Church Fathers argued in multiple places, be a gateway to the sin of lust. We can easily see, in these days of such salacious websites as PornTube and Skypegirls.com, the relationship between drunkenness and debauchery. It is perhaps curious that the Church, which holds wine at the center of its most sacred ceremony, did not choose to list drunkenness as a deadly sin—even above and beyond gluttony. To be sure, getting drunk is portrayed as negative behavior throughout the cultures of the world, but it is curious that it never made the "top seven" sins.

Renaissance gluttony was often depicted in art, such as the tapestry "Gluttony" by Dutch artist Pieter Coecke van Aelst. Other artists who used gluttony as a motif include Pieter Bruegel the elder and Heironymous Bosch, and the theme became a favorite in emblem books of the 17th century.[13] Perhaps the most infamous depiction is in Bosch's *The Last Judgement* where the fate of the glutton is nothing if not disgusting: a glutton is forced to drink from a barrel of latrine sewage while other gluttons are cooked on spits or sautéed in frying pans. In Bruegel's engraving of *Gula* (gluttony), "The sin is personified by a woman in the dress of a Flemish burgher's wife. She is drinking from a jug. At her feet, her animal equivalent, a hog with ears and hind legs of a dog, gorges itself on turnips and carrots. During the Middle Ages, each deadly sin was associated with a familiar barnyard animal, to help people to remember what the sins were. A pig or hog represented gluttony."[14] The association grew from the pig's size and tendency to eat as much as is put in front of them, even to the point of fighting off other pigs for more food.

Although it has often been connected with overeating, since gluttony represents any situation in which the stomach is put at the center of attention, fasting and eating disorders might, ironically, be considered gluttonous behavior. Fasting has been symbolic of religious devotion since time in memoriam. "Down through the centuries, eating and fasting have been to Christians complex symbols and complex acts."[15] Because the Eucharist as the "bread of life" became central to the Catholic Mass, the act of consuming it became central to a mystical involvement with the Christian God. As a result, extreme fasting—in which only the Communion wafer and the wine are consumed—grew to be a sign of serious devotion. Gregory the Great wrote that fasting was making an offer to God. "It was to embrace hunger, to join with the vulnerability to famine that threatened all living things, in order to induce from the creator and provider of blessings the gifts of fertility, plenty, and salvation."[16] How, then, could fasting become a sin?

Perhaps it is when the individual is guilty of fasting as a sign of pride. Alan of Lille, the 12th century French theologian, argued that "abstinence must be inner and outer."[17]

> Fast is medicine to soul and body. It preserves the body from disease, the soul from sin. About its medicine effects, earthly and heavenly philosophy agree. If Adam had fasted in paradise . . ., he would not have been exiled into damnation.[18]

Similarly, for Muslims, fasting is a virtuous act, particularly during the month of Ramadan. In fact, Muslim tradition has it that if the individual would suffer or endure hardships, he or she is under no obligation to fast; fasting itself in such instances might be considered sinful behavior. Devout Christians who insist on the Communion wafer and wine as their only dietary intake might also be deemed as "crossing the line" from devotion to sin. Jews are doctrinally required to fast on only one day each year: Yom Kippur, the holiest day on the Jewish calendar; that fasting, intended to reflect devotion and selflessness, may also have originally been functional—Jews are expected to spend the entire day of Yom Kippur in synagogue.

Of course, I do not mean to suggest that devotional fasting and eating disorders such as anorexia and bulimia are on equal grounds. Eating disorders are psychological ailments that often involve body dysmorphia in which the individual experiences a persistent lack of recognition of the seriousness of low body weight because he or she sees his or her body in distorted and unrealistic ways. Nonetheless, the rise in eating disorders "coincides with an obsessive cultural focus on the body"[19] as well as an obsession with dieting. In a culture so focused on body image, one report suggests that as many as 45 million Americans are on a diet each year.[20] Whose problem is this?

The current cultural obsession with litigation has prompted some arguments that companies selling sugary drinks and fat laden treats be held liable for their customers' health lapses. Where does responsibility lie here and what about free will? If the responsibility is shifted off the shoulders of the individual and heaped onto the backs of corporations, it would seem that humanity is giving up, surrendering its free will and any hope of control over its future. I'm reminded of the *Seinfeld* episode when George Costanza decides he will start wearing sweatpants every day. "You know the message you're sending out to the world with these sweatpants?" Jerry asks him. "You're telling the world, 'I give up. I can't compete in normal society.'" In Disney's 2008 film *WallE*, human beings of the future have become so lethargic (and overweight as the result of dependence on technology) that they are unable to escape their recliners and require their "reality" be piped in via monitors; they are even fed by robotic arms, their own arms too heavy to lift food.

But this begs an entirely different—and much more difficult— question: is the glutton in fact gluttonous of his or her own free will or does some other factor compel him or her to gluttony? When we look to psychology for an answer, we are only helped so much. If gluttony is defined as "self indulgence," then free will would have to, inherently, be in play because indulging the self involves an active and not a passive decision. The individual actively indulges the self; thus, we could argue that same individual could choose not to indulge the self. The presence of choice implies free will, which would remove the blame from any outside agency—or corporation.

And yet, a few high profile lawsuits have been brought against major corporations in which the blame is laid upon them for an individual becoming ill or unhealthy. In 2002, two teenagers sued McDonald's Corporation: Jazlyn Bradley was 19 at the time, 5 feet, 6 inches and weighed 270 pounds; Ashley Pelman was 14, 4 feet, 10 inches and weighed 170 pounds. Bradley's father reportedly said he thought McDonald's was healthy food for his children. The suit alleged that McDonald's "engaged in a scheme of deceptive advertising" in order "to create the false impression that its food products were nutritionally beneficial and part of a healthy lifestyle if consumed daily." In February 2003, a federal judge threw out their lawsuit in which the girls claimed "the practices of McDonalds in making and selling their products are deceptive and that this deception has caused the minors who have consumed McDonalds' products to injure their health by becoming obese."[21]

Did someone force the girls to eat McDonald's food? Bradley said she ate an Egg McMuffin (300 calories) for breakfast and a Big Mac meal (with French fries and soda at approximately 1,000 calories) for dinner as her regular diet. Pelman preferred Happy Meals (with an average of 470 calories) and said she ate at the restaurant three or four times a week. Samuel Hirsch, their lawyer, said that the effects of McDonald's food on people's health were "a very insipid, toxic kind of thing." He also argued that the girls were not responsible for their own actions due to their age. Some studies have argued that constant exposure to fast food—via advertising in all media and the ever present "golden arches" every few blocks—is brainwashing Americans into eating poorly. A 2010 study by the Rudd Center for Food Policy & Obesity at Yale University suggests that increased television advertising of fast food has resulted in increased consumption by elementary school children.[22] The report found that between 25 and 28 percent of the products advertised to adolescent Americans are food. Investigators note that companies had pledged, after a 2006 initiative from the Better Business Bureau, to pull back on such advertising or at least advertise "better-for-you" foods to children under 12. Nonetheless, childhood obesity in the United States has risen from 13.9 percent in 1999 to 18.5 percent in 2016.[23]

We might refer for an analogue to the recent history of cigarettes, which quickly moved from advertising endorsements by medical doctors (and the Flintstones) to warnings on packaging from the Surgeon General that are now larger than the company logos—all in the course of less than 50 years. Should a Big Mac come with a warning on the box? Increasingly, jurisdictions now require calorie figures be posted in menus alongside items so that the consumer can make informed choices—Filet-O-Fish (410 calories and 20 grams of fat) or garden salad (15 calorie with 0 grams of fat). The message is confusing if not hypocritical: "We want you to be healthy, so you decide between this tasty calorie heavy meal and this bland but healthy salad." This is especially difficult when the "healthy choice" is more expensive than the less healthy "value meal."[24] Even the package encourages the former (any McDonald's devotee, no matter how young, can easily pick out the ubiquitous logo and packaging).[25] When The Cheesecake Factory was recently chided for selling the "unhealthiest meal in America," the company responded that it offers a variety of dishes for all of its customers.

In her short discussion of gluttony, novelist Francine Prose often equates obesity with gluttony. She spends time recounting the national statistics on rising obesity, particularly in children, and claims they can give us some insight into gluttony in America. However, it is a gross error to make that equation, that is, it might be true that all gluttons are obese, but it is equally untrue that all obese persons are gluttons. No one can argue that Americans as a whole are not getting fatter, but does that consequently mean that

Americans are becoming more gluttonous?

One excellent indication of what Prose calls "our schizophrenic attitude toward gluttony" occurs each year around 12:03 A.M. on New Year's Eve. After an evening of revels, including extensive, often excessive, food and drink, the first television commercials to air after "the ball drops" are invariably for Weight Watchers, Jenny Craig or some new fitness machine.[26] We move from gluttonous revelry to repentant asceticism literally with the stroke of the clock. It's enough to make the New Year snap back on itself.

Gluttony can also be an occasion for humor, intended or not. I recall a college screening of Federico Fellini's 1969 film of Petronius's ancient Roman literary orgy, *Satyricon*. The audience of college students were beside themselves throughout with laughter as we watched the players gorge themselves on everything from food to drink to sex, Fellini having been heavily influenced by the art of Peter Bruegel. The gluttonous behavior was so extreme that our only reaction was laughter.[27] Petronius's name is invoked by Robert Burton in the chapter on "Quantity of Diet" in his 1628 *Anatomy of Melancholy*, what is essentially the first early modern self-help book, where Burton purports to outline every possible cause for melancholy, what we today commonly refer to as depression. The book, which Dr. Samuel Johnson used to keep on his nightstand, is a romp through the physical, the environmental and even the historico-religious: one reason given for feeling sad is that Adam and Eve, our grandparents, sinned in the Garden of Eden, and we have yet to really get over it.

Burton gives extensive space to the quality of diet, noting in various places that, for example, "all venison is melancholy" and "generally, all such meats as are hard of digestion breed melancholy."[28] In an extended section, Burton addresses gluttony as "quantity of diet a cause" of possible depression. He writes that for such people "Belly is God. They wear their brains in their bellies, and their guts in their heads."[29] He does, however, admit that overindulgence in food and drink has become "the fashion of our times": "what were vices are now considered virtues."[30]

The most recent *DSM5* explicitly states that "obesity is not considered a mental disorder." However, "binge-eating disorder," as "distinct from obesity," is assessed both by quantity and context of eating. The guide explains that "a quantity of food that might be regarded as excessive for a typical meal might be considered normal during a celebration or holiday meal." Thus, binge-eating disorder is characterized by excessive intake of food during a "discrete period of time." Your uncle George who packs away the turkey and pumpkin pie at Thanksgiving therefore is neither binge-eating nor gluttonous as a result of context.

Current cultural attitudes toward gluttony in religiously-based diet books also argue for a food disorder in lieu of an explicit sin. Christian titles such as *What Would Jesus Eat?*, *The PrayFit Diet*, and *The Hallelujah Diet* are not alone; Jewish diets include *Secrets of a Kosher Girl* and *How to Succeed on Any Diet: A Jewish and Friendly Guide to Dieting & Exercise*, while *Buddha's Diet: The Ancient Art of Losing Weight without Losing Your Mind* encourages timely and mindful portion control, rather than abstinence from eating. None of these offerings suggests that obesity is equivalent to gluttony and is a sin. In *Food for Life: The Spirituality and Ethics of Eating*, L. Shannon Jung suggests gluttony is "a sin to which we become insensitive through complicity—a complicity that knows we stand to benefit from such gluttonous policies as cheap food, export subsidies, market penetration, and exploitation of the poor."[31]

Perhaps it is easier to wrap our minds around the concept of gluttony in the 21st century if we move away from focusing only on food. I would like to suggest that gluttony today can take different forms. Americans have increasingly—and quickly—become gluttons of another commodity: information. The speed with which information is processed has increased steadily. Computing power seems to increase exponentially on an almost daily basis.[32] Processor rates, hard drive capacities, portable and wearable devices—all have contributed to a gluttonous onslaught of data, and it seems Americans cannot get enough.

As one example we can consider the changing ways in which Americans have received news. In the earliest days of the republic, news was delivered from town to town on horseback. The speed of the news cycle was in direct relation to the speed of a horse. And the volume of news was essentially what could be carried in the rider's pack. Early newspapers were one pagers crammed with details both important and banal.[33] The earliest American newspaper, *The Boston NewsLetter*, which began publishing on April 24, 1704, was a single page, printed on both sides and issued weekly. Much of its news was sensational—pirates captured— but it also detailed English politics and local events such as fires, deaths, and even sermons. The news cycle was slow. Compare this with today's saturation.

News—"fake" and otherwise—comes at us with blazing speed and in overwhelming volume. Social media, cell phones, 24-hour cable news, online news, and newspaper sites, not to mention traditional printed newspapers and magazines, now make being "out of the loop" a true anomaly, if not a stigma. And Americans cannot get enough. In addition to at least three major cable news networks (the oldest of them, CNN, went on the air in 1980), there are now apps that deliver "breaking news" directly to one's smartphone or Apple Watch. This gluttonous flood of information can be overwhelming. Some call themselves "news junkies"; others swear off watching news for periods in fits of abstinence (or asceticism).

In the 1986 fantasy comedy *Short Circuit*, a robot named "Johnny 5" requires continual "input" in the forms of visual and verbal stimuli. In one especially prescient scene, Number 5 is rifling through volumes from a bookshelf (encyclopedias, dictionaries), as if he is eating the information, looking to sate himself, until the shelves are empty. He pauses, looks at Ally

Sheedy's character, and says "more input." In the sequel, *Short Circuit 2*, Johnny 5, spies the "World's Biggest Bookstore" on the street in New York City and exclaims, "major input!" We cannot get enough.

Is this gluttony? It is if we believe that gluttony is defined by over satiation, regardless of whether it is food or information. "Data glut." "Data overload." In 1997, David Shenk called it "data smog."[34] In fact, magazines and bookshelves are currently filled with pieces on our "addiction to technology." Recent titles include Daniel Levitin's *The Organized Mind:*

Thinking Straight in the Age of Information Overload, Bill Kovach and Tom Rosenstiel's *Blur: How to Know What's True in the Age of Information Overload*, and Daniel Kahneman's influential study *Thinking, Fast and Slow*.

In *The Cyber Effect*, forensic cyber psychologist Mary Aiken argues that technology is "designed to addict" and that it encourages impulsivity and thus can lead to erratic, violent, and often irrational behavior. The increased amount of information can leave us bloated and even sickened by the scourge called FOMO ("fear of missing out"). This gluttony of information has left human beings constantly anticipating and wanting more, like a panting dog waiting for the tennis ball to be thrown again. The dog doesn't know when it will be thrown, only that it will be thrown at some point, leaving him constantly on guard and focused only on that, unable to appreciate the world around him (if you just looked away to refresh your email, you are the panting dog). This is the result of gluttony—an ongoing obsession with the object at hand and an inability to appreciate anything other than the object itself, whether that is food or data. We see it too in the teenager obsession with capturing every aspect of existence on their phone so that it can be posted to social media. They seem unable to appreciate the event, focused instead on recording and "sharing" it. If you don't believe me, watch a group of teenagers go through an art museum, phones in hand, quickly, barely pausing to study the art but leaving with dozens of photos that document the visit but seem to ignore the actual experience.

Perhaps the epitome of a gluttony of input in our time comes in the form of binge-watching television shows, a practice that only began in the early 2010s with the growth of digital streaming. As early as 1854, the word "binge" referred to excessive drinking. By the mid-1990s, online Usenet discussion groups began talking about the idea of binge-watching to catch up on television shows.[35] Studies have begun to show the negative psychological effects of binge-watching, and college students (notorious for procrastination) often indicate their habit of binge-watching a television show all night as an excuse for not writing a paper. Some will say there is nothing wrong— ethically, morally—with binge-watching and that it is merely the latest cultural phenomenon. But if that is the case, I ask, then why is it called "binge" watching, that is, using a pejorative word as a descriptor?

A 2015 University of Texas study found incidence of binge-watching correlated with depression, loneliness, and obesity.[36] In the 2013 MacTaggart Lecture (an annual media lecture in the United Kingdom), now disgraced Hollywood star Kevin Spacey spoke of the viewers of his Netflix show *House of Cards*: "If they want to binge—as they've been doing on 'House of Cards'— then we should let them binge."[37] *House of Cards* was the first episodic television show released all at once, making mass consumption possible. A more recent survey by Patient.info shows those aged 18–24 were five times more likely to feel lonely and three times more likely to feel depressed as the result of binge-watching.[38] The British study also indicates other "hidden dangers" of binge-watching that include obesity, sleeplessness, and eye strain. The summer before he started college, Eli Susser watched the first two seasons of *Lost* (49 episodes, about 40 hours) in just two weeks: "I barely left my couch," he said.[39] This type of gluttonous viewing behavior is, I would argue, not much different than devouring an entire box of Hostess Twinkies (20 cakes: 2,700 calories, 90 grams of fat and 3,600 mg of sodium) in a single sitting. Neither behavior seems healthy, either psychologically or physically.

Journalist Brandon Baker[40] offers six reasons why people binge-watch: (1) they seek an improved viewing experience, (2) they seek a sense of completion; (3) they seek cultural inclusion and fear being left out of conversation regarding pop culture; (4) they succumb to convenience; (5) they fear being left behind and want to catch up; and (6) they desire relaxation and nostalgia. It is also interesting that, with more shows produced by Netflix and Amazon, screenwriters have begun to construct narrative in order to feed the viewers' desire to binge. Episodes blend into one another; Netflix will allow you to conveniently move from one episode to the next without doing anything, even allowing you to skip the opening credits, if desired, so you can get right to the meat of the show.

Binge-watching can, of course, also serve as a stress reliever. However, the same thing that happens after binge-eating will often be experienced by the binge-watcher. The crash. Psychologists call it "situational depression." "When we substitute TV for human relations we disconnect from human nature and substitute for [the] virtual."[41] In a 2017 study published in the *Journal of Clinical Sleep Medicine,* more than 80 percent of young adults identify themselves as binge-watchers.[42]

Technology, however, provides us with a world of infinite and endless choices. One online meme jokes, "You have reached the end of the Internet," something, of course, not possible. "Facebook has an endless feed; Netflix automatically moves on to the next episode in the series; Tinder encourages users to keep swiping in search of a better option."[43] This gluttony of choice has led to a "tyranny of choice" in which the act of "choosing is traumatic" in itself.[44] The grocery store cereal aisle is an ideal example; hundreds of choices, from lowfat granola to high sugar generic brands, can cause the consumer to freeze like deer caught in headlights, paralyzed by an overabundance of choice, resulting in the purchase of whatever is "easy" and "quick," the decision too complicated to consider.

Technology overload is a viral topic online—a Google search results in more than 41,000 hits—with a complaint most often appearing in the boardroom now reaching the bedroom. A San Francisco–based company named "Digital Detox" offers retreats to give "individuals the freedom and permission they need to truly unplug and decompress. Participants put aside their digital arm to recharge, gain perspective, and reevaluate their relationship with digital technology."[45] The blanket promise is that "Digital Detox can help reduce anxiety, stress, depression, tech dependency, fatigue, and information overload." "Disconnect," they say, "to reconnect." In this, we are back with the sentiments of D. H. Lawrence[46] and Paul Valéry, both of whom lamented the increasing lack of humanity in human beings, a humanity that is overshadowed if we resign ourselves to overindulgence.

Chapter Five: Avarice

Three great forces rule the world: stupidity, fear and greed.

—Albert Einstein

"Greed is good." Thus spoke Gordon Gekko in Oliver Stone's seminal 1987 film *Wall Street*. An ode to the American greed of the 1980s, the film garnered an Oscar and a Golden Globe for its star Michael Douglas. The film chronicles the rise and fall of Bud Fox, the ambitious son of an airline worker, played by Charlie Sheen, who idolizes Gekko and hopes to work for him, only to buckle under unethical and illegal insider training that ultimately leads him from his window office in handcuffs. The film presents Gekko as an inversion of God, a satanic figure who preaches the antithesis of the golden rule. Even *Wikipedia* notes that Gekko is the symbol of "unrestrained greed." In the iconic speech delivered to a group of stockholders, Gekko preaches, "Greed, in all of its forms—greed for life, for money, for love, knowledge— has marked the upward surge of mankind." In Gekko's philosophy, greed is an evolutionary marker of humanity.[1]

Writing in *The New York Times* in 2017, novelist Francine Prose called greed "the deadly sin that is currently ruling our society."[2] In 1838's *Democracy in America*, Alexis de Tocqueville thought that Americans were "almost sad in their pleasures" because they "never stop thinking about the goods they do not possess."[3] Americans, he wrote, have a "taste for material well-being" that makes them perpetually unhappy with what they have in the quest for what they do not yet possess.[4] Desire as the cause of suffering recalls the Four Noble Truths of the Buddha, which teach that attachment to what we desire causes our suffering and unhappiness.

Phyllis Tickle, the American religious writer, calls greed "the most social and by extension the most political of the sins."[5] Also called "avarice" (from the Latin *avaritia* meaning greed or inordinate desire), greed is one of the oldest sins to be delineated and is one of the very few to be explicitly named in the Bible. Indeed, the New Testament gospels are littered with invectives against greed and wealth. But what does the Old Testament have to say on the matter? Some of the earliest references to greed appear in the story of David and Nathan in 2 Samuel in the parable of the ewe lamb, a tale that follows the account of David's lust for Bathsheba. In the parable, told by the prophet Nathan, a rich man has "many flocks and herds," while a poor man has "but one little ewe lamb." A traveler visits the rich man, and instead of taking one of his own flock, he takes the poor man's single ewe lamb and prepares it for the traveler's meal. David rebukes the man only to have Nathan conclude, "Thou art the man." Conventional readings of the parable cast David as the rich man with Uriah (Bathsheba's husband) as the owner of the ewe lamb (Bathsheba) that David steals in an impetuous but calculated act of lust.[6] But the tale also gives us a view of a man already blessed with wealth and prosperity who only wants more and, more pointedly, wants what someone else already has.

Literary representations of greed are too numerous to count—from the New Testament's Mammon to Shakespeare's Shylock to Nikolai Gogol's *Dead Souls* in which the main character searches small towns to buy souls. I will focus here quite arbitrarily on two: Geoffrey Chaucer's medieval Pardoner and novelist Saul Bellow's modern American failure, Tommy Wilhelm. Chaucer's 14th-century tale of a Pardoner in *The Canterbury Tales* is perhaps the prototypical narrative on avarice in Western literature. A Pardoner was a person licensed to sell papal pardons and indulgences who roamed the English countryside in the Middle Ages, traveling from town to town on horseback in order to hear confessions and grant pardons. The practice was, by the time of Chaucer, highly corrupt, as Chaucer's own Pardoner attests. He claims to have papal authority and sells holy relics such as a supposed piece of the veil of the Virgin Mary.

Perhaps more surprising to Chaucer's reader is the Pardoner's forthrightness regarding his motivation.[7] Although he claims his theme is always the same—"*Radix malorum est cupiditas*" ("money is the root of all evil")—he doesn't actually care about those to whom he preaches: "I preach of nothing but covetous."[8] And he has seen success as an avaricious Pardoner, claiming to have made each year "a hundred marks" (about $10,000 2018 USD). The Pardoner's tale involves three drunk friends who go in search of Death, whom they feel has wrongly taken one of their companions. In their quest, they are diverted when they discover a treasure of gold coins and decide to make off with it under the cover of darkness and then divide the wealth. Secretly, they each devise a way to murder the others to claim the treasure for their own. As a medieval *exemplum* (a moral anecdote), the tale ends with all three dead at each other's hands. The Pardoner concludes his tale with "O cursed sin of all cursedness!" warning the reader to be "wary of the sin of avarice!" The Pardoner's Tale would later be adapted to the 1948 film *The Treasure of the Sierra Madre*, in which Humphrey Bogart, Walter Huston, and Tim Holt prospect for gold in Mexico only to engage in conspiracies against one another.[9] Bosley Crowther's *New York Times* review noted, "One might almost reckon that [John Huston, the film's director] has filmed an intentional comment here upon the irony of avarice in individuals and in nations today,"[10] and the film remains standard viewing in college ethics courses.

In Saul Bellow's 1956 novel *Seize the Day*, the greed of mid-century America percolates until it drives Tommy Wilhelm to the edge of sanity. Wilhelm is a failed businessman hoping to get some financial help from his retired and wealthy physician father. In the process, Wilhelm connects with Dr. Tamkin, a questionable investor who calls himself a psychologist. Wilhelm's father, the retired Dr. Adler, ashamed of his son's failures, boasts that his son's "income was up in the five figures" to which Tommy disgustedly thinks, "How they love money. They adore money! Holy money! Beautiful money! It was getting so that people were feeble-minded about everything except money."[11] It is, he continues, "the world's business."

Tommy comes to his father for help, but the old man is incapable of affection or empathy and only sees that Tommy wants his money: "I can't give you any money. There would be no end to it if it started. And I want nobody on my back. Get off! And I give you the same advice, Wilky. Carry nobody on your back."[12] Tamkin explains that "Moneymaking is aggression. People come to the market to kill. They say, 'I'm going to make a killing.' It's not accidental. Only they haven't got the courage to kill, and they erect a symbol of it. The money. They make a killing by a fantasy."[13] More often, such aggression results in emptiness as in the fable of the goose who laid the golden egg in which the countryman kills the goose only to discover the golden eggs are empty.

In the novel, Tommy Wilhelm is caught in a whirlwind of despair and financial exigency. He is desperate for a world in which wealth is not the only valued characteristic, but he himself is just as guilty of putting money at his center. He invests his last money in the commodities market by giving it all (including power of attorney) to Tamkin, only to have Tamkin vanish in the novel's closing pages. Now destitute—both financially and emotionally— Tommy stumbles into a funeral of a man he does not know. He prays that he be protected "against that devil who wants my life" and closes the novel in a flood of tears and water imagery suggesting both drowning and rebirth. This would seem to suggest that the modern American attitude toward greed can lead to one of three outcomes:

(1) Tommy's father, Dr. Adler, is a medical doctor living out his retirement years in a posh New York City hotel; he wants for nothing materially but seems to have no emotional affect; (2) Dr. Tamkin, Tommy's investment confidante, is a swindler who claims to have worked the market

"scientifically,"[14] telling Tommy, "There's also a calm and rational, a psychological approach";[15] (3) Tommy Wilhelm is a failure, who himself admits early in the novel, "A man is only as good as what he loves."[16] It is unclear whether Tommy is guilty of greed; instead, I think he is caught up in a greed-driven world, one in which money is the ultimate sign of success. In his desperation to fit into this world, a world he admits he feels disconnected from, he appeals to different money sources: his father, the market, Dr. Tamkin. But he realizes at the novel's end that the desire for money is fruitless as we all end up in death, Hamlet's "undiscovered country." As he begins to cry before the open coffin, he thinks, "A man—another human creature, was what first went through his thoughts."[17] The push to the precipice brings Tommy Wilhelm to confront his own mortality and, with it, his own humanity. In a letter to Samuel Goldberg, Bellow wrote of his own "valuable illumination about money, thanks to *Seize the Day*. I've learned the true value of a dollar. It's about two cents, on my scale. We need money on account of our vices. But after all, vice isn't everything."[18] Elsewhere, Bellow wrote, "I don't know how to enjoy money, anyway. Haven't a clue, and never have had. What do you do with it?"[19]

This confused American attitude toward money has been evident since the earliest days of the republic, evident in the Great Seal of the United States most conspicuous on the one-dollar bill. Designed by Charles Thomson in 1782, the seal has always seemed an anachronism: a symbol of American capitalism—the one-dollar bill—but imbued with great spiritual symbolism. What does this indicate about the founders' feelings on greed?

Charles Thomson's design of a pyramid of 13 levels leads up to the eye of Providence, that is, the eye of God. The pyramid is said to be the symbol of America's "strength and duration."[20] But the pyramid does not reach all the way to the eye; instead, there is a large gap just between the top and the eye. Etched into the base, the year 1776, in addition to being the year of the founding of the country, adds up to 21, the age of reason. Reason can lead one to the divine, but in order to reach the eye, one must take a leap of faith across a chasm. The pyramid represents the concrete world, while the eye of God represents the more abstract concept of divinity and eternity; to be sure, there is a wide gap between the two. The image asks its bearer to reconcile the desire for divine knowledge with the capitalist fabric of the country.

The establishment of a pyramid by which one reaches the eye of God recalls the Tower of Babel, an image of greed and desire in Genesis (of course, one is also reminded of that story as a tale of pride—a tale that has also been summoned in discussions of the doomed fate of the Twin Towers[21]). Archetypally, the pyramid symbolizes the desire of human beings to leave the earth and reach up to the divinity. In ancient Egypt, the pyramid was a symbol of wealth and power. In the case of the pyramid on the Great Seal, the 13 steps symbolize the 13 original colonies, but this is in essence a broken pyramid called a frustum, a pyramid without a point. A pyramid with an unfinished top (one without a cap) symbolizes unfinished work, in this case implying the ongoing growth (financial and spiritual) of the country. The image is ironically overseen by the Latin motto *Annuit Coeptis*, meaning "He approves our undertakings"—a divine endorsement, it would seem, of avaricious behavior. As such the Great Seal is indicative of the American conflict between being human and being ruthless. Indeed, selflessness and greed rarely coexist. In his analysis of the seal in *The Power of Myth*, Joseph Campbell says, "What destroys reason is passion. The principle passion in politics is greed. That's what pulls you down."[22] As secularism became the backbone of the country, the culture's focal point shifted from the cathedral in the Middle Ages; today's city has its financial center as its focus.

The acquisition of wealth is indeed a calculated and often well-planned process (unless you win the lottery). One might argue it is a rational process, but reason and money will not bring one to the eye of God nor to understanding and knowledge. Given the imagery on the dollar bill, reaching that height requires faith and trust, and it is faith and trust that are most lacking in one who is greedy. Moliere's Harpagon (in *The Miser*) knows no trust. Shakespeare's Shylock (in *Merchant of Venice*) has his faith only when it is convenient for his purse. In fact, greed seems given to the abandonment of faith and trust and an increase in paranoia and insecurity—characteristics of what psychologists' standard handbook, the *Diagnostic and Statistical Manual of Mental Disorders (DSM5)*, calls "hoarding disorder."[23]

A 1938 *Economic Journal* article discusses hoarding exclusively in the context of economics, evoking the earliest uses of the word in English in a 10th-century sermon by Aelfric where it is without negative connotation and is synonymous with amassing of wealth: "*Hordiað eowerne goldhord on heofenum*" ("Hoard up your gold hoard in heaven").[24] So, hoarding in Old English merely seems to denote that acquisition of wealth in heaven, while greed (*gitsung* in Old English) is the *excessive* acquisition of wealth on earth. Again, we find that the key to sin is not merely the act itself—physical love, eating—it is engaging in the act to excess.

Perhaps the modern history of hoarding begins with the story of the Collyer brothers, Homer and Langley, who were literally crushed by their possessions in their Harlem apartment in March 1947. Their story, and the syndrome it coined,[25] represented "a paradigm shift in hoarding as a curious abnormality."[26] These "two eccentric brothers," as *The New York Times* called them, were both graduates of Columbia University and were descendants of one of New York City's oldest families. After their mother's death, the brothers continued to live together in the Harlem brownstone they inherited and were eventually found dead amidst 120 tons of debris including baby carriages, old food, potato peelers, bowling balls, photos of pinup girls, more than 25,000 books, 8 live cats, 14 pianos, and countless bundles of newspapers and magazines. All of the material was virtually worthless with the only items of value auctioned for less than $2,000. Their story remains a mystery to this day: why were they hoarding mounds of useless items? Why had they become so reclusive? Homer was discovered on March 21, 1947, but his brother Langley would not be discovered until April 8, only 10 feet from where Homer had died but inside a two foot wide tunnel.[27] The Collyer brothers' story can be read as an *exemplum* for the modern reader, like Chaucer's tale was for the medieval.

Several studies have indicated that those with hoarding disorder, as the *DSM5* calls it, may have an increased tendency to anthropomorphize objects. Thus the accusation that "people who hoard appear to find it difficult to define the boundary between 'who they are' and 'what they own.'"[28] Another study indicates that those who anthropomorphize money are more generous in giving to charities.[29] I would argue then that those who are financially greedy regard money only as an object. There is some evidence that humanizing objects (hoarding) and money (greed) makes one more likely to donate or give them away, while viewing them as purely material chattel might cause one to be less empathetic and thus more desirous of keeping items.

Because it is frowned upon to enjoy excess while others have little to nothing, greed becomes a moral question. But how do we differentiate as a society between "wealthy" and "greedy"? Oftentimes, the two terms are conflated, and that is unfortunate. The most significant differentiation is that many times the wealthy are also philanthropic. Bill Gates, founder of Microsoft, has a net worth of $91 billion, but in 2009, Gates and Warren Buffett (currently worth more than $89 billion) founded The Giving Pledge, whereby they and other billionaires pledge to give at least half of their wealth to philanthropy. As of 2018, 175 pledgers have signed onto the agreement. It is difficult to imagine the fictional Gordon Gekko, for whom greed is "good," being one of them.

Hoarding itself has, ironically, become big business. Companies such as 1800-Got-Junk will haul away unwanted items; clients in the television commercial merely have to point at an item for it to disappear. On their website, the company calls itself the "unofficial sponsors of spring cleaning." Not only are there popular television series (*Hoarders* on A&E, TLC's *Hoarding: Buried Alive*, and *Hoarders: Family Secrets* on Lifetime), there are shelves of self help books designed to help those with hoarding tendencies. Perhaps the largest movement has been the KonMari method of organizing and separating from one's material items.

KonMari was born of the mind of Marie Kondo, a Japanese woman who claims to have tidying in her blood; she spent five years as a priestess in a Shinto shrine and opened her own consulting business at age 19. The popularity of Kondo's philosophy grew from the overwhelming success of her book, *The LifeChanging Magic of Tidying Up: The Japanese Art of Decluttering and Organizing*, first published in Japanese in 2011. The basic principle is to look at items and ask whether they "spark joy"; if the answer is negative, the individual is encouraged to get rid of it through either donation or discard. In 2015, *Time* magazine named her one of its "100 most influential people," and the book has sold more than 6 million copies in some 30 countries. *Fast Company*, the business magazine, predicts the home organization market will be worth almost $12 billion by 2021 with Marie Kondo's brand at its center.[30]

KonMari would seem to be a direct reaction to a culture drowning in its own stuff, and although her method does not advocate giving away money that does not "spark joy," one could easily see the practice extrapolated to money in the form of charitable giving. Following from Gordon Gekko's "upward surge of mankind," some studies claim that greed is evolutionary, that being greedy may increase access to resources and thus give the individual an evolutionary advantage.[31] But greed does not stop at money or material goods.

In his "Natural History of the Planet," Tim Flannery notes that human beings are "selfish, greedy beings" who continue to exploit the world's natural resources for their own gain.[32] We need only to look at the ways that humanity has treated the planet's natural resources to appreciate the presence of greed as a marker of human activity. Not only have the effects of global warming and climate change influenced everything from access to clean water to terrorist activity, the continued effects of the industrial age consume disproportionate amounts of natural resources and energy, plundering our natural landscape. The growth of cities, developed like modern-day monuments to Mammon, has made human prosperity possible all the while ignoring the detrimental effects on the world and humanity itself, including pollution, population congestion, crime, and the very manipulation of the environment to suit humans' needs.

On the opposition side, biologist Frans de Waal has recently argued that "Greed is out, empathy is in." In his 2009 book *The Age of Empathy*, de Waal suggests, in response to Richard Dawkins's famous theory of the "selfish gene," that "Genes can't be any more 'selfish' than a river can be 'angry,' or sun rays 'loving.' Genes are little chunks of DNA. At most, they are 'self promoting,' because successful genes help their carriers spread more copies of themselves."[33] De Waal later suggests that the majority of humanity is "altruistic, cooperative, sensitive to fairness, and oriented toward community goals."[34] Nonetheless, in a 2016 Pew Research poll, 57 percent of Americans surveyed felt that Americans are greedy.[35]

Greed can also be a reaction to life situations, such as the reactions of those who lived through the Great Depression or who survived the Nazi concentration camps. As one example, we can look at Art Spiegelman's masterful graphic novel, *Maus*, recalling his adult understanding of his parents' behavior in keeping even the smallest piece of string. Spiegelman's father, Vladek, a survivor of the camps, lives with his second wife Mala, who complains, "He's driving me crazy! He won't even let me throw out the plastic pitcher he took from the hospital room last year!" "He's more attached to things than to people!"[36] At another point, Vladek picks up some telephone wire: "It's good for tying things" he tells Art, to which Art responds "You ALWAYS pick up trash! Can't you just BUY wire?" His father answers, "Pssh. Why always you want to buy when you can FIND?"[37] Art comes to realize that his father's collecting and reluctance to throw anything out can be traced to his years in the camps when every material item might have come in handy. It is not that a piece of telephone wire sparks joy for Vladek; his materialism is entirely pragmatic.

In this case, Vladek's hoarding is also a coping mechanism to deal with memories and fear. Some studies have even looked at what is called "memory hoarding" as an obsessive-compulsive disorder. Perhaps Vladek is doing just the opposite—an attempt to hoard material goods to further repress memories. If Vladek can fill his existence with "stuff," he will have no figurative room to remember. And avoidance of painful memories— the opposite of memory hoarding—has been central to Holocaust survivors. I recall the women working at our neighborhood bakery in the Bronx. Each summer, when shortsleeve work shirts were in order in this non–airconditioned store, I noticed the numbers tattooed on their arms. I didn't know what those numbers were until I got to college—the Holocaust was not something widely discussed by the survivors in my neighborhood in the 1970s. The memories were, if not repressed, then at least suppressed.

In his memoir of time spent in a concentration camp at Auschwitz, Primo Levi repeatedly recalls hoarding situations in the camp. But, as Frederic Homer notes, "The Germans artificially manufactured scarcity in the Lager," and Levi himself writes, "A fortnight after my arrival I already had the prescribed hunger."[38] "If a prisoner chose to survive, he must supplement the given provisions by guile and theft."[39] The kind of hoarding found in the camps is of a very different variety than, say, the Collyer brothers'. The treatment in the camps basically removed the identity of the prisoners, stripping them of their selves and reducing them to either the resignation of death or a competition for life. To an outside observer, what appeared to be hoarding was actually a survival instinct. And this instinct did not cease after the camps were liberated. Many Holocaust survivors appear on the surface to be hoarders: the woman who has a closet full of string and brown paper from packages; the man who refuses to throw out old screws, even if they are tarnished with rust.[40] But retaining rubber bands is different from the raw acquisition and accumulation of money.

The truth is that, regardless of how you slice it, the majority of wealth in the world is held by very few. A 2018 Oxfam report indicates that the world's richest 1 percent hold 82 percent of the world's wealth.[41] The greedy person lives in a state of perpetual subjectivity in that he or she seems unable to appreciate the needs and desires of others. Instead, he or she wants to keep everything for himself or herself, regardless of whether he or she needs it or not. He or she is naturally selfish and self centered. The image of the greedy individual parallels that of the glutton—think Jabba the Hutt in the Star Wars saga, a bloated and repulsive creature who focuses only on the desire for more. Greed is distorted vision in which everything is reduced to a material good to be acquired and cached away. The greedy see the world only as a sponge for what can be wrung out of it. We currently see this degree of shortsightedness in discussions related to practices such as fracking and the various other ways humans continue to extract finite resources from the earth. Human beings are hoarding the world's resources without regard for either future inhabitants or the sustainability of the earth itself.

By the turn of the 21st century, the bigwigs of Wall Street had become the poster children for greed. The economic crisis of 2008, in which millions lost their homes and the Dow Jones Index lost 33 percent of its value, set in motion the third longest U.S. recession since World War II. Almost in direct response to Gordon Gekko, British investment fund manager Nicola Horlick writes, "The events in the financial markets since the middle of 2007 and the banking crisis of 2008 into 2009 have demonstrated that greed is not good."[42] Then chairman of the Federal Reserve Alan Greenspan faulted "infectious greed" for the crisis. Given the devastating effect of that crisis on millions of people, it is difficult to disagree. And here is perhaps the best illustration of the effect that greed has not just on the greedy individual but on those around the individual. Journalist Jane Mayer writes of "dark money" and how the global billionaire culture, stoked by "the radical right," transformed to "the 1 percent" and was subsequently vilified in the media and movements such as "Occupy Wall Street."[43] In 2017, when the investment firm Charles Schwab asked how much money is required to be considered "wealthy," respondents said it is an average of $2.4 million, "nearly 30 times the actual median net worth of U.S. households."[44] A majority of Americans surveyed in 2012 said that inequality is "an acceptable part of our economic system," a number that has also increased since the late 1990s.[45] So, there appears to be a disconnect between societal stereotypes regarding greed and wealth and actual societal attitudes.

Greed encourages rash behavior in the name of expediency and immediate gratification. As John Meadowcraft writes, "There is nothing inherently virtuous about an economy that only satisfies people's needs."[46] I recall when we bought our second house after moving to Troy, New York, in the summer of 2004, before the financial crisis. Our realtor encouraged us to purchase houses that, in the end, were about $50,000 above what we could really afford on a professor's salary. "Don't worry," he told me, "I've got a mortgage guy for you." That "mortgage guy," with whom I only spoke by phone, also encouraged us to apply for a mortgage about $75,000 above what we felt comfortable with. Luckily, I had sound intuition and called an old friend, also a realtor, to ask him for advice. I still recall talking to him by phone: "What should I do?" I asked. "Run," he said. It was clear that something was not above board here. I never called the realtor again, and he never tried to contact me. We ended up purchasing a home we felt comfortable affording. Four years later, the market collapsed, and thousands of homeowners were "under water," that is, they owed more on their homes than the homes were worth. Both the realtor and the mortgage broker stood to make a lot of money off my potential foolishness, but I would have been the one to suffer the consequences of their greed a few years later.

Greed also encourages inequality—economic and otherwise. More than 3 billion people live on less than $2 a day. Larry Ellison, founder and CEO of the Oracle Corporation, spent more than $250 million on his yacht, money that could have fed 25 million children under the age of five for a year;[47] as of this writing, Ellison's net worth exceeds $62 billion. Making money is not wrong. Making money is not a sin. But it would seem that when the acquisition of that money produces the kind of gross inequality and poverty we currently witness, something is wrong.

As has been a question with each of our sins, I wonder whether greed is an acquired trait. Is it a learned behavior or is one born with it? In the many rags-to-riches stories we have at our disposal, we see the impoverished move to the wealthy, and with that move comes a polar shift in attitudes toward money and material goods. Those born with the famed silver spoon in their mouth know no different and struggle to appreciate the mediocre financial existence of the majority of the population. Watch an episode of *Keeping Up with the Kardashians* (currently in its 15th season!) if you don't believe me. The *Los Angeles Times* calls the show a "Hollywood version of The Brady Bunch— the harmless high jinks of a loving blended family against a backdrop of wealth and famous connections."[48] But, writing in *The Washington Times*,

Jessica Chasmar said that the show "illustrates our nation's moral, spiritual and cultural decay."[49]

This brings us to an interesting intersection with the work of evolutionary biologists such as E. O. Wilson and psychologists such as Steven Pinker who make various claims about the evolutionary nature of altruism and whether greed is natural to human beings. In *Better Angels*, Pinker defines biological altruism: "behavior that benefits another organism at a cost to oneself."[50] To be sure, Pinker links all types of altruistic activity to varying degrees of sympathy or empathy. Wilson sees "eusociality" in which societies—human and nonhuman—work together for the betterment of the entire group, most notably in a division of work and the attitudes toward reproductive and childrearing behaviors.[51] It would appear that evolution does not favor selfish people.

Human beings cannot claim greed as only their own. For example, wolverines (whose scientific name, *Gulo gulo*, is derived from the Latin word for gluttony) have been described as playground bullies. Once "wolverines have consumed all they can fit into their stomachs, and then they try to spoil any leftovers so that other predators and scavengers can't eat them. This fits part of our description of greed. It's not just about acquiring things; it's about having more than others have."[52] Studies have shown that those who display greed or have greedy tendencies often lack empathy. They are unable to "walk in the shoes" of others, unable to see the world from others' points of view, essentially stuck in a loop of subjective response. Pinker notes, "The research gives teeth to the speculation that humanitarian reforms are driven in part by an enhanced sensitivity to the experiences of living things and a genuine desire to relieve their suffering."[53] One study suggests that watching the Kardashians is making people more selfish and antisocial.[54]

As a candidate, Donald Trump described himself as a "very greedy person": "I like money. I'm very greedy. I'm a greedy person. I shouldn't tell you that, I'm a greedy—I've always been greedy. I love money, right?"[55] However, in a 1990 interview with *Playboy* magazine, he said "I don't think I'm greedy," and cited his giving to charities: "I gave away the royalties from my book." In the same interview, he referred to Leona Helmsley, the so-called queen of mean who was sentenced to 16 years in prison for tax evasion, as "a truly evil human being" who was guilty of "much more than greed." During her trial for tax evasion, a maid reported that Helmsley had once said, "We don't pay taxes; only the little people pay taxes." It is noteworthy that at her sentencing, Judge John M. Walker said that Helmsley had been motivated by "naked greed."[56]

During the campaign, Trump also accused Hillary Clinton of being "greedy as hell" as the reason she wanted to be president.[57] Trump repeatedly claimed that he was "greedy for the United States," that is, "We're going to grab and grab and grab. We're going to bring in so much money and so much everything."[58] "I don't do it for the money": the first sentence in Trump's 1987 best seller *Art of the Deal.* This from a man who refused to release his tax returns that would disclose his true wealth, causing wild speculation that his claimed wealth of $3 billion may actually be much lower.

I doubt anyone would disagree that greed, contrary to Gordon Gekko's statement, is a bad thing. The more difficult issue for the 21st century is the role of honestly gotten wealth in the morality of humanity. How are we to balance the increasing economic divide, and just how might the wealthy 1 percent increase their moral standing by resisting the forces of greed in lieu of the forces of charity and compassion?

Chapter Six: Envy

Hatred is active, and envy passive dislike; there is but one step from envy to hate.

—Johann von Goethe

When I was six years old, in a fit of envy for what I perceived as favorable attention given to my younger three-year old brother, I hit him in the head with a block. Not my finest moment. I took one of our building blocks, a rather heavy, pale oblong piece of wood and hit him across the forehead causing a gaping wound that began bleeding over the front of his face. I believe he required six stitches. Until we were both well into our thirties, our mother still believed the story that "the block fell off the shelf and hit him in the head." I received no punishment.

******

"And when they were in the field, Cain rose up against his brother Abel, and killed him."[1] Thus, ends the prototypical story of envy in the Old Testament. Ignoring God's warning that "sin is couching at the door," Cain slaughters his brother in a rage of envy. Asked where his now-dead brother is, Cain famously responds, "Am I my brother's keeper?" For the murder of his brother, not for his envy of him, Cain is exiled and destined to live with the mark of sin on his forehead, what became called the "curse of Cain."

The Bible tells that God favored ("had regard" for) Abel's sacrifice over that of his brother, causing Cain to become "very angry." More notably, the text tells that "his countenance fell." The *Oxford English Dictionary* defines countenance as "appearance, aspect, look," but it more contextually defines it as "bearing, demeanour, comportment." Cain's countenance here indicates not only his anger but his self esteem and his self image as regards his place in the world next to his brother. In the hierarchy that was the world, Cain viewed himself as lower than his brother Abel whom he envied for his love and regard by God.

His anger is related to his envy, and both lead to his abandonment by God and, ultimately, to his slaying of his brother. As psychologist Rein Nauta puts it, "Cain would rather be actively guilty than passively ashamed."[2] Many pastoral interpretations of the Cain and Abel story deem Cain initially ashamed that his sacrifice is not accepted by God. That shame leads him to envy, which leads him to murder. What of the relationship between shame and envy? Indeed, shame and envy can lead to violence—we have to only look at the myriad school shooters of the past two decades to see this.[3] In several instances, the shooter is reported as having been scorned or rejected by a potential romantic liaison or peer group, only to result in feelings of shame. The shooter then feels uncontrollable envy (and hatred) for others, viewing the world as an unjust place in which he has been unfairly cast as an alien. This alienation leads to shame, and "shame appears similar to envy in the sense that it also involves a sense of inferiority."[4] All of this envy leads to impotence, frustration, and ultimately destruction.

Envy is not jealousy.[5] "In envy, one is envious of what another, in one's eyes unjustly possesses."[6] The words have long been confused, so much so that lexicographer Bryan Garner feels the need to make the distinction in his *Garner's Modern American Usage*,[7] though I would argue his distinction between rivalry and resentment is not especially helpful. Envy is a more deeply felt emotion and longer lasting than jealousy; envy is visceral, while jealousy is intellectual. As essayist Joseph Epstein writes, "Envy doesn't tend to remind you of the dignity of humankind."[8] In fact, envy is perhaps the most reviled of the seven deadly sins since it is rooted in several of the other six: envy is part pride, part lust, part greed, and perhaps most egregiously sliding the individual into pure solipsism. Envy is the ultimate focus on self; unlike pride, envy does not reflect inflated sense of self but instead a lack of sense of self. The envious person has an undeveloped or underdeveloped sense of self-causing him or her to desire what others have to fill gaps in his or her personal self.

Envy can be so strong that it has the power to change one's physical appearance: we describe someone as "green with envy." Envy positions itself as an obstacle to happiness. Aristotle argued that the goal of life is happiness (*eudomania*), but he also suggested that happiness differs for every person "like pleasure, wealth, or honour."[9] The problem with envy is that it is easy to argue that embracing feelings of envy actually contributes to my desire to be happy. So, how can that be bad? Envy is indeed a human urging (do nonhuman animals envy? Darwin thought so), but it is one of the few sins discussed that can cause recoil in the bearer. For example, Paul Valéry's Monsieur Teste notes his feelings of envy: "In the past—some twenty years ago—anything above the ordinary achieved by another man was for me a personal defeat. At that time I could see nothing but ideas stolen from me! How stupid!"[10] Elsewhere, Valéry writes of the "light of envy," which, like "the light of disgust" and "the light of pride," can be very bright.[11] "Every strong passion kindles its own light, illuminates and brings out vividly all that can arouse or stimulate it, in the sum of things present."[12] "Shortcomings," he writes, "positively dazzle" in that they blind us to reality. Indeed, envy has the very ability to cause us to ignore all that is right and beautiful in lieu of our own feelings of emptiness.

Literature provides us with ample examples of envious behavior. In *Paradise Lost*, Milton's Satan is envious of all other beings—if he can't be happy, no one will be. The envious one drags down the envied. When he first sees Adam and Eve in Eden, he can hardly believe his eyes: "O Hell! What doe mine eyes with grief behold."[13] His envy of the pair and their ideal state compels him to revenge; he even notes that he "could love" the pair under different circumstances and then vows to either live with the pair in Eden, bring them with him to live in Hell, or destroy them. As mystery writer Dorothy Sayers[14] writes of envy: "At its best, Envy is a climber and a snob;

at its worst, it is a destroyer—rather than have anybody happier than itself, it will see us all miserable together."[15]

Avarice is the desire to have what one wants but does not have. Envy is not necessarily the possession but is instead the desire itself. In her 1957 work "Envy and Gratitude," psychoanalyst Melanie Klein writes, "Envy is a most potent factor in undermining feelings of love and gratitude at their root."[16] Aristotle said, "Envy is pain at the sight of such good fortune as consists of the good things already mentioned; we feel it towards our equals; not with the idea of getting something for ourselves, but because the other people have it."[17] The key to understanding envy is to see it as a feeling of injustice.[18]

Human beings seem to have an innate faith in natural justice—a belief that, in the end, "the truth will out" and justice will be served. Envy arises when that faith in natural justice either lags or is not present at all or when experience proves that natural justice fails to work. "All mythology harps on Justice."[19] Our faith in justice is integral to the averting of envy. If we remain secure in our faith that universal justice persists, we have no reason to feel envious of others, safe in the assumption that in the end everything will equal out. But, as our parents and so many others have told us, the world is in reality not a fair place.

Perhaps the most significant issue in discussion of envy is equality. Most believe that because "all men are created equal," this means that all should have the same opportunities and material goods. This, however, is erroneous and is at the root of so much divisiveness, from the quarrel over the corner office by coworkers to the vicious war over water rights between two countries. Equality is a mirage because it implies that everyone is equal regardless of merit. We should instead aim for equity. Let me explain what I mean by the difference.

Equity implies fairness, while equality has us treat everyone the same without consideration for the contexts of need, ability, or merit. We should aim for an equitable society, one which facilitates fairness, not equality. In a work environment, merit pay is awarded to the employee who has seen greater success than his or her peers; this is not equality, it is equity. It is fair that the first employee receives the merit pay increase; if the situation were equal, both would receive (or not) the increase, regardless of their work outcomes. To argue for equality in such a situation would only encourage resentment and poor work ethic with even more harmful outcomes.

Equality demands that everyone be on equal ground, while equitability distributes reward in line with worth. I would love to be 6 feet, 2 inches, 175 pounds, with deep blue eyes and wavy blond hair. It is absurd for me to be envious of Robert Redford for his looks because we are not equals. We might be potentially equitable if my acting skills were on par with his (which they are not), but we will never be equals in appearance.

The desire for equality evokes envy. Equality is at play when the child complains that his twin brother has more cookies. "It's not fair," he proclaims. What he really means is, "that's not just." He and his brother have no discernible difference in quality; they are the same age and have been engaged in the same activities all day. Why does one brother get more than the other? When the one brother has completed more chores and receives more cookies, that is equitable. More reward for more work.

Equity is socialist; equality is democratic and capitalistic. Equity has associations with justice and fairness; equality means everyone is on the same level. Envy grows from the desire to be equal. As Epstein writes, "One of the evils of socialism was to eliminate, along with injustice, envy itself."[20] If all have the same amount and quality of goods, there would be nothing left to envy. Equitability ensures that all have the same access to goods in line with their station. If the corner office opens up, those with seniority should be given right of first refusal. Equality would require that everyone—from the most senior employee to the college graduate hired yesterday—be given an equal opportunity for the office. To be sure, the only way that envy is removed from this equation is to understand the qualifying phrase in my definition "in line with their station."

In a leaked 2004 memo, Prince Charles wrote, "What is wrong with people nowadays? Why do they all seem to think they are qualified to do things far above their capabilities?"[21] The English public was less than amused because this implied the royal endorsed a class structure in which everyone remains in their station. Most often, today, "station" in life is comparable to economic (salary, tax bracket) more than social status (birthright, ancestry). But I argue here that "station" is also tied to age, experience, and knowledge. The idea that birth determines station in life is indeed antiquated and antithetical to our modern sensibilities.

The business world has developed something called "equity sensitivity theory." However, as one of the theory's founders notes, "The theoretical notions advanced are relevant to any social situation in which an exchange takes place, whether the exchange be of the type taking place between man and wife, between football teammates, between teacher and student, or even, between Man and his God."[22] This is a justice theory in which equity is measured by comparing the ratio of contributions (or costs) to benefits (or rewards) for each person.[23]

How does this shake out for our discussion of envy? If we live in a truly equitable society, envy should not be a concern because members will understand that results are based in just and fair determinations. Of course, we do not live in such a society. Ours is a world riddled with inequity and injustice. The world seems rife at times with modern-day Cains envious of everyone from close relatives to absolute strangers. We live in a world of constant desire for what we do not yet have—a bigger house, a nicer car, a faster computer, a more attractive spouse, a more successful career. We indeed live in a world whose very fabric is sewn with the threads of Buddhist suffering as a result of desire.

Although John Rawls is often credited with its most extensive and eloquent modern discussion, the relationship between justice and envy is as old as the Greek philosophers. Aristotle writes that envy arises "if we can show that they have met with undeserved prosperity . . . and point out that they have unjustly received, or are receiving, or are about to receive many benefits."[24] But he does not look on such feelings with admiration: "For envy is very near to hatred."[25]

In his seminal *Theory of Justice*, first published in 1971, Rawls argues that envy "is not a moral feeling."[26] Instead, he posits that envy is part of human nature: "It is sufficient to say that the better situation of others catches our attention. We are downcast by their good fortune and no longer value as highly what we have; and this sense of hurt and loss arouses our rancor and hostility."[27] Rational individuals, Rawls argues, are not subject to envy, recalling earlier assertions that sin interrupts reason. Envy is the result of perceived injustice, and the world is wrought with what Rawls terms "benign envy," where "there is no ill will intended or expressed" as in "envying" someone for their happy marriage.[28] This does not mean that you want their happy marriage (or wish them an unhappy marriage), more that you admire their marriage. Benign envy becomes problematic when it metastasizes.

The cancer-like envy is the feeling that brings resentment, which Rawls argues *is* a moral feeling. Grudging, spite, and resentment are "collectively harmful."[29] In his landmark 1912 work *Ressentiment*, the German philosopher Max Scheler writes that *ressentiment* occurs on "a progression of feeling" that includes envy and spite,[30] though envy and spite have "specific objects." The word is the French translation of the English word "resentment" but carries a more moral connotation indicative of a hostility directed at the object of one's envy. *Ressentiment* is more holistic envy, more consuming, and is the result of those unable to negotiate "a moral self-conquest."[31] Scheler argues that in "a democracy which is not only political, but also social and tends toward equality of property," *ressentiment* should be slight.[32] The contemporary Western world would seem to qualify—with its "approximate equal rights . . . or formal social equality."[33] What has gone wrong? Much, I argue, is dependent on the *perception* of equal rights and social equality, not necessarily the *reality* of that theoretical framework. We tend to believe everyone in the United States has equal rights—our laws dictate as much— but the reality does not scan. If equal rights were reality and became the foundation of behavior, there would be no place for envy. In the introduction to *Democracy in America*, de Tocqueville writes of "the equality of conditions," which he sees as the "focal point" of understanding American society.[34] In fact, de Tocqueville writes that equality is the dominant feature of democratic societies; thus, envy would not be an issue in such societies. The United States, however, is a contradiction: a democratic society but one also rife with envious sentiment and behavior.

Rawls pinpoints the root of envy in a lack of self esteem: "Now I assume that the main psychological root of the liability to envy is a lack of self confidence in our own worth combined with a sense of impotence."[35] Envy also occurs when we feel powerless, either power that has been removed or power that never was. Impotence can cause envy. I might envy my neighbor because of his new car, but what I am really experiencing is powerlessness in that I do not have the means to purchase a similar car.

> Impotence or powerlessness constitutes an additional sense in which the blow to self esteem is undeserved. The blow is not simply mediated by an unjust basic structure, but the disadvantaged are also impotent to effect the necessary change through normal (and morally acceptable) channels, which include not only due political process, majority voting and lobbying, but also social agitation, collective action, civil disobedience and other legitimate

actions.[36]

The frustration that comes with envy via impotence results in Max Scheller's *ressentiment*: "a self poisoning of the mind."[37] This is the envy that holds a grudge, the envy that will not release its grip on the psyche, the envy that might turn one green.[38] It is also the envy that can be self destructive in that it demands that the holder of the grudge "stay in the victim role and perpetuate negative emotions associated with rehearsing the hurtful offense."[39] Envy is the bedrock of our contemporary victim culture.[40]

Some argue the envy is an adaptive evolutionary response. One study suggests that "the whole purpose of envy is to motivate you into action either by independently trying harder (envy) or by coveting and stealing what the other has (jealousy)."[41] Another argues that envy has "been shaped by selection to facilitate successful social competition for access to resources that affect fitness."[42] In 1872's *The Expression of Emotions in Man and Animals*, his foundational theory of emotion and expression, Darwin writes only that envy is one of many feelings that "can be detected by the eye";[43] socioevolutionary theory has posited that envy is part of the survival instinct.

At a professional conference I once attended, lunch was catered by the host university. The faculty participants and the higher level administrative participants were separated for the meal. The faculty soon discovered that their lunch came with conditions and restrictions not visited on the administrators. Faculty were permitted one can of soda and were served a buffet lunch on paper plates with plastic utensils. The administrators were also served a buffet lunch but with china plates and real silverware; drinks were unlimited. It was not until the faculty had realized this inequity that they became envious and, eventually, resentful. This was a situation in which the faculty participants had less power than the administrative participants, and that unlevel playing field was highlighted. Envy—and snide jokes about other now-magnified differences in how the groups were treated—pervaded for the rest of the conference in the form of a finitely timed grudge. The inequity had been highlighted and contributed to envy and even disgust. As Immanuel Kant defined it, envy is "a tendency to perceive with displeasure the good of others."[44] That "displeasure" hovered over the remaining days of the conference.

Nonetheless, envy traditionally has little place in a society members view as ultimately just. In Shakespeare's tragedy, one of the reasons that Hamlet acts as he does is not out of envy of Claudius (though the Freudians would disagree) but is instead due to his bleak view of justice. This is perhaps best explained by Claudius himself in his confession in Act 3:

In the corrupted currents of this world

Offence's gilded hand may shove by justice,

And oft 'tis seen the wicked prize itself

Buys out the law

This, even Claudius realizes, is not so in a divinely judged cosmology:

but 'tis not so above;

There is no shuffling, there the action lies

In his true nature

It is in fact Hamlet's view that there is no justice on earth that compels him to action:

But heaven hath pleased it so,

To punish me with this and this with me,

That I must be their scourge and minister.

He proclaims himself not envious of Claudius, although Rosencrantz and Guildenstern mistakenly assess him melancholic due to ambition, that is, his desire for the throne. Instead, he feels a divine appointment to represent justice on earth, to be "their scourge and minister," to exact justice on his uncle for murdering his father.

Freud and his protégé Ernest Jones did not agree.[45] First Freud and later and more completely Jones argued that Hamlet's Oedipus Complex, his envy of and desire to kill his father in order to fulfill his sexual desire for his mother, lay behind the play's raison d'etre. Never mind that I find this argument highly questionable,[46] nowhere in the play does Hamlet suggest envious feelings. In fact, the word "envy" appears in *Hamlet* only twice, both when Claudius discusses the impending duel between Hamlet and Laertes as when Claudius claims, upon hearing of Laertes's precision with his sword, Hamlet was "envenomed" with envy.[47]

In fact, it is rare to find envy as the motivating force in revenge tragedies of the English Renaissance; revenge in that drama is much more likely the result of vengeance in response to a criminal act.[48] Although he does mention envy in the *Poetics*, Aristotle does seem to imply that catharsis itself is purification of emotion from envy. "Envy," he writes, "is pain at the sight of such good fortune as consists of the good things already mentioned; we feel it towards our equals; not with the idea of getting something for ourselves, but because the other people have it."[49] With this, Aristotle transports us from the agora of the fourth century BCE to the cyberspace of the 21st century CE.

Perhaps the largest growth in the envy industry these days has been promulgated by the explosive nature of social media. Facebook. Twitter. Instagram. Snapchat. "FOMO." Fear of missing out. Sherry Turkle argued in 2014 that "the fear of missing out [had] become a fear of missing anything."[50] If we are friends on Instagram, I probably envy you. Never mind that most of what is posted on social media is posed or artificial in some way. Fourth graders compete to see who can get the most followers on Snapchat or the most likes on a Facebook post. This is, to be sure, an odd phenomenon in which the word "social" has taken on an entirely new meaning. Never before have human beings seemed so alone and at the same time so "social."[51] Our society seems obsessed with reinvigorating the importance of solitude for reflection and edification but is also worried at every turn that we will miss a notification on our phone. This only adds to feelings of envy as those who attempt to engage in solitude experience withdrawal in peculiar ways—not withdrawal from seeing and interacting with others but withdrawal from the rush of dopamine the brain receives when a post on Facebook is liked.

But, why is my friend getting so many "likes" for his photograph of his egg salad sandwich and everyone is ignoring my post about my flat tire? In her recent study *The Happiness Effect: How Social Media Is Driving a Generation to Appear Perfect at Any Cost*, Donna Freitas recalls an online survey of more than 700 college students in which they were asked to respond to a series of statements about how they feel about social media. Of the more than half who said social media makes them compare themselves to others, some said, "This makes me sad" or "It usually makes me feel bad about myself."[52] Another poignantly responded, "I try not to do this but I can't seem to help myself."[53] Our addiction to envy is being enabled by our dependence on technology. Technology has created an increasingly competition-driven and cut-throat culture in which everyone envies someone else.

Of course, this leads back to the vast discussion of the self I touched on in an earlier chapter and what it means to be a "self" in the modern world: a complete discussion is beyond the parameters of the present study, but I encourage the reader to explore discussions of self and identity in such wonderful writers as Luciana Floridi, Sherry Turkle, and Charles Taylor. Let me just frame Taylor's philosophy on the self, perhaps the most fully formed, as an example.

In *Sources of the Self*, Taylor sees the modern self as emerging from a clear moral context. We live in a morally-constructed universe, whether that construction comes from us or from a divine being. Thus, we conduct our selves in line with that moral structure. "This perversity can be described as a drive to make ourselves the centre of our world, to relate everything to ourselves, to dominate and possess things which surround us."[54] We run the risk of not only narcissism but of a pure subjective existence in which "it's all about me." In such a construction, envy would be a causal and necessary consequence. This does not, however, mean that Taylor is endorsing envy as a way of life. The key is to become an adept self evaluator and to develop the ability to step outside of self and develop and retain a degree of objectivity. This will permit the individual to look at himself or herself in the mirror and see more than just his or her superficial reflection. This will result in a multidimensional identity, one in which the individual is able to exist in the world but also have the ability to step outside of that existence and achieve a degree of self realization, what Taylor calls "radical reflexivity." What seems to have happened instead is what Sherry Turkle calls the "edited self." Individuals are so caught up in their online image and how they appear to others that they obsess over refining that online persona to the detriment of working on Taylor's "radical reflexivity."

Social media not only discourages "radical reflexivity," but also negates it. With its lightning speed, its cacophony of voices, and its distortion of the facts, social media outlets encourage not only body dysmorphia but identity dysmorphia, that is, a disconnect between who one is in reality and who one is online. Social media becomes a Petri dish for envy. Never mind the inherent loss of privacy, life online is even more a simulation than Jean Baudrillard imagined. In his 1981 treatise *Simulacra and Simulation*, Baudrillard argued that modern existence has become a simulation— an imitation of the real world. A development of Plato's "Allegory of the Cave," Baudrillard's idea is that much of what we currently experience as "real" in the world is in fact a simulation of reality, whether that be Disney World or virtual reality. We are caught up, Baudrillard writes, in "the endlessly reflected vision."[55] To be sure, life experienced in the world of social media is at least once removed from reality with virtual reality blurring the lines even more. It is also ripe for the ugly practice of constantly comparing oneself and one's achievements to others. On Facebook and Instagram, it seems that everyone else is having a better life than I am. Although we are currently witness to the greatest accessibility to knowledge in human history, one in which there has been "an exponential increase in common knowledge,"[56] that access seems to have bred not collegiality and collaboration but feelings of resentment.

Michael Kinsley wrote about Internet envy on Slate.com as early as 1999. "Internet envy" (almost a syndrome in and of itself) is pandemic in the online community. Multiple studies show that social media can foster feelings of envy, particularly in teenagers. When I look at your posts and photos on Facebook, posts in which your life appears ideal, I experience pangs of Internet envy. Over time, this can develop into feelings more hostile and angry. A 2017 study concluded that consumers using Instagram experience feelings of envy causing them to pay more for a product they envied someone else possessing.[57] Envy also makes money for its enablers.

Most of us have grown up with some status symbol popular in our teens. Whether the Swatch Watch of the 1980s, the newest Nike sneakers of the 2000s, or the latest iPhone of the 2010s, envy of those possessing those symbols has only been magnified online. Instagram and Snapchat feed viewers a constant stream of "famous" people either directly or indirectly hawking wares. YouTube has birthed an entire category of "influencers," people (many in their teens) paid by companies to endorse or promote their products, encouraging the viewer to envy the influencer, causing them to eventually spend money. And the envy does not stop at clothing, makeup, or electronics. The number of people coming into plastic surgeons and asking for "the Kylie Jenner" (lip enhancement; $500–2,000) or "the Kim [Kardashian] Butt" (buttock implants; $4,000–5,000) increased dramatically in recent years, even in girls as young as 14. "Dr. Simon Ourian, the Los

Angeles based doctor who shot to fame because of his association with the Kardashians (Kim Kardashian Snapchats from his office), called the Kardashian-Jenner clan both individually and as a unit the 'biggest influencing power force behind any concept that happens on social media' today."[58] Some plastic surgeons have even begun using social media as a platform to attract and retain patients with some running contests offering free treatments.[59] The increasing availability and use of online filters to alter one's appearance on social media have only served to increase instances of what some have called Snapchat dysmorphia, a term the *Facial Plastic Surgery* journal of the American Medical Association recently identified as a valid ailment, which allows the individual to not only add floppy puppy ears to a photo but to smooth out skin, make teeth whiter, or reposition eyes.[60] Patients come to plastic surgeons for corrective surgery to make them look more like their online representations, ripe with envy of perceived perfection online.

Social media influencers can prey on the selfie generation quite easily, quite often, and from just about anywhere in the world. The selfie generation is the logical realization of Christopher Lasch's "culture of narcissism." *Time* magazine in fact named "You" as its 2006 Person of the Year. The Internet put self obsession into everyone's pocket, facilitating a daily and deeper focus on the external self almost to the point of destroying the inner self. Much of the blame for that destruction can be found in feelings of envy that can at times be palpable. The impulse to compare my situation to yours is human nature, but Benjamin Franklin thought envy was an obstacle to "true happiness."[61] A 2008 Gallup poll asked Americans if they were "angry that others have more than they deserve." In the current context of the online universe, this comparison is almost always a losing game.[62] If my Facebook updates are read by no one, can I be said to be alive? Without "interactive stimuli," we fall into "a state of reflective passivity indistinguishable from nonexistence."[63] My breakfast will never look as savory as yours in that Instagram post. My evening sitting on the couch will never compare on Snapchat to your backstage experience at the Taylor Swift concert. Living in this online world can only stoke my envy and cause bitter feelings.

Bitterness, resentment, and envy are perhaps some of the most vitriolic emotions one can experience. Perhaps those feelings are natural to human beings, but it is the continued seeding and reseeding of such feelings that ultimately detract from our humanity. As Hamlet counsels his mother to not continue sleeping in his uncle's bed: "Do not spread the compost on the weeds."

Chapter Seven: Sloth

We excuse our sloth under the pretext of difficulty.

—Quintillian

In the mid-1970s, my father was once pulled over by a State Trooper on the New York State Thruway for driving his 1966 Chrysler Newport too slowly. Many roads now post both maximum and minimum speeds. I cannot imagine getting a "speeding ticket" for not driving fast enough; however, the current New York State fine for driving too slowly is $195. How can doing anything slowly be illegal? How can it be a sin?

In his schema for the seven deadly sins, Gregory the Great conflated two sins on Evagrius Ponticus's list into one: he combined acedia (mental sloth or apathy) and sadness into sloth. Although, with the development of modern psychology and the growing understanding of mental illness, it would be absurd to regard sadness as a sin, I believe that acedia is a better description than sloth for our final sin. Acedia has long implied listlessness or lethargy, what teens sometimes call "a case of the blahs." It is easy to see how this condition morphed first into melancholy and then into depression, but I doubt that Prozac is the cure for acedia. But whether it is boredom,[1] depression,[2] or laziness,[3] the condition of "the blahs" seems to reach far and wide in the 21st century. It is estimated that more than 16 million American adults, almost 7 percent of the population, experience a "major depressive episode" at least once a year.[4] Depression affects almost 13 percent of the U.S. population aged 12–17 with a growing number being put on antidepressive medications each year.[5] And depression is peripherally related to sloth, as depression can get caught in a cycle with apathy and disinterestedness.

It was only fitting in the composition of this book that I left sloth as the final sin to discuss. Although I think it is one of the more prevalent of the seven deadly sins in our culture today, I do not think it is the most harmful. It is humorous that most books on Amazon.com related to "sloth" are written for children, either about the animal or just about the joys of being slow, like the animal. A culture that encourages stillness and slowing down also discourages laziness. We cannot seem to make up our minds.

Acedia has been the curse of modern life since the end of World War I. In the shadows of the Great War, a generation of thinkers regarded acedia as the decline of Western culture. By the time T. S. Eliot published *The Waste Land* in 1922, he could write not only that April, the month of rebirth, is the "cruelest month" but call London an "Unreal City" and observe the desolation of the modern intellectual landscape: "Here is no water but only rock/Rock and no water and the sandy road." Our most astute scholar on the topic of sloth is Siegfried Wenzel, whose masterful *The Sin of Sloth: Acedia in Medieval Thought and Literature* provides a thoroughly readable and accessible overview of the subject. Wenzel notes that *acedia* was not invented by monks but instead "had a long history in Greek literature, from a work attributed to Hippocrates down to Hellenistic writers."[6] In fact, discussions of *melancholia* (a type of deep sadness or gloom) and acedia run through the writings of the ancient Greek philosophers, including Aristotle and Galen.[7]

Sloth has an interesting history. Hamlet might be said to suffer more from acedia than from melancholy, at least early in the play, when he first appears on stage dressed in mourning black and laments his "too, too sullied flesh":[8] "How weary, stale, flat, and unprofitable/Seem to me all the uses of this world!"[9] This is not sloth; it is not laziness; it is more indicative of existential despair. To be sure, he is mourning the recent death of his father, but this is a kind of hopelessness associated with depressive disorders, the characteristics for which sound more like acedia and are described in the *DSM5:*

1. Depressed mood most of the day, nearly every day, as indicated by

either subjective report (e.g., feels sad, empty, hopeless) or observation made by others (e.g., appears tearful). (Note: In children and adolescents, can be irritable mood.)

2. Markedly diminished interest or pleasure in all, or almost all, activities most of the day, nearly every day (as indicated by either subjective account or observation.)

3. Significant weight loss when not dieting or weight gain (e.g., a change of more than 5% of body weight in a month), or decrease or increase in appetite nearly every day. (Note: In children, consider failure to make expected weight gain.)

4. Insomnia or hypersomnia nearly every day.

5. Psychomotor agitation or retardation nearly every day (observable by others, not merely subjective feelings of restlessness or being slowed down).

6. Fatigue or loss of energy nearly every day.

7. Feelings of worthlessness or excessive or inappropriate guilt (which may be delusional) nearly every day (not merely self-reproach or guilt about being sick).

8. Diminished ability to think or concentrate, or indecisiveness, nearly every day (either by subjective account or as observed by others).

9. Recurrent thoughts of death (not just fear of dying), recurrent suicidal ideation without a specific plan, or a suicide attempt or a specific plan for committing suicide.

Several of these are also "symptoms" of modern life. How many suffer from insomnia, fatigue, distraction, and lack of self worth?

For the monastic world, where acedia was in effect "born," this meant withdrawal from the monastic community, lack of desire for devotion and work (*ora et labora*, "pray and work" is generally identified as the motto of the

Rule of St. Benedict). As historian Andrew Crislip explains, in writers such as the seventh-century Syriac mystic Joseph Hazzaya, acedia is pictured as a great weight from under which it is difficult to move—"a burdensome disease on all my limbs."[10] It is perhaps easy to understand why monks living apart from the bustle of daily society or, in some cases, living a reclusive, eremitic life might be more susceptible to acedia, which can include both physical and psychological illness. In fact, many of the writers make a significant distinction between psychological (or spiritual) acedia and physical acedia. John Cassian, in his *Institutes*, writes that acedia can cause sloth: "[Acedia] causes him [a monk] to be slothful when it comes to any kind of work."[11] After cataloging idle behavior cited from Paul, Cassian clearly puts forward the idea that acedia is at the root of other sinful behavior: "You see how many conditions sprout from one disgraceful vice, and how serious and wicked they are."[12] Acedia is "the root cause of so many vices."[13]

As Jean-Louis Guez de Balzac, the French author whose letters made him famous, wrote in 1665, "Solitude is fine but you need someone to tell that solitude is fine."[14] After all, as every college freshman in Sociology 101 learns, humans are social animals. In *Politics*, Aristotle wrote that "man is by nature a social animal." In Chapter 4 of *Descent of Man*, Darwin asserts "man is a social animal," which Darwin notes we see in humanity's "dislike of solitude, and in its wish for society beyond that of his own family."[15] In Genesis, God says, "It is not good that the man should be alone."[16] Solitude can be a beautiful thing, but human beings usually function better in groups. It is not surprising then that two of the remedies for acedia prescribed by Jean-Charles Nault (the contemporary Benedictine writer) are "prayer and work."[17] Nault prescribes a balance between the two. In a more secular arena, we might merely substitute "reflection" for "prayer" and note the balance between "alone time" and community. One of the most common topics in today's business world is "work/life balance."[18] Many are tagged with "workaholic," while others are called "dead weight." As we have seen is so typical in discussions of sin, the middle way—moderation—is desirable.

This balance is difficult to attain, as technology continues to confuse the meaning of the word "social." Children begin understanding the world "in terms of what they know best: themselves."[19] Adults graduate from this stage of development when they begin realizing empathy. Technology has enabled a kind of stalling in the childlike stage so that some fail to develop empathy and the true understanding of their relationship to other human beings. These are the people whose definition of being "social" is having a thousand friends on Facebook. They are, as Turkle put it in her 2011 book, "alone together."[20]

Envy and sloth almost seem antithetical. Envy consistently says, "I want what you have," while Sloth says, "leave me alone." In his rule for monks, St. Benedict cautions against being "a loafer."[21] Elsewhere the monks are warned that "Idleness is the soul's enemy,"[22] that if one is so "slothful that he will not or cannot meditate or read," he should be given work to keep him busy.[23] Of course the Bible famously instructs that "Idle hands are the devil's workshop."[24] Inertia, both physical and psychological, is the enemy. Physical inertia is the inability to move. Psychological inertia may be worse because it implies an indisposition to change and implies a stagnation of spirit. As Romantic poet William Blake wrote in *The Marriage of Heaven and Hell*, "Expect poison from standing water." Standing water is not only a literal breeding ground for diseases like Malaria and Dengue Fever; in some folklore, a dream of standing water is an indication of sloth, bad luck, and even death.[25]

Although he is credited with the origin of the idea of the seven deadly sins, Evagrius Ponticus was most concerned in his text with "the demon of *acedia*"—mental or physical slothfulness. He saw it at the root of many other sins, possibly the "commander" of the other sins.[26] Sloth, in Evagrius's work, is more like apathy than laziness. The monk struck by acedia looks "constantly towards the windows, to jump out of the cell, to watch the sun to see how far it is in from the night hour, to look this way and that."[27] Acedia also builds "dislike for the place and for [the monk's] state of life itself."[28] It is easy here to see how acedia and sadness were eventually conflated as sloth by Gregory the Great. Evagrius famously calls sloth "the noonday demon" (of Psalm 91) because it attacks when the sun is at its highest and the day at its hottest. In the 2001 account of his own depression, *The Noonday Demon*, Andrew Solomon concluded that "the opposite of depression is not happiness but vitality," in essence the antithesis of inertia.[29] Sloth grows from inertia and becomes boredom, and boredom can then develop into depression. Paul Valéry wrote, "Boredom is the feeling one has of being a creature of habit and living in a state of *conscious nonexistence*, as though one had a faculty of perceiving one *is* not, does not exist at all. In the last resort boredom is the response of like to like."[30] The French term is *ennui* and is related to the Modern English word "annoy." One experiencing acedia has folded his boredom into inertia to the point of feeling *ennui* at life.

No coincidence that acedia continues to be one of the greatest dangers in monastic life. Evagrius is writing of acedia as it directly relates to the cenobitic life and not any type of secular existence, and Gregory's attempt to reclassify the seven deadly sins forced him to modify the monastic drudgery of acedia to the more universal experience of sloth. How ironic that it is also quite prevalent in modern life. While living a solitary existence with little to no external stimulation seems given to acedia, how can those engaged in modern life—with its 24/7 news cycle—be prone to it as well? In a world in which silence is almost extinct, it is surprising that modern acedia seems epidemic.[31]

Let me suggest a hypothetical case study in modern acedia: the online addict. He sits for hours on end in front of a screen, typing on a keyboard or twiddling a joystick, interacting with either disconnected bodies or fictitious beings. He scorns physical human contact, his metabolism slows, his weight increases, his sleep is erratic, and his mind is unfocused on anything other than the pixels on the screen. It is only in the confines of a virtual world that he "exists," if it is indeed to be called existence. He ceases serious intellectual engagement and reflection and thrives instead on being fed an electronic IV of sounds and images to stimulate his stagnating mind.

This addiction to technology is not currently recognized as such in the *DSM5*, but the American Psychological Association does suggest "Internet gaming disorder" in the appendix with its nine characteristics including "loss of interest" in other activities. The topic appears on magazine covers from *Newsweek* to *People*, from *Time* to *Psychology Today* almost every month. Psychologists claim that Internet addiction "exploded when the Internet went mobile" with the iPhone in 2007.[32] A 2012 National Institutes of Health study suggested that 8.2 percent of Americans and Europeans present characteristics of Internet addiction.[33] Although there is as yet no single definition for "Internet addiction," its chief characteristic is excessive time spent online, but the spiritual and psychological effects might be extensive. Other than with the growing development of so-called wearables (e.g., AppleWatch, FitBit), time spent online is by nature time spent alone and still—the type of environment conducive to sloth and acedia.

My reading of the sin of sloth sees it as a transgression of apathy or boredom. In a study of boredom, Peter Toohey, professor of classics at the University of Calgary, writes that "in its modern phrase," "acedia becomes a strange conjunction of depression . . . and a doubt in the goodwill of the world itself."[34] In 1621's *The Anatomy of Melancholy*, Robert Burton writes that there is "nothing is so odious . . . as sloth and negligence."[35] Sloth can present in so many different forms in a modern world seemingly obsessed with continual movement. We are perpetually told that physical exercise is important— many are addicted to it and so spend hours in the gym. We are also told that regular mental exercise is important—and so we download a "brain game" app on our smartphone. But actual physical and psychological movement seem rare. Movement implies change. It implies moving forward. Sloth is the inability or desire to change.

In the closing scene of Woody Allen's 1977 film *Annie Hall*, Alvy Singer and Annie break up: "A relationship, I think, is like a shark. You know? It has to constantly move forward or it dies. And I think what we got on our hands is a dead shark." Constant movement, forward or back, indicates life. In the aptly titled "Proverbs of Hell" in *The Marriage of Heaven and Hell*, William Blake encourages movement and action:

The road of excess leads to the palace of wisdom.

He who desires but acts not, breeds pestilence.

The busy bee has no time for sorrow.

Technology invites us to be more idle as it increasingly provides us with devices and processes to make life easier and supposedly "more efficient." In this case, efficiency breeds apathy. Technology makes us lazy.

When remote controls for televisions were first introduced by Zenith in 1950, they were called "Lazy Bones." A 1951 advertisement for the $30 product calls it "miraculous." The 2012 *Washington Post* obituary of Eugene J. Polly, the inventor in 1955 of the first wireless remote control, notes not everyone was thrilled with his new device: it was sometimes blamed for contributing to obesity and sparking marital spats.[36]

We can now receive a massive amount of entertainment without ever leaving the living room sofa, as the Internet has brought us streaming video and audio. First run movies are now piped directly to our tablets— so much for the night out at the movie theater, and never mind the trip to the now defunct neighborhood video store. The viewer can now remain cocooned in his or her house and receive all of his or her entertainment beamed directly to a television or computer screen. Of course, some of this is continued fallout from the attacks on 9/11 after which cable television burst with shows on home decorating and baking as Americans harbored a bunker mentality.

Even eating has become a field for acedia. New services such as GrubHub, DoorDash, and UberEats make it possible to have just about any restaurant's food delivered right to your door. A colleague likes the ease of having lunch delivered right to her office, even though the restaurant is perhaps 500 yards from her door. Online shopping has exploded notions of brick and mortar retail with shopping malls closing at an alarming rate, some being converted into apartment complexes and megachurches while others might be usefully transformed into housing for the homeless. A 2017 report from Credit Suisse predicted that 20–25 percent of American malls would close within five years with online sales, allowing shopping from the cushy sloth of your living room sofa, growing from 17 percent in 2017 to a predicted 35 percent in 2030.[37]

Again, as Alvy Singer says in *Annie Hall*, "It's important to make a little effort once in awhile." While the pace of daily living has increased with lightning speed, our actual movement forward as a species seems to have slowed dramatically. We seem mired in delusion and never ending "navel gazing"; we have become Narcissus entranced by our own image in the lake. Technology has transformed the ways we receive information, from how we buy books to how we get news, essentially dooming the actions of going to a bookstore or even reading a physical newspaper (personally, I view the black ink on my fingers from my daily *New York Times* as a badge of honor in this day of electronic subscriptions). This is nothing to say how technology has interrupted our connections to each other and encouraged a new kind of apathetic human race.

We live at a time when sentiments of empathy run through the mission statements of many universities and corporations. Technology bullied empathy to the back of the room, so much so that people now have to be told explicitly to practice compassion. It is much easier to spend Saturday afternoon on the couch playing video games than it is to go out and work at a homeless shelter, help to clean a local park, or even just spend some quality time with a loved one, *sans* technology. And human beings are increasingly about ease. In an 1889 speech called "The Strenuous Life," Theodore Roosevelt said, "A mere life of ease is not in the end a very satisfactory life, and, above all, it is a life which ultimately unfits those who follow it for serious work in the world."[38] He goes on to prescribe that we "boldly face the life of strife."

Technology has also dramatically changed the paradigm of education—both for the better and the worse. When I was an undergraduate, I spent hours in the campus library with wooden card catalog drawers, flipping through cards and savoring the joys of serendipity. Online library catalogs do not encourage that activity; in fact, most make it impossible. The use of the "reference section" at the library, combing through books to find the right article, fact, or reference, has declined so much that most university libraries have done away with the "reference section"—"it's all online" and discoverable from anywhere, anytime, with little effort. And my sloth is encouraged; how many times I have "googled" something instead of getting up from my chair to look up the same information in a book not 15 feet from my desk. Technology feeds on human inertia like an *Ouroboros*.

Some of my fondest child memories involve the summers my family spent in South Fallsburg, New York, north of New York City, at a bungalow colony called "Cooper's." It was small—perhaps 10 families—with no communal dining facility, no camp, just a pool and space to roam. As an adult, I would often ask my mother, "What did I *do* all day?" Adult me would have been bored silly with the slow pace of living. My mother responded, "You played with your trucks. You dug in the dirt. You walked in the woods.

You went in the pool." Add to this the horror of the analog world of the 1970s. There was no television that could get reception, just an AM radio on which I could get WABC, the New York City top 40 station I listened to endlessly. I think this is more than nostalgia; it is the realization that technology has increased the speed of daily life and inundated us with a constant barrage of data, information, and pseudo entertainment. But we are being sold a bill of goods—the benefits do not necessarily outweigh the costs.

When I began writing on sloth, a friend emailed me a photo of a sloth. But sloth as a human sin long predates the appellation of the animal. First referred to in literature in 1526 by Spanish historian Gonzalo Fernández de Ovideo y Valdés,[39] three-toed sloths, known for their painstaking slowness, have been on this planet for almost 64 million years. Their lack of speed is part of their survival, as it requires less energy than moving fast. That, combined with sharp hooklike fingers, serves to protect them from predators. Combined with camouflage, their slowness defends them. Sloths live exclusively in trees, coming down to the ground only about once a week to defecate. The sloth is perfectly adapted for the quiet life in the trees, but somewhat curiously they are not especially lazy, just slow (though they can move three times as fast in the water). Contrary to the popular stereotype, recent studies show that sloths are actually quite smart, though it seems unlikely that any will be earning a Nobel Prize anytime soon.[40]

Swiss psychiatrist Carl Jung suggests that "a person leading a lazy and inactive life" might be "particularly prone to the compulsion of libido, that is to all kinds of fears and involuntary constraints."[41] This is what the monastic authors were most concerned with—the ways in which acedia can become a "gateway drug" for other sin. In the modern world, the devils are metaphorical and perhaps more powerful as they masquerade as progress; actor Dan Aykroyd claims the Internet is "the devil's gateway."[42] He is joking, but technology has always been feared as an agent of evil. Long after Socrates feared the danger that writing posed to memory, in the 15th century, Johannes Trithemius lashed out against the new invention of the printing press. In his 1492 work *De laude scriptorum manualium* (*In Praise of Scribes*), Trithemius lamented the death of the art of the scribe (most of whom were monks) and worried that the printing press would become an excuse for the sloth of monks.[43]

Much of the psychology research and scholarship on the subject of laziness refers to school children and issues related to education. But what of the laziness of adults? Our culture perceives laziness as a choice, while acedia is deemed more pathological. Laziness is a habit, while acedia is a mental health issue. In *The Moviegoer*, Walker Percy's 1962 National Book Award winning novel, Binx Bolling is certainly guilty (he is the embodiment of Catholic guilt in the novel) of a laziness in need of spiritual salvation. He is able to escape his laziness and begin a quest for the meaning of his life and a search to discover his true inner self, thus rising to become the novel's hero. A quite different case of acedia can be found in Albert Camus's novel *The Stranger* in which the title character Meursault kills an Arab on the beach in French Algiers only to defend himself by saying essentially "the sun was in my eyes." Meursault's apathetic take on the absurdity of modern existence is reflected in his nonchalant attitude toward his mother's death: "Mama died today. Or maybe, yesterday; I can't be sure." The French refer to this as *l'ennui morbide* or deadly boredom.[44]

Jungian psychologist James Hillman calls acedia "the heavy sloth of depression, the drying despair of melancholy."[45] Avoiding acedia is about directing energy and controlling focus. No surprise, then, that practices such as yoga and meditation highlight the importance and connection of physical movement to spiritual wellness and psychological health. No surprise, either, that to counterbalance acedia, people have often taken to the other extreme, unable to slow down and experience life, overworried that reflection and contemplation might instead foster acedia and sloth. The result is a species that has taught itself speed is the indicator of a life well lived.

Conclusion

Sin is no longer the concern it was when Gregory the Great was writing around the year 600 CE. As the fabric of the world changed its hue from devoutly religious to liberally humanistic, moving from sacred to profane, the very nature of morality changed with it. No longer concerned with notions of divine justice and eternal punishment, humanity adjusted its focus from the hereafter to the here and now. Combined with confusion over the composition of the self, we discover an increasingly narcissistic culture in which the self is not only the center of the individual but the center of society. This ethos—most dramatically altered with the onslaught of personal technology in the late 20th century—signals a fundamental change in attitudes toward responsibility in contemporary society.

Indeed, in a culture in which blame is often referred from the individual to just about any external source possible, human beings have come to confuse subject with object and increasingly lack levels of empathy necessary for collaboration and compassion. Having turned over too much power to the technology it invented, humanity is now in danger of relinquishing its agency, resulting in intellectual and spiritual impotence and, in several cases, a shifting of responsibility to the technology itself.

The year 1918 saw the end of World War I and brought a fundamental shift in the intellectual landscape. Given the dramatic changes in the past 100 years, it is unclear just where we are headed. What will we as *Homo sapiens* look like in 2118? If, as many futurists believe, the singularity is nearer than we think, how will our very existence be changed once we can download and upload our consciousness, our memories (and our minds)? Do we run the risk of becoming amoral beings, lacking emotion and connection to one another, existing as Fritz Lang's drone-like workers do in the opening to *Metropolis*? Or will we instead become highly-developed consciousnesses without conscience?

It is not as if we have not been warned. Thoughtful humans have been wondering about this for centuries, starting with Socrates's warning in *Phaedrus* that writing will damage human memory and most recently with Yuval Noah Harari's prediction that Dataism will "conquer the world":

> Dataism thereby threatens to do to *Homo sapiens* what *Homo sapiens* has done to all other animals. Over the course of history humans created a global network and evaluated everything according to its function within that network. . . . The lives and experiences of all other animals were undervalued because they fulfilled far less important functions, and whenever an animal ceased to fulfil any function at all, it went extinct. However, once we humans lose our functional importance to the network, we will discover that we are not the apex of creation after all.[1]

The flag having been raised, it should come as little surprise that, unchecked, humanity has kept pressing ahead, all the while not realizing (or wanting to realize) that what it once saw as progress was an illusion, that we gave up too much to gain too little. With it, we have run the danger of sliding down the slippery slope. Technological progress has increasingly skewed morality, distorted notions of sin, and contorted notions of right and wrong.

The most basic human principles are now in question. It seems almost unthinkable that the U.S. Congress has had to introduce several bills that would have outlawed cloning human beings.[2] While ethicists debate the moral ambiguities, science has blindly marched forward, undoubtedly already having developed the laboratory procedures necessary to make genetic copies of human beings. As should happen more often, the Congress has agreed (at least legally) to wait until the philosophical complexities of the issue have been worked out. More often than not, this is not the case. Driverless cars are not only in production but have been tested on public roadways, often ending in disaster. As one example, in March 2018, an Arizona woman riding her bicycle was killed by a self-driving Uber car. We have the technology to build and manufacture driverless cars; should we? We need time to reflect because, as philosophy professor Michael Patrick Lynch has written recently, "Acceptance without reflection is dangerous."[3]

Nonetheless, the last 100 years have forced us to reexamine our very existence on this planet. So much so that even the definitions of our most basic concepts are now called into question. What is truth? What is life? What is sin? However, if we cease even attempting to clarify and hone our language, we will have truly given up. Therefore, it is imperative that we keep moving, motion being a sign of life and potential change. And we can never relinquish the potentiality of the species to anyone or anything. As such, the pushback at the demagogues and dictators of our world cannot cease. The standard for moral behavior must be established and retained, and those who would violate that standard through acts of sin— however we might define it— must not be permitted to thrive. Human beings are naturally moral animals, as Robert Wright puts it, but human beings also require a system of checks and balances. As in democratic government, the human psyche is composed of faculties that, while not biologically based, are in constant discussion and negotiation, but they require some standard of moral behavior against which to measure actions. That standard is socially developed, based on the prevailing mythologies of the culture, whether religious or not.

The definition and codification of sin are old practices. Gregory the Great's seven deadly sins were a convenient way for the Church to counsel (and control) its members in the Middle Ages. It was a system that prevailed in Western thought well into the Renaissance. With the Enlightenment and increasing stress on the individual, standards for moral behavior moved from external verification to internal monitoring. Increasingly in our world, it is no longer the case that people check their morals with an external authority; instead, morality is an individual choice, and sin is not just a matter of public action but of private intention.

What this means for the culture is as yet unclear. Morality is always changing as the result of shifts in historical, social, economic, and philosophical contexts. For the moment, we are at a potential tipping point. We can either invest in humanity by rededicating ourselves to morality, empathy, and compassion, or we can continue on the downward spiral of increasing moral decay we are currently riding; it is the much feared slippery slope. Once humanity has begun that descent, it will be extraordinarily difficult to regain its footing.

This is a defining moment. We sit at a precipice, at the top of the slippery slope. We still have the power to prevent the slide, and it is that power that is not only vital for the future of humanity, but it is what makes us human. Some thinkers, including Paul Valéry and D. H. Lawrence, both of whom I have referenced throughout this work, felt that post–World War I humanity was at a similar point. Both seemed to express hope that humanity could halt the skid, regain its equilibrium, and move forward. Instead, we sank into a second world war, a cold war, an age of frightening and potentially catastrophic nuclear arms, and, finally, an age of simulated war—all once again demeaning our humanity.

In post–World War II America, journalist Victor Cohen published a book looking forward to *1999: Our Hopeful Future*. In this research-based prediction of the future, Cohen summarizes his view from 1956, a view that could easily be recycled today:

> Man's world is perilous and his future uncertain, but I believe we are
> justified in optimism based on real things that are now happening; on trends
> we can now see if we only look; on today's facts rather than fears. I believe
> we are justified in optimism based on the premises that the automatic era
> will give us more income, more leisure and more time to think; that there
> is a very good chance that we will actually use a little of this time to learn

and think.[4]

No one would, I think, accuse me of optimism, but I do have some of the same confidence Cohen voices. In particular, I hope that technology will do what Vannevar Bush had thought it could in his 1945 essay: give us more time to conduct high level thinking and focus on facts rather than fears, on truths rather than false claims.

If we consider the changing role of sin in our culture, we also realize that we need to engage in much more self regulation and self control than we have in recent history. The focus needs to be the more diligent investigation of our internal selves as related to other selves (Jung's "collective unconscious"). With that tenet in mind, the occurrence of sin of all kinds may not be eradicated—that may not be possible given the human condition—but it could be reduced. Perhaps then we can fulfill the prescription in the closing lines of T. S. Eliot's 1922 poem *The Waste Land* taken from the Hindu Upanishads:

Datta. Dayadhvam. Damyata. ("Give. Compassion. Control.")

In the Upanishads, the phrase is uttered by Lord Vishnu and is understood to mean: be charitable (overcome greed), have mercy (overcome anger), and have self restraint (overcome lust and gluttony).

Our intention is as important as our action. "After all, we live most of our time alone, and the biggest part of our life is the silent yet busy stream of our private thoughts."[5] To disregard the weight of intention is to disregard the entire interior life humanity has spent millennia developing. Our human existence is a blend of the physical and the spiritual. To deny or disregard the spiritual in lieu of the purely physical would be incredibly harmful to us as a species. Carl Jung wrote, "It is an almost ridiculous prejudice to assume that existence can only be physical."[6] Indeed, technology stresses the physical almost to the entire exclusion and dismissal of the spiritual.[7] Valéry predicted "a terrible future" for us in which "the machine, with its demands, will subject even the most lighthearted, most elusive, to its disciplines. It records and it foresees; it regulates and hardens."[8] I am far from a Neo-Luddite, one who is phobic about any modern technology, but I am concerned about the effect technology has had and continues to have on our spirituality, on our humanity, and as a result on our notions of sin.

We live in a culture that is increasingly narcissistic, divisive, and bitter. As we regress into tribalism, sins such as envy and greed are magnified. Every group seems guilty of excessive pride, all while the individuals that make up those groups are dragged into acedia and gluttony. A culture incapable of dealing with its own sexuality too often falls into patterns of lustful behavior that oftentimes escalate to violence and destruction.

Valéry wrote, "The seven deadly sins are the seven *pure* colors of the spectrum in the Good Man's soul."[9] If we can hold fast to the middle way, carefully negotiating our way down the median, then all the colors of sin can counterbalance each other. We *can* be empathetic and compassionate toward each other while balancing our complex inner selves with the exterior personae we manage on a daily basis. Our future as humane beings depends on that balance.

Notes

Introduction

1. D. H. Lawrence, Studies in Classic American Literature (Harmondsworth: Penguin, 1977), 90–91.

2. Paul Valéry, Analects, trans. Stuart Gilbert (Princeton, NJ: Princeton University Press, 1970), 457.

3. "Rabbi" means "teacher," and rabbis are not always ideal pastoral counselors, but this one was equally adept at parsing Hebrew scripture and giving career advice.

4. Deuteronomy 6:9.

5. For an introduction, see Lee McIntyre, Post-Truth (Cambridge: MIT Press, 2018).

6. Emil Brunner, Man in Revolt: A Christian Anthropology, trans. Olive Wyon (Philadelphia: Westminster Press, 1939), 43.

7. Brunner, Man in Revolt, 43.

8. I hesitate to use the phrase "New Age religion" since "religion" usually refers to an organized belief system, whereas New Age intentionally lacks universal structure.

9. Paul Valéry, "Remarks on Intelligence," in his The Outlook for Intelligence, trans. Denise Folliot and Jackson Matthews (New York: Harper, 1962), 75.

10. The current Catechism of the Catholic Church: "Sin is a personal act. Moreover, we have responsibility for the sins committed by others when we cooperate in them." Catechism of the Catholic Church, http://www.vatican.va/ archive/ENG0015/_INDEX.HTM (accessed August 1, 2018).

11. Steven Pinker, The Blank Slate: The Modern Denial of Human Nature (New York: Viking, 2002), 174.

12. Ibid., 175.

13. José Ortega y Gasset, Man and Crisis, trans. Mildred Adams (New York:

W.W. Norton, 1958), 75.

14. Jean-Paul Sartre, Being and Nothingness, trans. Hazel E. Barnes (London: Routledge Classics, 2009), 574. For an astute study of Sartre's ideas on sin, see Kate Kirkpatrick, Sartre on Sin: Between Being and Nothingness (Oxford: Oxford University Press, 2017).

15. Sartre, Being and Nothingness, 709.

16. Pinker, Blank Slate, 175.

17. Gasset, Man and Crisis, 203.

18. "President Bill Clinton on Monica Lewinsky, #MeToo and Whether His Apology Was Enough," Today,

https://www.today.com/news/president-bill-clinton-monica-lewinsky-metoo-whether-his-apology-was-t130189

(accessed June 5, 2018).

19. Pinker, Blank Slate, 176.

20. "When you were slaves to sin, you were free from the control of righteousness."

21. Genesis 1:26. All references to the Bible are to the Revised Standard Version.

22. Genesis 3:12.

23. Genesis 2:17.

24. Genesis 3:1.

25. Genesis 3:6.

26. See Peter Millican, "Hume's Fork, and His Theory of Relations," Philosophy and Phenomenological Research, 95, no. 1 (2017): 3–65.

27. Tom Wolfe, "Sorry, But Your Soul Just Died," Independent, February 2, 1997.

28. 1903's The Great Train Robbery appears to be the first film to employ the convention on film.

29. Genesis 3:14.

30. Pinker, Blank Slate, 179–80.

31. Valéry, Analects, 548.

32. Robert Wright, The Moral Animal: Evolutionary Psychology and Everyday Life (New York: Vintage, 1994), 330.

33. Julia Annas, The Morality of Happiness (New York: Oxford University Press, 1993), 12.

34. The "Middle Way" is also central to the teachings of the Buddha.

35. Aristotle, Nicomachean Ethics, in The Complete Works of Aristotle, ed. Jonathan Barnes (Princeton, NJ: Princeton University Press, 1984), 1751, §1109a1.

36. C. G. Jung, Aion: Researches into the Phenomenology of the Self, trans. R. F. C. Hull (Princeton, NJ: Princeton University Press, 1959), 25, §47.

37. Josef Pieper, The Concept of Sin, trans. Edward T. Oakes (South Bend, IN: St. Augustine's Press, 2001), 49.

38. Charles Darwin, The Descent of Man (New York: Penguin, 2004), 121.

39. Ibid., 130.

40. Wright, The Moral Animal, 344.

41. Ibid.

42. E. O. Wilson, The Meaning of Human Existence (New York: Liveright), 2014, 179.

43. Wright, The Moral Animal, 313.

44. Frederick Norris, "Evagrius of Pontus (345–399)," in The Encyclopedia of Early Christianity, ed. Everett Ferguson (New York: Garland, 1998), 405.

45. Gabriel Bunge, Despondency: The Spiritual Teaching of Evagrius Ponticus on Acedia, trans. Anthony P. Gythiel (Yonkers, NY: St. Vladimir's Press, 2012), 17.

46. Kevin Corrigan, Evagrius and Gregory: Mind, Soul and Body in the Fourth Century (Farnham: Ashgate, 2009), 73.

47. Ibid., 75.

48. Evagrius of Pontus, Evagrius of Pontus: The Greek Ascetic Corpus, trans. Robert E. Sinkewicz (Oxford: Oxford University Press, 2003), 66–69.

49. Ibid., 74.

50. Ibid., 76.

51. Ibid., 78 (by way of 1 Timothy 6:10).

52. Ibid., 80.

53. Ibid., 81.

54. Ibid.

55. Ibid., 83.

56. Ibid., 86.

57. Ibid., 87.

58. Ibid.

59. See "The Testaments of the Twelve Patriarchs, the Sons of Jacob the Patriarch," in The Old Testament Pseudepigrapha, ed. James H. Charlesworth (New York: Doubleday, 1983), volume 1, 783.

60. Ibid.

61. Ibid.

62. Stephan C. Kessler, "Gregory the Great (c. 540–604)," in Handbook of Patristic Exegesis: The Bible in Ancient Christianity, ed. Charles Kannengiesser (Leiden: Brill, 2006), 1336–68.

63. Mark DelCogliano, Moral Reflections on the Book of Job, by Gregory the Great (Collegeville: Liturgical Press, 2014), 17.

64. Jean Leclerq, The Love of Learning and the Desire for God (New York: Fordham University Press, 1982), 27.

65. Ibid., 26.

66. Donald Capps, Deadly Sins and Saving Virtues (Philadelphia: Fortress Press, 1987), 64. Capps also argues that the sins can be correlated to develop- mental age, reminiscent of Erik Erikson's stages of virtue outlined in his Insight and Responsibility.

67. This is the so-called Guidonian hand, used in countless musical texts throughout the Middle Ages.

68. Albert Camus, The Plague, trans. Justin O'Brien (New York: Vintage, 1956), 54.

69. Grace Whistler, "'Saints without God': Camus's Poetics of Secular Faith," Scandinavian Jewish Studies, 29, no. 1 (2018): 54.

70. Wolfe, 9.

71. Ibid.

72. In Hemingway's 1926 novel The Sun Also Rises, Bill asks Mike "How did you go bankrupt." "Two ways," Mike answers, "Gradually and then suddenly."

73. Gasset, Man and Crisis, 31.

74. Siegfried Wenzel, "The Seven Deadly Sins: Some Problems of Research," Speculum 43, no. 1 (1968): 21.

75. Valéry, Analects, 345.

76. Karl Menninger, Whatever Became of Sin? (New York: Hawthorn Books, 1973), 17.

77. Jung, Aion, 25.

78. Gasset, Man and Crisis, 24, §48.

79. Ibid., 35.

80. Ibid., 186.

81. D. H. Lawrence, Apocalypse (New York: Penguin, 1931), 22.

82. Ibid., 47.

83. Ibid., 49.

Chapter One: Pride

1. Oxford English Dictionary definition.

2. D. H. Lawrence, Phoenix II: Uncollected, Unpublished, and Other Prose Works by D.H. Lawrence (New York: Viking, 1968), 72.

3. Although this quotation is generally attributed to Jung across the Inter- net,

I find no source for the quotation.

4. Valéry, Analects, 513.

5. John Cassian, The Institutes, trans. Boniface Ramsey (New York: The Newman Press, 2000), 255.

6. Gregory the Great, Morals on the Book of Job, xxxi.45, http://www.lectionarycentral.com/gregorymoraliaindex.html (accessed March 2, 2018).

7. Julius Müller, The Christian Doctrine of Sin, trans. William Pulsford (Edinburgh: T&T Clark, 1852), 1.177.

8. Phillip Cary, Augustine's Invention of the Inner Self: The Legacy of a Christian Platonist (New York: Oxford University Press, 2000).

9. Sarah Spence, Texts and the Self in the Twelfth Century (Cambridge: Cambridge University Press, 1996).

10. Brian Stock, The Integrative Self: Augustine, The Bible, and Ancient Thought (Philadelphia: University of Pennsylvania Press, 2017).

11. See Saul Brody, "Reflections on Yvain's Inner Life," Romance Philology 54 (2000–2001): 277–98.

12. Ibid.

13. Charles Taylor, Sources of the Self, The Making of the Modern Identity (Cambridge, MA: Harvard University Press, 1989), 116.

14. Jung, Aion, 9.

15. Taylor, Sources of the Self, 131.

16. Ibid., 129.

17. Charles Taylor, The Ethics of Authenticity (Cambridge, MA: Harvard University Press, 1991), 4.

18. Alexis De Tocqueville, Democracy in America, trans. Arthur Goldhammer (New York: The Library of America, 2004), 484.

19. Taylor, Sources of the Self, 130ff.

20. Taylor, Ethics of Authenticity, 4.

21. Ibid., 26.

22. See Peter J. Burke and Jan E. Stets, Identity Theory (Oxford: Oxford University Press, 2009).

23. Taylor, Ethics of Authenticity, 45, emphasis added.

24. Martin Bloomfield, Seven Deadly Sins: An Introduction to the History of a Religious Concept, with Special Reference to Medieval English Literature (East Lansing: Michigan State University Press, 1967), 75.

25. Ibid.

26. Ibid.

27. D. H. Lawrence, "We Need One Another," in Phoenix: The Posthumous Papers, ed. Edward McDonald (New York: The Viking Press, 1964), 190.

28. Jung, Aion, 23.

29. See Maurice Merleau-Ponty, The Phenomenology of Perception, trans. Colin Smith (London: Routledge and Kegan Paul, 1962).

30. http://www.gutenberg.org/ebooks/1676.

31. Taylor, Sources of the Self, 115.

32. Ibid., 116.

33. C. G. Jung, Answer to Job, trans. R. F. C. Hull (Princeton, NJ: Princeton University Press, 1958), para. 716.

34. Emanuel Swedenborg, Secrets of Heaven §149:2, https://www.swedenborg.com/wp-content/uploads/2015/08/NCE_SecretsofHeaven2_portable.pdf (accessed April 1, 2018).

35. Mary Beard surveys these issues in her recent How Do We Look: The Body, The Divine, and the Question of Civilization (New York: Liveright, 2018).

36. Albert W. Fields, "Milton and Self-Knowledge," PMLA 83, no. 2 (1968): 392.

37. On the single sexuality of the original human being, see Phyllis Trible, God and the Rhetoric of Sexuality (Philadelphia: Fortress Press, 1978); and Carol

Meyers, *Rediscovering Eve: Ancient Israelite Women in Context* (Oxford: Oxford University Press, 2013).

38. Plato, Phaedrus, in *The Collected Dialogues*, ed. Edith Hamilton and Huntington Cairns (Princeton, NJ: Princeton University Press, 1989), para. 246f.

39. Richard Rolle, *The Fire of Love*, trans. Clifton Wolters (New York: Penguin, 1972), 70.

40. Ibid., 81.

41. Lily B Campbell, *Shakespeare's Tragic Heroes* (London: Methuen, 1961), 103.

42. Oscar Wilde, "The Soul of Man under Socialism," in *The Artist as Critic: Critical Writings of Oscar Wilde*, ed. Richard Ellmann (New York: Vintage, 1969), 263.

43. Jessica Tracy, *Take Pride: Why the Deadliest Sin Holds the Secret to Human Success* (Boston: Houghton Mifflin, 2016).

44. See Caroline Walker Bynum, *Jesus as Mother: Studies in the Spirituality of the High Middle Ages* (Berkeley: University of California Press, 1982); and Christa Grössinger, *Picturing Women in Late Medieval and Renaissance Art* (Manchester: Manchester University Press, 1997).

45. Philo, *Philo Volume 1*, trans. F. H. Colson and G. H. Whitaker (Cambridge, MA: Harvard University Press, 1929), 265.

46. Philo, *The Decalogue*, in *The Works of Philo Complete and Unabridged*, trans.

C. D. Yonge (Peabody, MA: Hendrickson, 1993), 519.

47. 2 Baruch 54:15.

48. Moses Maimonides, *The Guide of the Perplexed*, ed. Shlomo Pines and Leo Strauss (Chicago: University of Chicago Press, 1963), 154–56.

49. Perspectives on Myths & Sacred Texts, https://www.pbs.org/moyers/faithandreason/perspectives1.html (accessed May 1, 2018).

50. Stephen Greenblatt, The Rise and Fall of Adam and Eve (New York: W.W. Norton, 2017), 34.

51. See Theresa Sanders, Approaching Eden: Adam and Eve in Popular Culture (Lanham, MD: Rowman & Littlefield, 2009).

52. John Milton, Paradise Lost, in The Riverside Milton, ed. Roy Flannagan (Boston: Houghton Mifflin, 1998), 4.516 (cited hereafter as PL with book and line number).

53. See Arthur O. Lovejoy, The Great Chain of Being (Cambridge: Cambridge University Press, 1964).

54. PL, 10.145.

55. PL, 9.908.

56. PL, 9.915.

57. PL, 9.997.

58. Ulrich Steinvorth, Pride and Authenticity (New York: Palgrave Macmillan, 2016), 30.

59. Reinhold Niebuhr, The Nature and Destiny of Man, Volume One: Human Nature (New York: Scribner's, 1964), 200.

60. Ibid., 179.

61. Valéry, Analects, 519.

62. The test was conducted on July 16, 1945. Less than three weeks later, on August 6, the bomb was dropped on Hiroshima.

63. "Man is a monster who expends all his energy on safeguarding and increasing his monstrosity. If he is the lord of creation this is due to his powers of destruction. Man can create only at the expense of the rest of creation" (Valéry, Analects, 479).

64. J. Robert Oppenheimer, "Prospects in the Arts and Sciences," in The Open Mind (New York: Simon and Schuster, 1955), 141.

65. Ibid.

66. Valéry, Analects, 521.

67. It is interesting to note that Berners-Lee's current project, Solid, "aims to radically change the way Web applications work today, resulting in true data ownership as well as improved privacy" (https://solid.mit.edu/). The initial democratic goal of the World Wide Web was a decided lack of ownership in an effort to engage more people in knowledge-building.

68. See, for example, Mark Bauerlein, The Dumbest Generation: How the Digital Age Stupefies Young Americans and Jeopardizes Our Future (New York: Penguin, 2008).

69. See lyrics to her song "Napoleon."

70. Christopher Lasch, The Culture of Narcissism: American Life in an Age of Diminishing Expectations (New York: W.W. Norton, 1979), 12.

71. Daniel Sarewitz, "Saving Science," New Atlantis (2016). http://www.the newatlantis.com/publications/saving-science.

72. "Stem Education Is Vital—But Not at the Expense of the Humanities," Scientific American, October 1, 2016.

73. Sarewitz, "Saving Science."

74. Alexander Langlands, Craeft: An Inquiry into the Origins and True Meaning of Traditional Crafts (New York: W.W. Norton, 2018), 343.

75. Quoted in Sarewitz, "Saving Science," 28.

76. Martin Heidegger, The Question Concerning Technology and Other Essays, trans. William Lovitt (New York: Harper, 1977), 16.

77. Ibid., 27.

78. Ibid., 35.

79. Sarewitz, "Saving Science."

80. Artemis Project, http://www.breastcancerdeadline2020.org/about-the-deadline/artemis-project.html (accessed August 1, 2018).

81. Geoffrey Chaucer, "The Franklin's Tale," in The Canterbury Tales (London: Penguin, 1970).

82. The phrase is Ophelia's in her council to her brother, Laertes, in Shakespeare's Hamlet.

Chapter Two: Lust

1. The Fall, 6–7.

2. Eusebius, The History of the Church from Christ to Constantine, trans. G. A. Williamson (New York: Penguin, 1989), 186.

3. It is worth noting that in his study of Origen, Jean Danielou glosses over the incident, remarking only "He afterwards admitted that he had been wrong on that point." Origen, Jean Danielou, trans. Walter Mitchell (New York: Sheed and Ward, 1955), 13.

4. Peter Brown, The Body and Society: Men, Women, and Sexual Renunciation in Early Christianity (New York: Columbia University Press, 1988), 26–27.

5. See Richard Finn, Asceticism in the Graeco-Roman World (Cambridge: Cambridge University Press, 2009), esp. chapters 1 and 2; see also Asceticism, ed. Vincent L. Wimbush and Richard Valantasis (New York: Oxford University Press, 1998); on Jewish practices specifically, see M. Lazarus, The Ethics of Juda- ism, trans. Henrietta Szold (Philadelphia: The Jewish Publication Society of America, 1900), 246–56.

6. Philo, Moses I and II, in Philo, trans. F. H. Colson (Cambridge, MA: Harvard University Press, 1984), 2.68.

7. Quoted in Brown, Body and Society, 31.

8. Ibid., 162.

9. Eusebius, 183.

10. An Etymological Dictionary of the Latin Language (London, 1828), https://archive.org/stream/anetymologicald00valpgoog/anetymologicald00valpgoog_ djvu.txt (accessed March 1, 2018).

11. See Joan E. Taylor, The Essenes, the Scrolls, and the Dead Sea (New York: Oxford University Press, 2012).

12. Ferdinand Pratt, The Theology of the St Paul, trans. John L. Stoddard

(Westminster: The Newman Bookshop, 1926), 2.469–70.

13. For an exhaustive study of Church writing on fornication, see John F. Dedek, "Premarital Sex; The Theological Argument from Peter Lombard to Durand," Theological Studies 41, no. 4 (1980): 652–60.

14. "CK 'banned' ad," October 19, 2006, https://www.youtube.com/watch?v=vZVk21Pco-c (accessed September 1, 2018).

15. "Carl's Jr. Paris Hilton Commercial 2014 I Love Texas," September 21, 2014, https://www.youtube.com/watch?v=z1xGF5MusCk (accessed September 1, 2018).

16. The first documentary appeared in 1979 with a fourth edition in 2010.

17. Greg M. Smith, Beautiful TV: The Art and Argument of Ally McBeal (Austin: University of Texas Press, 2007), 51.

18. Michel Foucault, The Use of Pleasure: The History of Sexuality, Volume 2 (New York: Vintage, 1985), 20.

19. Ibid.

20. Pratt, 2.52.

21. Brown, Body and Society, 47.

22. See Franklin Chamberlain Porter, "The Yecʿer Ha," Yale Biblical and Semitic Studies (1901): 93–94. Nonetheless, Porter concludes "The soul is the man" (93).

23. Plato, "Laws" in The Collected Dialogues (Princeton, NJ: Princeton University Press, 1989), 8 para. 840.

24. 1 Corinthians 6:9.

25. Philip Ariès, "Homosexuality in Ancient Rome," in Philippe Ariès and Andre Bejin, eds., Western Sexuality: Practice and Precept in Past and Present Times, trans. Anthony Forster (Oxford: Oxford University Press, 1985), 37.

26. See also John Boswell, Christianity, Social Tolerance, and Homosexuality (Chicago: The University of Chicago Press, 1980), 341–45.

27. Marilyn B. Skinner, Sexuality in Greek and Roman Culture (New York: Blackwell, 2005).

28. 1 Corinthians 11:9 and Ephesians 5:22.

29. Elaine Scarry, The Body in Pain: The Making and Unmaking of the World (New York: Oxford University Press, 1985).

30. See Elaine Pagels, The Gnostic Gospels (New York: Vintage, 1979).

31. See Wendy Doniger, "Medical and Mythical Constructions of the Body in Hindu Texts," in Religion and The Body, ed. Sarah Coakley (Cambridge, UK: Cam- bridge University Press, 1997), 167–84.

32. 2 Samuel 11:2.

33. 2 Samuel 11:4

34. 2 Samuel 11:15.

35. 2 Samuel 11:27.

36. 2 Samuel 11:27.

37. 2 Samuel 12:9.

38. Zucker and Reis 74.

39. 2 Samuel 12: 13.

40. J. Cheryl Exum, "Desire, Love, and Romance in the Hebrew Bible," Oxford Research Encyclopedia of Religion,

http://religion.oxfordre.com/view/10.1093/acrefore/9780199340378.00 1.0001/acrefore-9780199340378-e-54 (accessed April 1, 2018).

41. Sukkah 52a and 52b. The other things the Lord "repents that He had created them" are: Exile, the Chaldeans, and the Ishmaelites. The author goes on to note that it is due to lust that women were ordered to be separated from men in the synagogue seats.

42. James Kugel, The Ladder of Jacob: Ancient Interpretations of the Biblical Story of Jacob and His Children (Princeton, NJ: Princeton University Press, 2006), 81.

43. Talmud Shabbat 55b:6.

44. H. Hirsch Cohen, "David and Bathsheba," Journal of Bible and Religion, 33, no. 2 (1965) 142–48.

45. Ibid.

46. Alexander Izuchukwu Abasili, "Was It Rape? The David and Bathsheba Pericope Re-examined," Vetus Testamentum, 61 (2011): 1–15.

47. G. G. Nicol, "The Alleged Rape of Bathsheba: Some Observations on Ambiguity in Biblical Narrative," Journal for the Study of the Old Testament, 73 (1997): 43–53.

48. See, for example, R. M. Davidson, "Did David Rape Bathsheba? A Case Study in Narrative Theology," Journal of Adventist Theological Society, 17 (2006): 81–95.

49. Wayne Craven, "The Iconography of the David and Bathsheba Cycle at the Cathedral of Auxerre," Journal of the Society of Architectural Historians, 34, no. 3 (1975): 226–37.

50. Craven, "Iconography," 236.

51. Frank Chamberlin Porter, The Yeçer Hara: A Study in the Jewish Doctrine of Sin (New York: Scribner's, 1901).

52. Brown, Body and Society, 9.

53. Simon Blackburn, Lust: The Seven Deadly Sins (New York: Oxford University Press, 2004), 24–25.

54. Plato, Laws VI, 783.

55. Brown, Body and Society, 38.

56. Ibid.

57. Ibid., 40.

58. Ovid, The Art of Love, trans. Rolfe Humphries (Bloomington: Indiana University Press, 1957), 1.9.

59. Andreas Capellanus, The Art of Courtly Love, trans. John Jay Parry (New York: Columbia University Press, 1990), 193.

60. Constant J. Mews has edited The Lost Love Letters of Heloise and Abelard:

Perceptions of Dialogue in Twelfth-Century France (New York: St. Martin's Press, 1999).

61. The Letters of Abelard and Heloise, trans. Betty Radice (New York: Penguin, 1974), 51.

62. Ibid., 52.

63. Ibid., 68.

64. Ibid., 69.

65. See Aquinas's Summa Theologica, Prima Secundae Partis, q.18.

66. See Catherine Belsey, Desire: Love Stories in Western Culture (Oxford: Blackwell, 1994), esp. chapter 5.

67. Thomas Aquinas, Summa Theologica, Suppl. q.65, a. 4.

68. Ibid., q. 153.

69. Carole Straw, "Gregory's Moral Theology: Divine Providence and Human Responsibility," in A Companion to Gregory the Great, ed. Bronwen Neil and Mat- thew Del Santo (Leiden: Brill, 2013), 177–204.

70. Hamlet, 1.2.145–47.

71. Helen Vendler, The Art of Shakespeare's Sonnets (Cambridge, MA: Harvard University Press, 1997), 552.

72. He said he had "committed adultery in my heart many times."

73. Romans 1:24.

74. Jung, Aion, 24.

75. Hamlet, 2.2.

76. Uta Ranke-Heinemann, Eunuchs for the Kingdom of Heaven: Women, Sexuality, and the Catholic Church, trans. Peter Heinegg (Garden City: Doubleday, 1990), 11.

77. See Tom W. Smith, "A Report: The Sexual Revolution?" The Public Opinion Quarterly, 45, no. 3 (1990): 415–35.

78. The family viewing hour was deemed unconstitutional by Judge Warren J. Ferguson in November 1976. The concept persisted well into the 1980s

with shows like The Cosby Show and Happy Days headlining the 8pm
schedule. For a full accounting of the "family viewing hour" saga, see
Geoffrey Cowan, See No Evil: The Backstage Battle over Sex and Violence
on Television (New York: Simon and Schuster, 1978).

79. "Family Viewing Time," Museum of Broadcast Communications,
http://www.museum.tv/eotv/familyviewin.htm (accessed August 1,
2018).

80. Steven Hall, "Fashion Brand Uses Men's Lust for Female Nudity to
Promote Itself across Social Media," AdRants,

https://www.businessinsider.com/vicomte-a-uses-lust-in-social-media-
promotion-2013-12 (accessed August 1, 2018).

81. Foucault, 6.

82. For a lucid discussion, see Christa Grössinger, Picturing Women in Late
Medieval and Renaissance Art (Manchester: Manchester University Press,
1997).

83. Canto 5 of Dante's Inferno, where the lustful are punished, is characterized
by birds who are helpless against the wind and whose piercing cries are
perpetual.

84. In Sin and Fear, Jean Delumeau mentions that even "the legality of the
various sexual positions" was fodder for priestly contemplation when it
came to assessing the severity of the sin of lust (216).

85. Jean Delumeau, Sin and Fear: The Emergence of a Western Guilt Culture
13th-18th Centuries, trans. Eric Nicholson (New York: St. Martin's Press,
1990).

86. See Peter N. Stearns, American Cool: Constructing a Twentieth-Century
Emotional Style (New York: New York University Press, 1994), esp.
chapter 2, "Victorian Style."

87. The phrase indicates a resurgence of interest that began with the social
media boom around 2012.

88. Aria Darcella, "Edward Enninful's Seven Deadly Sins, with Naomi

Campbell, Kate Moss, & More,"

https://vmagazine.com/article/edward-enninfuls-seven-deadly-sins-with-naomi-campbell-kate-moss-more/ (accessed February 1, 2018).

89. Augustine, Concerning the City of God against the Pagans, trans. Henry Bettenson (New York: Penguin, 1972), 577.

90. For a few case studies, see "Internet Sex Addiction: Case Studies and Treatment," Psychology Today,

https://www.psychologytoday.com/us/blog/mindful-sex/200808 /internet-sex-addiction-case-studies-and-treatment (accessed March 1, 2018).

91. Terence G. Kardong, Benedict's Rule: A Translation and Commentary (Collegeville: The Liturgical Press, 1996), 64.55.

92. Kardong, Benedict's Rule, 64.55.

93. Jean Kilbourne, Can't Buy Me Love: How Advertising Changes the Way We Think and Feel (New York: Simon and Schuster, 1999), 259.

94. One estimate has porn films making $15 billion while much online porn is free. "The porn industry makes more money than Major League Baseball, the NFL, and The NBA combined." "How Big Is the Porn Industry?"

https://medium.com/@Strange_bt_True/how-big-is-the-porn-industry-fbc1ac78091b (accessed February 1, 2018).

95. "How Big Is the Porn Industry?"

96. "2014 Crime in the United States," FBI, https://ucr.fbi.gov/crime-in-the-u.s/2014/crime-in-the-u.s.-2014/tables/table-1 (accessed February 1, 2018).

97. Ted Gup, "On the Subject of Lust, Donald Trump Is No Jimmy Carter," New Republic, October 10, 2016.

98. Paul Bloom, "The Ways of Lust," New York Times, December 1, 2013, SR12.

Chapter Three: Anger

1. Paul Valéry, "The Crisis of the Mind," in The Outlook of Intelligence (Princeton, NJ: Bollingen), 23.

2. Jared Lanier, inventor of many virtual reality platforms, has recently denounced the power of social media and its destruction of the individual in Ten Arguments for Deleting Your Social Media Accounts Right Now (New York: Henry Holt, 2018).

3. "Charlie Chaplin: Laughing at Modernism," Crystal Bridges Museum of American Art, https://crystalbridges.org/blog/charlie-chaplin-laughing-at-modern ism/ (accessed March 1, 2018).

4. Roger Ebert, Roger Ebert's Movie Home Companion: 400 Films on Cassette, 1980–85 (New York: Andrews, McMeel & Parker, 1985), 209.

5. Valéry, Analects, 55.

6. "Controlling Anger before It Controls You," American Psychological Association, http://www.apa.org/topics/anger/control.aspx (accessed September 1, 2018).

7. Mary P. Nichols, "Aristotle's Defence of Rhetoric," Journal of Politics, 49, no. 3 (1987): 657–77.

8. Michael Michelini, "The Differences between East and West in Terms of Culture and Education, Global from Asia,

https://www.globalfromasia.com/east- west-differences/ (accessed March 1, 2018).

9. Lucius Annaeus Seneca, Anger, Mercy, Revenge, trans. Robert A. Kaster and Martha C. Nussbaum (Chicago: The University of Chicago Press, 2010), 23–25.

10. See Erich Neumann, Depth Psychology and a New Ethic, trans. Eugene Rolfe (New York: Putnam, 1969).

11. Ibid., 14.

12. Ibid., 20.

13. Ibid., 25.

14. Ibid., 29.

15. Ibid., 67.

16. Ibid., 70.

17. Ibid.

18. Ibid., 72.

19. "George Carlin—Unmasked with George Carlin," https://www.youtube.com/watch?v=s-clvDxl8qI (accessed April 1, 2018).

20. Ibid., 77.

21. Ibid., 85.

22. Ibid., 84.

23. Ibid., 90.

24. Ibid., 91.

25. Aristotle, Nicomachean Ethics, in The Complete Works of Aristotle, ed. Jonathan Barnes (Princeton, NJ: Princeton University Press, 1984), 1777.

26. Ibid., 1755.

27. For most cogent discussions of this topic, see the ongoing work of Martha C. Nussbaum.

28. Pinker, The Blank Slate, 307.

29. See D. M. T. Fessler, "Madmen: An evolutionary perspective on anger and men's violent responses to transgression," in M. Potegal, editor, International handbook of anger: Constituent and concomitant biological, psychological, and social processes (New York: Springer, 2010), 361–81.

30. Pinker, The Blank Slate, 317.

31. Shantideva, The Way of the Bodhisattva (New York: Shambhala, 1997), 78.

32. Augustine, Concerning the City of God against the Pagans, trans. H. S. Bettenson (New York: Penguin, 2003), 169.

33. M. C. McCarthy, "Divine Wrath and Human Anger: Embarrassment Ancient and New," Theology Studies 70, no. 4 (2009), 865.

34. Ibid., 848.

35. Proverbs 29:11.

36. Ephesians 4:26.

37. W. C. Mattison, III, "Jesus Prohibition of Anger (MT 5:22): The Person/ Sin Distinction from Augustine to Aquinas, Theological Studies, 68, no. 4 (2007), 839–64.

38. A. T. Hanson, The Wrath of the Lamb (London: SPCK Publishing, 1957), 36–40; MacGregor, passim.

39. Galen, On the Passions and Errors of the Soul, trans. P. W. Harkins (Columbus OH: Ohio State University Press, 1963), 32.

40. Galen, 31.

41. Aristotle, Rhetoric, in The Complete Works of Aristotle, ed. Jonathan Barnes (Princeton, NJ: Princeton University Press, 1984), 2195.

42. McCarthy, "Divine Wrath and Human Anger," 861.

43. Ibid., 857.

44. Judith M. Lieu, Marcion and the Making of a Heretic: God and Scripture in the Second Century (New York: Cambridge University Press, 2015).

45. M. Aloysia, "The God of Wrath?" Catholic Biblical Quarterly, 8, no. 4 (1946), 407–15.

46. David Powlison, "Anger, Part 1: Understanding Anger," Journal of Biblical Counseling, 14, no. 1 (1995), 4.

47. Bruce Edward Baloian, Anger in the Old Testament (New York: Peter Lang, 1992).

48. Genesis 4:5.

49. Matthew Richard Schlimm, From Fratricide to Forgiveness: The Language and Ethics of Anger in Genesis (Winona Lake, IN: Eisenbrauns, 2011).

50. Schlimm, 197.

51. Genesis 4:6–7.

52. Regina Schwartz, The Curse of Cain: The Violent Legacy of Monotheism (Chicago: University of Chicago Press, 1997), 5.

53. Quoted in Ibid., 31.

54. Genesis 6:7.

55. Ibid., 18.

56. Genesis 4:12.

57. Genesis 4:7.

58. Genesis 8:1.

59. Genesis 8:21.

60. Ibid.

61. Exodus 20:5.

62. Exodus 34:14.

63. Gary Heiron, "Wrath of God (OT)," The Anchor Bible Dictionary, ed. David Noel Freedman (New York: Doubleday, 1992), 991. For discussion of the Numbers verse "God is not like humans," see the opening chapter of Mark Sheridan, Language for God in Patristic Tradition: Wrestling with Biblical Anthropomorphism (Downers Grove, IL: IVP Academic, 2015).

64. Exodus 32:19.

65. Exodus 32:33.

66. Exodus 32:34.

67. Exodus 33:11.

68. Dennis. J. McCarthy, "Covenant in the Old Testament: The Present State of Inquiry," Catholic Biblical Quarterly, 27, no. 3 (1965): 217–40.

69. 1 Samuel 12:15.

70. 1 Samuel 12:24, 25.

71. Leviticus 26:17.

72. Genesis 3:24.

73. Leviticus 26:40, 42.

74. Lactantius, De Ira Dei (A Treatise on the Anger of God), ed. P. Schaff, 395, https://www.ccel.org/ccel/schaff/anf07.html (accessed September 1, 2018).

75. Michael C. McCarthy, "Divine Wrath and Human Anger: Embarrassment

Ancient and New," Theology Studies, 70, no. 4 (2009): 845–74.

76. Lactantius, De Ira Dei, 395.

77. Ibid., 406.

78. The phrase refers to Origen's prescription that one way to read the Bible is "spiritually," that is, allegorically.

79. Augustine, City of God, 643.

80. Genesis 4:5.

81. Genesis 4:6.

82. Genesis 4:7.

83. Schwartz, The Curse of Cain, 2.

84. Ibid., 3.

85. P. W. Van der Horst, "Philo van Alexandrie over de torn Gods," in A. de Jong, editor, Kleine Encyclopedie van de Toorn (Utrecht, NL: Utrechtse Theologische Reeks 21, 1993): 77–82.

86. Judges 2:1–4.

87. Judges 2:4.

88. Rudolf Otto, The Idea of the Holy, trans. J. W. Harvey (London: Oxford University Press, 1958).

89. Ibid., 19.

90. Elie Wiesel, The Trial of God, trans. Marion Wiesel (New York: Shocken, 1979); see also Henry Maitles, "Surviving the Holocaust: The Anger and Guilt of Primo Levi," Journal of Genocide Research, 4, no. 20 (2002): 237–51.

91. 2 Samuel 6: 6–8.

92. 2 Samuel 6:6.

93. 2 Samuel 6:7.

94. Numbers 32:13.

95. Deuteronomy 32:19.

96. Psalms 89:30; Isaiah 47:6.

97. Jung, Aion, 59.

98. John Hick, Evil and the God of Love (Norfolk, UK: Collins, 1966).

99. Anthony T. Hanson, The Wrath of the Lamb (London: SPCK Publishing, 1957), 3.

100. Mark 3:5.

101. Matthew A. Elliott, Faithful Feelings: Rethinking Emotion in the New Testament (Grand Rapids, MI: Kregel, 2006), 214.

102. Ibid.

103. Ibid.

104. Matthew 3:7.

105. C. H. Dodd, The Epistle of Paul to the Romans (New York: Harper and Brothers, 1932), 22.

106. For more on God's zeal in the Old Testament, see Martin Hengel, The Zealots: Investigations into the Jewish Freedom Movement in the Period from Herod I until 70 A.D., trans. David Smith (Edinburgh: T&T Clark, 1989), chapter 4.

107. See Martin Hengel, The Zealots: Investigations in to the Jewish Freedom Movement in the Period from Herod I until 70 A.D., trans. D. Smith (Edinburgh, T&T Clark, 1989).

108. Stephen Voorwinde, "Jesus and Anger: Does He Practice What He Preaches?" 31,

https://www.baylor.edu/content/services/document.php/235701.pdf (accessed August 1, 2018).

109. John 2:17.

110. Voorwinde, 31.

111. Ibid., 32.

112. G. H. C. MacGregor, "The Concept of the Wrath of God in the New Testament," New Testament Studies, 7, no. 2 (1961): 102.

113. Ibid., 104.

114. Ibid., 100.

115. Milton, Paradise Lost, 3.406–7.

116. Ephesians 4:26.

117. James Denney, "Anger," in Dictionary of Christ and the Gospels, ed. J. Hastings (New York: Scribner's, 1906), 60.

118. Joel 3:12.

119. Isaiah 2:10.

120. Hanson, 170.

121. Ibid., 180.

122. Babylonian Talmud, Eruvin, 65b.

123. The 1755 earthquake, which may have killed as many as 100,000, is most notable for having birthed the formal study of theodicy (the balance of divine goodness with the existence of evil) in philosophy and religion.

124. Seneca, 36.

125. Ibid., 42.

126. Pinker, Better Angels, 8–10.

127. Aristotle, 2195.

128. Ibid.

129. Billy Joel, "Prelude/Angry Young Man," https://www.billyjoel.com/song/preludeangry-young-man-6/ (accessed September 1, 2018).

130. Grace Vogel, "Last Year's Women's March Arose out of Anger; This Year There's a Plan," Weekender, September 24, 2018, http://www.dailycal.org/2018/01/28/last-years-womens-march-arose-out-of-anger-this-year-theres-a-plan/ (accessed October 1, 2018).

131. Constance Grady, "2017 Was the Year of Women's Anger, Onscreen and Off," Vox, December 21, 2017, https://www.vox.com/2017-in-review/2017/12/21/16776708/2017-womens-anger-womens-march-reckoning-handmaids-tale-alias-grace-big-

little-lies-three-billboards (accessed October 1, 2018).

132. Will Bunch, "An Oxymoron of Anger and Joy, Women's March Doesn't Know What's Next. That's the Beauty of It," Inquirer, January 20, 2018, http://www.philly.com/philly/columnists/will_bunch/philadelphia-womens-march-2018-draws-large-crowd-parkway-20180120.html?arc404=true (accessed October 1, 2018).

133. Susan Opotow, "Aggression and Violence," in The Handbook of Conflict Resolution, ed. Morton Deutsch and Peter T. Coleman (San Francisco: Jossey-Bass, 2000), 411.

134. Bertrand Russell, "The Expanding Mental Universe," ed. Robert E. Egner and Lester E. Denonn, The Basic Writings of Bertrand Russell (London: Routledge, 2009), 371.

135. Ibid.

136. Ibid., 372.

137. Pinker, Better Angels, 572.

138. Frans de Waal, The Age of Empathy: Nature's Lessons for a Kinder Society (New York: Random House, 2009).

139. Mencius, Mencius, trans. D. C. Lau (London: Penguin, 1970), 6A.6.

140. See Militarism, Sport, Europe: War without Weapons, ed. J. A. Mangan (London: Frank Cass, 2003); see also, Nigel B. Crowther, Sport in Ancient Times (Westport, CT: Praeger, 2007).

141. Dan P. McAdams, "The Mind of Donald Trump," Atlantic, June 2016, https://www.theatlantic.com/magazine/archive/2016/06/the-mind-of-donald- trump/480771/ (accessed August 1, 2018).

142. Michael Kimmel, Angry White Men: American Masculinity at the End of an Era (New York: Nation Books, 2017), 19–20.

143. Howard Zinn, A People's History of the United States 1492-Present (New York: Harper Collins, 1998), 321.

144. For a very insightful study, see Martha C. Nussbaum's recent book, Anger and Forgiveness: Resentment, Generosity, Justice (New York: Oxford

University Press, 2016).

145. Audrey Gelman, "The People's Champ: Elizabeth Warren on Breaking Boundaries," Cut, https://www.thecut.com/2018/06/elizabeth-warren-interview.html (accessed September 1, 2018).

146. Jeffrey W. Swanson, Nancy A. Sampson, Maria V. Petukhova, Alan M. Zaslavsky, Paul S. Appelbaum, Marvin S. Swartz, and Ronald C. Kessler, "Guns, Impulsive Angry Behavior, and Mental Disorders: Results from the National Comorbidity Survey Replication (NCS-R)," Behavioral Sciences and the Law, 33, no. 2–3 (June 2015), 199–212.

147. This is a theme in Pankaj Mishra, Age of Anger: A History of the Present (New York: Farrar, Straus and Giroux, 2017).

148. The stories are recounted in Stephen Jay Gould, The Mismeasure of Man (New York: W.W. Norton, 1981).

149. Valéry, Analects, 591.

150. Ibid., 592.

151. Nussbaum, Anger and Forgiveness.

Chapter Four: Gluttony

1. Shantideva, The Way of the Bodhisatva (New York: Shambhala, 2006), 75.

2. When I was in Wales in the late 1990s, we walked past a restaurant with a sign in the window: "Eat As Much As You Like" for under six pounds. American restaurants make it a contest: "All You Can Eat."

3. Equivalent to about $6 million in 2018 USD.

4. For a readable account of Birdseye, see Mark Kurlansky, Birdseye: The Adventures of a Curious Man (New York: Doubleday, 2012).

5. The name "tv dinner" itself implies lethargic consumption as one "feeds" while being entertained by the television.

6. Jonathan Rees, Refrigeration Nation: A History of Ice, Appliances, and Enterprise in America (Baltimore: Johns Hopkins University Press, 2013), 162.

7. Ibid.

8. The logo of colored balloons is said to have been inspired by an International Balloon Race held at the Indianapolis Speedway witnessed by Elmer Cline, a marketing executive with Taggart Baking.

9. Amy Bentley and Hi'ilei Hobart, "Food in Recent U.S. History," in Food in Time and Place: The American Historical Association Companion to Food History, ed. Paul Freedman, Joyce E. Chaplin and Ken Albala (Oakland, CA: University of California Press, 2014), 165–87.

10. Nicholas Carr, "In the Kingdom of the Bored, the One-Armed Bandit is King," in his Utopia Is Creepy and Other Provocations (New York: W.W. Norton, 2016), 217.

11. Rees, Refrigeration Nation, 169.

12. Ibid., 166.

13. See Jennifer Meagher, "Food and Drink in European Painting, 1400–1800," MET,

https://www.metmuseum.org/toah/hd/food/hd_food.htm(accessed November 1, 2018).

14. David Haslam and Fiona Haslam, Fat, Gluttony and Sloth: Obesity in Medicine, Art and Literature (Liverpool: Liverpool University Press, 2009), 154.

15. Caroline Walker Bynum, Holy Feast and Holy Fast: The Religious Significance of Food to Medieval Women (Berkeley: University of California Press, 1987), 32.

16. Ibid., 33.

17. Ibid., 44.

18. Quoted in Ibid.

19. Susie Orbach, Bodies (New York: Picador, 2009), 89.

20. "Weight Management," Boston Medical Center,

https://www.bmc.org/nutrition-and-weight-management/weight-management (accessed August 1, 2018).

21. "Pelman v. McDonald's Corp," Justia US Law,

https://law.justia.com/cases/federal/district-courts/FSupp2/237/512/2462869/ (accessed October 1, 2018).

22. Tatiana Andreyeva, Inas Rashad Kelly, and Jennifer L. Harris, "Exposure to Food Advertising on Television: Associations with Children's Fast Food and Soft Drink Consumption and Obesity," Economic and Human Biology, 30 (2011); see also Rudd Report: Trends in Television Food Advertising, 2010.

23. "The State of Obesity," State of Obesity.org, https://stateofobesity.org/childhood-obesity-trends/ (accessed November 1, 2018).

24. See Kelly L. Haws, Kevin L. Sample, and Rebecca Walker Reczek, "Why Is Healthy Food So Expensive? Maybe because We Expect It to Be," Washington Post, January 5, 2017, https://www.washingtonpost.com/posteverything/wp/2017/01/05/why-is-healthy-food-so-expensive-maybe-because-we-expect-it-to-be (accessed August 1, 2018).

25. A 2007 report noted that children would choose the McDonald's packaging, regardless whether it contained French fries or carrots (Thomas N. Robinson, Dina L. G. Borzekowski, Donna M. Matheson, and Helena C. Kraemer, "Effects of Fast Food Branding on Young Children's Taste Preferences," Archive of Pediatric and Adolescent Medicine, 161, no. 8 [2007]: 792–97.)

26. It is interesting to note that the "first American weight watchers were much less concerned with fatness than they were with gluttony" (Hillel Schwartz, Never Satisfied, 27).

27. For a general discussion of gluttony in the ancient world, see Susan E. Hill, Eating to Excess: The Meaning of Gluttony and the Fat Body in the Ancient World (Santa Barbara: Praeger, 2011).

28. Burton, 191.

29. Ibid., 197.

30. Ibid., 198.

31. L. Shannon Jung, Food for Life: The Spirituality and Ethics of Eating (Minneapolis: Fortress Press, 2004), 71.

32. Detailed statistics can be found in Luciano Floridi's fine work The Fourth Revolution: How the Infosphere Is Reshaping Human Reality (New York: Oxford University Press, 2014), particularly the opening chapter.

33. For an excellent overview, see Andrew Pettegree, The Invention of News: How the World Came to Know about Itself (New Haven, CT: Yale University Press, 2014), esp. chapter 8.

34. David Shenk, Data Smog: Surviving the Information Glut (New York: HarperCollins, 1997).

35. Ben Zimmer, "Keeping a Watch on 'Binge-Watching,'" ThinkMap Visual Thesaurus, https://www.visualthesaurus.com/cm/wordroutes/keeping-a-watch-on- binge-watching/ (accessed June 1, 2018).

36. Yoon Hi Sung, Eun Kang, and Wei-Na Lee. "A Bad Habit for Your Health? An Exploration of Psychological Factors for Binge-Watching Behavior," American Association for the Advancement of Science (AAAS), Paper Presented at the Annual Meeting of the International Communication Association 65th Annual Conference, Caribe Hilton, San Juan, Puerto Rico, May 21, 2015.

37. "Kevin Spacey: James MacTaggart Memorial Lecture in Full," Telegraph, https://www.telegraph.co.uk/culture/tvandradio/10260895/Kevin-Spacey-James-MacTaggart-Memorial-Lecture-in-full.html (accessed June 1, 2018).

38. Sarah Jarvis, "Binge Watching and Your Health," Patient.info, https://patient.info/binge-watching-and-your-health (accessed June 1, 2018).

39. Scott Eidler, "TV Shows Online Transforms a Generation's Viewing Habits," Washington Post, March 21, 2011, https://www.washingtonpost.com/entertainment/television/tv-shows-

online-transforms-a-generations-viewing-habits/2010/12/07/ AFt23I2C_story.html?utm_term=.111f0e71fcd1 (accessed May 1, 2018).

40. Brandon Baker, "Infrequently Asked Questions: Why Do We Binge-Watch?" Philly Voice, July 27, 2016,

http://www.phillyvoice.com/infrequently-asked-questions-why-do-we-binge-watch/ (accessed June 1, 2018).

41. Dr. Judy Rosenberg cited in Danielle Page, "What Happens to Your Brain When You Binge-Watch a TV Series," NBC News,

https://www.nbcnews.com/better/health/what-happens-your-brain-when-you-binge-watch-tv-series-ncna 816991 (accessed July 1, 2018).

42. Liese Exelmans and Jan Van den Bulck, "Binge Viewing, Sleep, and the Role of Pre-Sleep Arousal," Journal of Clinical Sleep Medicine, 13, no. 8 (2017): 1001–8.

43. Adam Antler, Irresistible: The Rise of Addictive Technology and the Business of Keeping Us Hooked (New York: Penguin, 2017), 3.

44. Renata Salecl, The Tyranny of Choice (London: Profile, 2011), 60.

45. "Digital Detox Retreats," http://digitaldetox.org/retreats/# (accessed August 1, 2018).

46. See essays in D.H. Lawrence, Technology, and Modernity, ed. Indrek Manniste (New York: Bloomsbury, 2019).

Chapter Five: Avarice

1. See Robert H. Frank, The Darwin Economy (Princeton, NJ: Princeton University Press, 2011), where Frank attempts to extrapolate Darwin's theory of natural selection and apply it to the world of economics.

2. Francine Prose, "What Book Would You Recommend for America's Current Political Moment?" New York Times Sunday Book Review, May 14, 2017, 39.

3. Alexis de Tocqueville, Democracy in America, trans. Arthur Goldhammer (New York: Library of America, 2004), 625.

4. Ibid., 626.

5. Phyllis A. Tickle, Greed: The Seven Deadly Sins (New York: Oxford University Press, 2004), 23.

6. See David Daube, "Nathan's Parable," Novum Testamentum, 24, no. 3 (1982): 275–88.

7. See Joyce E. Peterson, "With Feigned Flattery: The Pardoner as Vice," Chaucer Review 10, no. 4 (1976): 326–36.

8. Modern English translations of Chaucer are my own.

9. The film was based on a 1927 novel by the same name.

10. Bosley Crowther, "'Treasure of Sierra Madre,' Film of Gold Mining in Mexico, New Feature at Strand," New York Times, January 24, 1948, L11.

11. Saul Bellow, Seize the Day (New York: Penguin, 2003), 36.

12. Ibid., 55.

13. Ibid., 69.

14. Ibid., 9.

15. Ibid., 10.

16. Ibid.

17. Ibid., 117.

18. Saul Bellow, Saul Bellow: Letters, ed. Benjamin Taylor (New York: Viking, 2010), 151.

19. Ibid., 166.

20. Richard S. Patterson and Richardson Dougall, The Eagle and the Shield: A History of the Great Seal of the United States (Washington, DC: Department of Foreign Services, 1976), 85.

21. Numerous commentators have, since the late 1960s, remarked the hubris of the building of the Twin Towers. See, for example, Will Self, "Will Self on the Meaning of Skyscrapers—from the Tower of Babel to the Shard," Guardian, March 26, 2015.

22. Joseph Campbell made this point throughout his career and work.

23. For an overview, see Randy O. Frost and Gail Steketee, Stuff: Compulsive

Hoarding and the Meaning of Things (New York: Houghton Mifflin, 2010).

24. Joan Robinson, "The Concept of Hoarding," Economic Journal, 48, no. 190 (1938): 231–36.

25. In modern firefighting parlance, a "Collyers' Mansion" refers to a home of hoarders filled with trash and debris.

26. Scott Herring, The Hoarders: Material Deviance in Modern American Culture (Chicago: The University of Chicago Press, 2014), 162.

27. For more on the Collyer brothers, see Franz Lidz, Ghosty Men: The Strange but True Story of the Collyer Brothers, New York's Greatest Hoarders (New York: Bloomsbury, 2003).

28. Clifford quoted in Herring, 177.

29. Xinyue Zhou, Sara Kim, and Lili Wang, "Money Helps When Money Feels: Money Anthropomorphism Increases Charitable Giving," Journal of Consumer Research 44 (2018): 158–163.

30. Katharine Schwab, "Marie Kondo Got You to Toss Your Stuff. Now She Sells $89 Boxes," Fast Company, July 24, 2018,

https://www.fastcompany.com/90206505/marie-kondo-got-you-to-toss-your-stuff-now-she-sells-89- boxes (accessed August 1, 2018).

31. Bin-Bin Chen, "An Evolutionary Life History Approach to Understanding Greed," Personality and Individual Differences 127 (2018): 74–78.

32. Tim Flannery, Here on Earth: A Natural History of the Planet (New York: Atlantic Monthly Press, 2010), 218.

33. Frans de Waal, The Age of Empathy, 39.

34. Ibid., 162.

35. Richard Wike, Jacob Poushter, Hani Zainulbhai, "As Obama Years Drawn to Close, President and U.S. Seen Favorably in Europe and Asia," Pew Research Center, June 29, 2016,

http://www.pewglobal.org/2016/06/29/as-obama-years-draw-to-close-president-and-u-s-seen-favorably-in-europe-and-asia/ (accessed June 1, 2018).

36. Art Spiegelman, Maus I: A Survivor's Tale: My Father Bleeds History (New York: Pantheon, 1986), 93.

37. Ibid., 116.

38. Frederic D. Homer, Primo Levi and the Politics of Survival (Columbia: University of Missouri Press, 2001), 25.

39. Ibid., 25–26.

40. See, for example, Luke Tress, "For Many Holocaust Survivors, Effects of Wartime Starvation Still a Plague," Times of Israel, May 3, 2016, https://www.timesofisrael.com/for-many-holocaust-survivors-wartime-starvation-still-a- daily-torment/ (accessed June 1, 2018); and Judy Bolton-Fasman, "The Messi- ness of Hoarding and Motherhood," Jewish Forward, March 7, 2016, https://forward.com/sisterhood/335305/the-messiness-of-hoarding-and-motherhood/ (accessed June 1, 2018).

41. Katie Hope, "'World's Richest 1% Get 82% of the Wealth,' Says Oxfam," BBC News, January 22, 2018, https://www.bbc.com/news/business-42745853 (accessed August 1, 2018).

42. Alexis Brassey and Stephen Barber, eds., Greed (New York: Palgrave, 2009), xiii.

43. Jane Mayer, Dark Money: The Hidden History of the Billionaires behind the Rise of the Radical Right (New York: Doubleday, 2016).

44. Kathleen Elkins, "Here's How Much Money Americans Think You Need to Be Considered Rich," CNBC, June 21, 2017, https://www.cnbc.com/2017/06/21/ how-much-money-americans-think-it-takes-to-be-considered-rich.html (accessed June 1, 2018).

45. Robert Frank, "Poll: The Rich Deserve Their Wealth," CNBC, July 12, 2012, https://www.cnbc.com/id/48160711 (accessed June 1, 2018).

46. In Barber 7.

47. Alexis Brassey and Stephen Barber, "Introduction to Greed," Greed, ed. Alexis Brassey and Stephen Barber (New York: Palgrave, 2009), 3.

48. Harriet Ryan and Adam Tschorn, "The Kardashian Phenomenon," Los Angeles Times, February 19, 2010,

http://articles.latimes.com/2010/feb/19/entertainment/la-et-kardashian19-2010feb19 (accessed June 1, 2018).

49. Jessica Chasmar, "Kardashian Culture Is Killing America," Washington Times, January 3, 2013,

https://www.washingtontimes.com/news/2013/jan/3/kardashian-culture-is-killing-america/ (accessed June 1, 2018).

50. Steven Pinker, The Better Angels of Our Nature: Why Violence Has Declined (New York: Viking, 2011), 583.

51. See E. O. Wilson, The Social Conquest of Earth (New York: Liveright, 2012).

52. Nathan H. Lents, "Wolverines Give Insight into the Evolution of Greed," Visionlearning, December 17, 2014,

https://www.visionlearning.com/blog/2014/12/17/wolverines-give-insight-evolution-greed/ (accessed March 1, 2018).

53. Pinker, Better Angels, 590.

54. Sarah Knapton, "Keeping Up with the Kardashians May Make Viewers Cold-Hearted towards Poor, Study Suggests," Telegraph, August 1, 2018, https://www.telegraph.co.uk/science/2018/08/01/keeping-kardashians-may-make-viewers-cold-hearted-towards-poor/ (accessed August 10, 2018).

55. Hill, https://thehill.com/blogs/ballot-box/gop-primaries/265335-trump-im-very-greedy (accessed June 1, 2018).

56. Factbase, https://factba.se/trump (accessed June 1, 2018).

57. Factbase, June 3, 2016, https://factba.se/trump (accessed June 1, 2018).

58. Factbase, February 23, 2016, https://factba.se/trump (accessed June 1, 2018).

Chapter Six: Envy

1. Genesis 4:8.

2. Rein Nauta, "Cain and Abel: Violence, Shame and Jealousy," Pastoral Psychology, 58 (2009), 67.

3. I think here of the cases where a high school boy was bullied or spurned by a girl—the shame felt escalates to envy of others, leaving the individual feeling impotent, the only power he yields resulting in violence. As Nauta writes, "When self-respect and self-esteem are fatally wounded, concern for others is of no consequence, for the only way to re-affirm one's own victimized self is by destroying those who were witness to its demise" (67).

4. Richard H. Smith and Sung Hee Kim, "Comprehending Envy," Psychological Bulletin, 133, no. 1 (2007): 53.

5. On the linguistic distinctions, see chapter 2 of Helmut Schoeck, Envy: A Theory of Social Behaviour (Indianapolis: The Liberty Fund), 1966.

6. Nauta, "Cain and Abel," 69.

7. "The careful writer distinguishes between these terms. Jealousy is properly restricted to contexts involving emotional rivalry; envy is used more broadly of resentful contemplation of a more fortunate person." Bryan A. Garner, Garner's Modern American Usage, 3rd ed. (New York: Oxford University Press, 2009), 488.

8. Joseph Epstein, Envy: The Seven Deadly Sins (New York: Oxford University Press, 2004), 19.

9. Aristotle, Nicomachean Ethics, 1731; for an extended study of envy in Aristotle, see Ed Sanders, Envy and Jealousy in Classical Athens: A Socio-Psychological Approach (New York: Oxford University Press, 2014), esp. chapter 4.

10. Paul Valéry, Monsieur Teste, trans. Jackson Matthews (Princeton, NJ: Princeton University Press, 1973), 17.

11. Valéry, Analects, 244.

12. Ibid.

13. Milton, Paradise Lost, 4.357.

14. In addition to countless mystery novels, Sayers translated Dante and wrote several Christian morality tracts.

15. Dorothy L. Sayers, The Other Six Deadly Sins: An Address Given to the Public Morality Council at Caxton Hall, Westminster, on October 23, 1941 (London: Methuen, 1941), 149.

16. Melanie Klein, "Envy and Gratitude," in Envy and Gratitude and Other Works 1946–1963 (New York: Delta Press, 1975), 176.

17. Aristotle, Rhetoric, 2211.

18. For a lucid and classic discussion of injustice, see Edmond N. Cahn, The Sense of Injustice: An Anthropocentric View of Law (New York: New York University Press, 1949).

19. Valéry, Analects, 87.

20. Epstein, Envy, 52.

21. Jennifer Carlile, "Prince Charles Complains about People Rising above their Station," NBCNews.com, November 24, 2004,

http://www.nbcnews.com/id/6519640/ns/world_news/t/prince-charles-complains-about-people-rising-above-their-station/#.W4_YjY68GGg (accessed January 1, 2018).

22. J. Stacy Adams, "Toward and Understanding of Inequity," Journal of Abnormal Psychology, 67 (1963): 422–36.

23. See Richard C. Huseman, John D. Hatfield, and Edward W. Miles, "A New Perspective on Equity Theory: The Equity Sensitivity Construct," Academy of Management Review, 12, no. 2 (1987): 222–34.

24. Aristotle, Rhetoric, 2312.

25. Ibid.

26. John Rawls, A Theory of Justice (Cambridge, MA: Harvard University Press, 1999), 467.

27. Ibid.

28. Ibid.

29. Ibid., 468.

30. Max Scheler, Ressentiment, trans. Louis A. Coser (Marquette: Marquette University Press, 1994).

31. Ibid., 6.

32. Ibid., 7.

33. Ibid., 8.

34. Alexis de Tocqueville, Democracy in America, 3.

35. John Rawls, Justice, 469.

36. Miriam Bankovsky, "Excusing Economic Envy: On Injustice and Impotence," Journal of Applied Philosophy, 35, no. 2 (2018): 257–59.

37. Scheler, Ressentiment, 4.

38. The Latin word invidia can be translated as both envy and grudge.

39. Charlotte van Oyen Witvliet, Thomas E. Ludwig, and Kelly L. Vander Laan, "Granting Forgiveness or Harboring Grudges: Implications for Emotion, Physiology, and Health," Psychological Science, 12, no. 2 (2001): 117–23.

40. See Conor Friedersdorf, "The Rise of Victimhood Culture," Atlantic, September 11, 2015,

https://www.theatlantic.com/politics/archive/2015/09/the-rise-of-victimhood-culture/404794/ (accessed June 1, 2018).

41. Vilayanur S. Ramachandran and Baland Jalal, "The Evolutionary Psychology of Envy and Jealousy," Frontiers in Psychology, 8.1619 (September 2017): 3.

42. Sarah E. Hill and David M. Buss, "The Evolutionary Psychology of Envy," in Envy: Theory and Research ed. Richard Smith (Oxford: Oxford University Press, 2008).

43. Charles Darwin, The Expression of the Emotions in Man and Animals (Chicago: University of Chicago Press, 1965), 261.

44. Quoted in Schoeck, Envy, 201.

45. See Ernest Jones, Hamlet and Oedipus (New York: W.W. Norton, 1949).

46. The Oedipus Complex argument is built on two errors: (1) reading into Hamlet's childhood, about which we know virtually nothing; and (2) over relying on performances, which are all inherently interpretations of the text.

47. Hamlet, 4.7.

48. See Charles A. Hallett and Elaine S. Hallett, The Revenger's Madness: A Study of Revenge Tragedy Motifs (Lincoln: University of Nebraska Press, 1981).

49. Aristotle, Politics, 2211.

50. Sherry Turkle, Reclaiming Conversation: The Power of Talk in a Digital Age (New York: Penguin, 2015), 146.

51. Sherry Turkle's earlier study was Alone Together: Why We Expect More from Technology and Less from Each Other (New York: Basic, 2011).

52. Donna Freitas, The Happiness Effect: How Social Media is Driving a Generation to Appear Perfect at Any Cost (New York: Oxford University Press, 2017), 41.

53. Ibid., 40–41.

54. Charles Taylor, Sources of the Self: The Making of Modern Identity (Cambridge, MA: Harvard University Press, 1989), 138–39.

55. Jean Baudrillard, Simulations, trans. Paul Foss, Paul Patton, and Philip Beitchman (N.p.: Semiotext[e], 1983), 144.

56. Luciano Floridi, The Fourth Revolution: How the Infosphere Is Reshaping Human Reality (Oxford: Oxford University Press, 2014), 42.

57. Saraniya Gunaseran and Haliyana Khalid, "How Envy Drives Consumerism on Instagram," PACIS 2017 Proceedings, 198,

https://aisel.aisnet.org/pacis2017/ 198/ (accessed March 1, 2018).

58. Rachel Strugatz, "Cosmetic Procedures: Kardashian-Drive, Millenal-Led," WWD, March 31, 2017, https://wwd.com/beauty-industry-news/beauty-features/kim-kardashian-kylie-jenner-drive-cosmetic-procedures-plastic-

surgery-10 852443/ (accessed March 1, 2018).

59. Sarah C. Sorice, Alexander Y. Li, and Jarom Gilstrap, "Social Media and the Plastic Surgery Patient," Plastic and Reconstructive Surgery, 140, no. 5 (2017): 1047–56.

60. S. Rajanala, M. B. C. Maymone, and N. A. Vashi, "Selfies—Living in the Era of Filtered Photographs," JAMA Facial Plastic Surgery, published online August 2, 2018.

61. Benjamin Franklin, "On True Happiness," 1785.

62. See S. T. Fiske, "Envy up, Scorn down: How Comparison Divides Us," American Psychologist, 65, no. 8 (2010): 698–706.

63. Nicolas Carr, "Raising the Virtual Child," in Utopia Is Creepy and Other Provocations (New York: W.W. Norton, 2016), 73.

Chapter Seven: Sloth

1. Peter Toohey, Boredom: A Lively History (New Haven, CT: Yale University Press), 2011.

2. Andrew Solomon, The Noonday Demon: An Atlas of Depression (New York: Scribner, 2001).

3. Mel Levine, The Myth of Laziness (New York: Simon and Schuster, 2003).

4. "Major Depression," National Institute of Mental Health, November 2017, https://www.nimh.nih.gov/health/statistics/major-depression.shtml (accessed June 1, 2018).

5. Ibid.

6. Siegfried Wenzel, The Sin of Sloth: Acedia in Medieval Thought and Literature (Chapel Hill: University of North Carolina Press, 1967), 6.

7. Peter Toohey, "Acedia in Late Classical Antiquity," Illinois Classical Studies, 15, no. 2 (1990): 339–52.

8. Hamlet, 1.2.129.

9. Ibid., 1.2.132.

10. Quoted in Andrew Crislip, "The Sin of Sloth or the Illness of the Demons?

The Demon of Acedia in Early Christian Monasticism," Harvard Theological Review, 98, no. 2 (2005): 143–69.

11. John Cassian, The Institutes, trans. Boniface Ramsey (New York: The Newman Press, 2000), 221.

12. Ibid., 223.

13. Ibid., 228.

14. Dissertations chrétiennes et morales (1665), XVIII: "Les plaisirs de la vie retiree."

15. Darwin, Descent of Man, 132.

16. Genesis 2:18.

17. See his The Noonday Devil: Acedia, the Unamed Evil of Our Times (San Francisco: Ignatius Press, 2015).

18. See Heather Boushey, Finding Time: The Economics of Work-Life Conflict (Cambridge, MA: Harvard University Press, 2016).

19. Sherry Turkle, Alone Together: Why We Expect More from Technology and Less from Each Other (New York: Basic, 2011), 27.

20. Turkle, Alone Together.

21. Benedict, Rule, 4.38.

22. Ibid., 48.1.

23. Ibid., 48.23.

24. Proverbs 16:27.

25. Patti Wiginton, "Water Folklore and Legends," ThoughtCo., March 21, 2018, https://www.thoughtco.com/water-element-folklore-and-legends-2561689 (accessed June 1, 2018).

26. Evagrius of Ponticus, The Greek Ascetic Corpus, trans. Robert E. Sinkewicz (New York: Oxford University Press, 2003), 9, 35.

27. Evagrius, 99.

28. Ibid.

29. Solomon, 443.

30. Valéry, Analects, 68.

31. Ironically, the most quiet place on earth, according to the Guinness Book of world Records, is a Microsoft research lab in Redmond, Washington, designed for audio testing. In fact, it is virtually impossible to find a natural place of quiet. For a comprehensive discussion of sound, see Hillel Schwartz, Making Noise: From Babel to the Big Bang & Beyond (New York: Zone Books, 2011).

32. Adam Alter, Irresistible: The Rise of Addictive Technology and the Business of Keeping Us Hooked (New York: Penguin, 2018), 256.

33. Hilarie Cash, Cosette D. Rae, Ann H. Steel, and Alexander Winkler, "Internet Addiction: A Brief Summary of Research and Practice," Current Psychiatry Reviews, 8, no. 4 (2012): 292–98.

34. Toohey, Boredom, 111.

35. Robert Burton, The Anatomy of Melancholy, ed. Floyd Dell and Paul Jordan- Smith (New York: Tudor, 1951), 40.

36. Emily Langer, "Eugene J. Polley," May 22, 2012,

https://www.washingtonpost.com/entertainment/tv/eugene-j-polley-engineer-who-invented-the-first-wireless-tv-remote-control-dies-at-96/2012/05/22/gIQAv4J4iU_story.html?utm_term=.547fd8c0d521 (accessed June 1, 2018).

37. Chris Isidore, "Malls Are Doomed: 255 25% Will Be Gone in 5 Years," CNN Money, June 2, 2017,

https://money.cnn.com/2017/06/02/news/economy/doomed-malls/index.html?iid=EL (accessed June 1, 2018).

38. Theodore Roosevelt, "The Strenuous Life,"

http://voicesofdemocracy.umd.edu/roosevelt-strenuous-life-1899-speech-text/ (accessed June 1, 2018).

39. Valdes called the sloth "the stupidest animal that can be seen in the world. So slow and heavy is he that it takes him all day to go fifty paces" (quoted in S. W. Britton, "Form and Function in the Sloth," Quarterly Review of

Biology 16.1 (March 1941), 13–34). Writing in 1825, Oliver Goldsmith thought the animal represented "an unfinished production of nature" (Britton 16).

40. Jason Bittel, "Sloths May Be Slow, But They're Not Stupid," National Geographic, March 1, 2018,

https://www.nationalgeographic.com.au/animals/sloths-may-be-slow-but-theyre-not-stupid.aspx (accessed June 1, 2018).

41. Jung, "Theory and Psychoanalysis" in Collected Works, 4 para. 474.

42. "Dan Aykroyd: The Internet Is the Devil's Gateway," Times of India, January 29, 2017,

https://timesofindia.indiatimes.com/entertainment/english/hollywood/news/Dan-Aykroyd-The-internet-is-the-devils-gateway/articleshow/55029167.cms (accessed June 1, 2018).

43. Johannes Trithemius, In Praise of Scribes (De Laude Scriptorum), trans. Roland Behrendt (Lawrence, KS: Coronado Press, 1974).

44. See L. Dupuis, "L'ennui morbide," Revue Philosophique de la France et de l'Etranger, 93 (1922): 417–42.

45. James Hillman, "Pathologizing: The Wound and the Eye," in Carl Gustav Jung: Critical Assessments, ed. Renos K. Papadopoulos (London: Routledge, 1992), vol. 3, 35.

Conclusion

1. Yuval Noah Harari, Homo Deus: A Brief History of Tomorrow (New York: Harper Collins, 2017), 400.

2. Most recently, a 2010 bill would have banned federal funding for human cloning, but the bill never passed the House of Representatives.

3. Michael Patrick Lynch, The Internet of Us: Knowing More and Understanding Less in the Age of Big Data (New York: Liveright, 2016), 11.

4. Victor Cohn, 1999: Our Hopeful Future (Indianapolis: The Bobbs-Merrill Company, 1956), 192.

5. D. H. Lawrence, "Thinking About Oneself," Phoenix: The Posthumous Papers of D.H. Lawrence (New York: Viking, 1964), 735–36.

6. C. G. Jung, Psychology and Religion (New Haven, CT: Yale University Press, 1938), 11.

7. See David F. Noble, The Religion of Technology: The Divinity of Man and the Spirit of Invention (New York: Penguin, 1999).

8. Valéry, Analects, 55.

9. Ibid., 252.

Index